THE KINGDOM OF WINTER

SARAH WOOD

THE
KINGDOM
OF
WINTER

MAGIC OF WORDS

Library of Congress Preassigned Control Number: 2019935743

ISBN-13 978-1-7329629-1-0

To Mum and Dad.
Thank you for inspiring me and keeping me motivated.
I couldn't have done it without you.
I love you!

THE
KINGDOM
OF
WINTER

SARAH WOOD

Prologue

Brilliant stars glittered overhead as a man stood in a small clearing surrounded by snow laden trees. Moonlight shone down, illuminating the clearing in cold silver light, as the man surveyed his surroundings. It looked like a scene from a painting, but he wasn't enjoying it at all. The wind rustled through the branches slightly and he turned quickly to scan the tree tops. When he realized it was only the wind, he relaxed; but only slightly. One would have thought he expected something horrible to come out of the bushes at any moment, instead of the friends he was expecting. A small rustle in the bushes behind him caused him to jump and turn around suddenly.

"Who's there?" he asked nervously.

The bushes parted and a man and woman walked quietly out, holding hands. They were both tall and regal with pale skin and shockingly white-blond hair. Both of them were wearing thick blue robes, and the man had a silver medallion around his neck. They contrasted severely with the small hunched man in thick robes of red and brown who had been waiting for them. He stood next to them, shaking slightly.

"Relax Garrin. No one's going to look for us way out here," the man said with smile that didn't quite reach his worried blue eyes.

"You never know who's watching, Robert. I know why we had to meet out here, but I'm not really used to holding councils out in the open like this." Garrin said with a nervous glance toward the sky.

"Sorry we're late, have the others left already?" Robert inquired.

"No, they're late too." Garrin answered in a worried tone.

"Has something happened?" the woman asked.

"Not that I know of. Yet." Garrin said not very reassuringly.

A few minutes later another woman strode into the clearing carrying a little girl of about two. The child's soft golden curls covered part of what looked like a small stuffed rabbit which she was clutching tightly.

"Marie! What is she doing here with you?" The other woman asked incredulously.

"I'm going to take her to the main land. It's not safe for her here." Marie replied quietly.

"You can't go! What about your kingdom!" Garrin said in distress.

"That's why I have a Council. They are more than capable of running Spring in my absence. Someday I hope we'll return but for now it's not safe for her," she attempted to explain.

The other three stared at her in disbelief. There was an awkward silence and then the pale woman spoke.

"How can you leave at a time like this? Your people will need you now more than ever. The Witch hasn't just escaped to run away. You know she's planning something!"

"What are you going to do with your little one then, Tira? Just leave him here while the darkness grows and swallows him?" Marie asked shortly.

"We already had to send him away to keep him safe." Tira said angrily. "You can't abandon your people, royalty is more than just a crown. You have a responsibility to protect them!"

X

"I have a responsibility to protect my daughter!" Marie answered hotly.

"You won't be keeping her safe by staying with her. Lilith wants us dead, our children are safer the farther they are from us. You don't think I wanted to go with my baby? You don't think it tore my heart out to send him away? I sent him with someone who can protect him because I know he'll be safer if he's not near me. Your selfishness will only endanger both her and your kingdom." Tira said coldly. Robert stepped closer to her and put a hand on her shoulder. She leaned into him slightly.

"You don't..." Marie started to retort. She stopped abruptly at the sound of someone crashing through the bushes towards them, and she held her child closer.

A man ran, limping into the clearing. He was short, with wild flame colored hair and large black glasses that were halfway down his nose. He bumped straight into Marie causing the little girl to begin crying as she was jostled in her mother's arms. He took a ragged breath running his fingers through his hair and shoving his glasses up to their proper place. His leg was bleeding from a large cut that went all down his left thigh. It looked deep, but he didn't pay it much attention.

"Watch out!" Marie snapped. Then she noticed the blood running down his leg and gasped. "What happened to your leg?"

"The Witch is on the move! I ran into one of her scouts.

She's on her way to Winter Castle."

Robert cursed under his breath and he and Tira ran out of the clearing.

"Are you certain Justin?" Garrin asked.

"Quite certain. Come on they'll need our help!" Justin replied all at once.

The two men started to leave, but then Justin turned around.

"Aren't you coming Marie?" he asked.

"No, I'm leaving Four Seasons until it's safe for my little girl." Marie said slightly guiltily. "I'll come back when it's safe," she assured him.

He just looked at her for a second longer and then turned to join the others. She watched as Justin limped off until he was out of sight. With a sigh she turned and carried her little girl out of the clearing in the opposite direction.

Chapter One

Ian sat on his bed in the hotel. The window was open and the air conditioning was on full blast, ruffling his already messy white-blond hair. The only thing about this that was unusual was that, outside, there was at least a foot of snow on the ground. He was, however wearing a large blue cloak and a scarf. The door to his room opened and a plump old lady in a fluffy white dress entered.

"Oh my goodness!" she shrieked. "What are you trying to do, catch pneumonia?"

Shoot!

"Umm no."

"What were you trying to do then?" she asked him.

"Nothing..." he said, looking guilty.

I am such a horrible liar. I hate lying.

"Hmph," the old lady snorted.

She bustled over and closed the window. The heater was turned on and the scarf confiscated. Then she turned to look at him.

"Now what were you really trying to do?" she asked him in a no nonsense voice.

"Nothing Nanna, really!" Ian said in what he hoped was a really convincing voice.

Not to his surprise, Nanna snorted again.

"Well, I just wanted to let you know that I'm going down to check the mail. I'll be back up in a couple of minutes. Don't do anything ridiculous while I'm gone."

Ian nodded. He waited till her back was turned to sigh and roll his eyes slightly.

Nanna left the room, muttering about irresponsible teenagers as she left. Actually Ian knew exactly what he was doing, leaving the window open; he did it a lot. He didn't like lying but for some reason he didn't want to explain why he liked feeling cold. It wasn't that he couldn't feel the cold, although he suspected that it didn't affect him like other people since other people didn't open their windows in the middle of winter. He just really liked it.

The reason Ian did this so often was to try and make it feel like home. He had been three years old when he had come to this place. Exactly twelve years had passed since then and he didn't remember much about his old home. All he remembered was that it was always cold there. He felt more connected to his past that way. He would sit and think and wonder about the home and maybe family he had left behind. He didn't know why he had been sent here at all but no matter how many times he asked, Nanna would never tell him anything. Even when they had to move very suddenly because of some sort of accident or another. Nanna seemed to think someone was trying to kill him, but Ian thought she was just a bit paranoid. Still, apparently he did attract danger since he had to admit that the amount of near misses he had wasn't really normal. When he was eight someone had tried to kidnap him from school and had ended up frozen on the playground. That was the last time he had gone to school which was fine by Ian. Other kids always made fun of him because of his pale skin and extremely light, practically white, hair anyways. When he was nine someone had almost backed into him in a parking lot. The car had stopped suddenly and it had been discovered later that the motor had frozen over. That was when Nanna had really started to get paranoid. After last year's episode of the brick nearly flattening his head he wasn't allowed out of the hotel on his own. It was a bit embarrassing to be escorted everywhere by a paranoid elderly woman. Especially because Nanna had a tendency to almost skewer people on the end of her umbrella if they attempted to talk to Ian. The only place she ever left him alone out in public was the library, and even that was only for a few minutes while she found her own books to read.

Actually, that's probably because nothing has ever happened to me in the library before.

Consequently he didn't really spend much time outside the hotel. Actually, he hadn't really wanted to lately. A week ago Ian had discovered how to freeze things. He had known he could freeze things, but it had only ever happened on accident. He had never been able to figure out how to do it intentionally before. Now, all his spare time, which was a lot, was devoted to practicing this newfound talent. He hoped if he froze something in front of Nanna then she would at least have to explain that.

Chances are that it won't work anyways, after all she didn't explain a thing when I froze a man's shoes to the playground. I wonder if I finally figured out how to work it because of this unusual winter. Winter isn't supposed to last till April. I wonder if something is wrong. Weather magic is really hard to control, especially for long periods of time, so it would have to be someone really powerful.

Suddenly a loud crashing noise interrupted his thoughts. Ian jumped and turned toward the noise. Standing in front of his now broken window was a girl at least five years older than himself, with long black hair and matching cold black eyes. She stood there staring at him with a satisfied smirk playing on her lips. She seemed to radiate an almost tangible aura of power.

She just jumped through my window. There's glass everywhere and she's not even cut! Who is she and what is she doing in my room? Nanna is going to lock me in the hotel vault after this. I'm going to have to live in a vault...Focus Ian! There is a creepy person in your room. Worry about the vault later.

She just sat there staring at him with a slightly amused look, like she knew she unnerved him and it was entertaining to her. Ian was suddenly reminded of a cat after it had cornered something.

Why do I suddenly feel like I'm the mouse here? How did she even get up here? My room is on the 11th floor! What is going on? She must be some kind of sorceress. Stars! There is a sorceress in my bedroom!

He had consistently avoided both the balcony and looking out the window because he really didn't want to see how high up he was. Just knowing he was all the way up on the eleventh floor was enough.

He took a deep breath and opened his mouth ready to yell for Nanna who was in the next room over.

Shoot! She went to get the mail. I wonder, could I get to the door without creepy sorceress lady noticing?

She smiled at him in a way that made him feel like a mouse again.

What are you supposed to do if a creepy sorceress breaks through your window anyways? If I can just get to the door without her noticing...Say something Ian! Anything. Just distract her.

"Who are you?" he asked quickly as he slowly backed toward the door.

"My name is Lillie." she said in a musical voice.

"Hi Lillie, what are you doing in my room?" Ian asked absently as he continued towards the door.

"I'm looking for you silly." she laughed eerily.

He stopped and looked at her in surprise.

Oh stars, she is so freaky! Why on Terramagus is she looking for me? Just my luck. I have an evil sorceress in my bedroom. I'm going to die and then Nanna is going to kill me! Although I'll already be dead so...No I am not dying today. I am getting to the door. Focus.

He began creeping backward again.

Lucky this hotel room isn't very big otherwise she'd have noticed by now. Unless she has already noticed and knows she can stop me before I get out...

Ian almost jumped when he finally felt the door knob press into his back. He casually put his hand behind his back, searching for the lock so that he could get out.

"Why are you looking for me?" Ian asked, focusing almost entirely on the lock that was jammed.

"Because you are the only one that stands between me and my crown, so I'll need to get rid of you," she said as if this were a quite obvious and normal thing to say.

"Oh, that's nice. Wait, what did you say?" Ian said as he actually registered the sentence.

Hearing someone say they are going to "get you out of the way" was not something that normally happened to people. Unfortunately it fit in just perfectly with the rest of his crazy life, right along with a paranoid guardian and falling bricks.

Why am I the only person in all of Terramagus to get locked in a hotel room with a crazy evil sorceress? What is she talking about, "in the way of her crown"?

"I'm in the way of your crown? You're going to do what to me? Wait, who are you?" Ian asked.

"Yes Ian, you're in the way of my crown so I'm going to destroy you." She said, smiling slowly.

I am going to die! Now would have been an extremely good time for Nanna to come in and check on me, not five minutes ago. Why hasn't she killed me already? I need to keep her talking so that I can get out of here.

"Why am I in the way of your crown?" Ian asked hurriedly.

As far as he knew, he was not anyone particularly important. As far as he knew didn't get him very far though. He didn't know much of anything about his past or his family, just that he remembered living somewhere cold.

She gave him a pitying look before she answered. "You're the Prince of Winter, Ian. Didn't you know? Too bad you won't live to enjoy it." Lillie said with a big smile.

Ian blinked at her in surprise.

What? No, she must be joking right? I couldn't possibly be a prince of winter. Winter isn't even a place, it's a season. No way. She's just trying to distract me so I don't call for help or get the door opened.

The strange girl smiled in obvious satisfaction at the look of confusion and shock on Ian's face.

"No more talking now little prince. I've rather enjoyed our little game, but your pitiful attempts to distract me are getting boring. You might as well step away from the door now."

She reached deliberately into her pocket just as Ian got the lock undone. He threw open the door as Lillie pulled a silver snowflake on a chain out of her pocket. She raised it in her hand and pointed at Ian.

"Say goodbye prince!" she cackled.

"Ahhh!"

He dropped down and felt whatever spell she had just used zip past his shoulder. Tucking into a clumsy roll he came up on his knees and took off running. A blast of blue light hit the wall behind where he had just been, leaving a big round hole in the wall.

Lillie's voice came floating down the hall after him. "There's nowhere to go little prince. No one here to save you now." She laughed gleefully.

Suddenly, the elevator at the end of the hall slid open with a sharp ping and Nanna stepped out. She seemed to freeze for a moment as she took in the scene before her, and then she charged down the hall, shoving Ian behind her as Lilith stalked forward lazily.

"You think you can stop me? You're old and out of practice. I'll get the prince in the end, but it would be amusing to kill you first." Lillie said. She swept her hand out and another blast of cold blue energy shot out, this time aimed at Nanna.

Ian shouted a warning, but Nanna didn't move. She raised one hand in front of herself, palm out and gestured up sharply. A thin milky white wall formed between herself and Lillie, and the incoming spell bounced off the barrier. Then she cupped her hands and a glowing white ball formed in her hands, solidifying until it looked like a large snowball of energy. She threw it at Lillie, and it landed inches away from her, exploding into a shower of white and electric blue sparks.

Nanna has magic sparking snowballs? I am never going to make her angry again! There has to be something I can do to help though...

 He pointed at Lillie's left shoe and concentrated hard. Her shoe froze to the ground as Lillie tried to dodge. She stumbled sideways and pulled her foot free but she was half a second too slow. She screamed and doubled over as another one of Nanna's snowball spells exploded into sparks on her forearm.

"Ohhhh!" she moaned.

Lillie turned towards Nanna and Ian.

"This isn't the end of this!" she vowed, still clutching her arm to her chest. "Someday I'll get rid of the little urchins, and then I'll rule Four Seasons forever!"

She spun around and disappeared into a flash of blinding blue light.

Then she was gone, leaving no trace behind except a lingering blue mist and a couple of new holes in the wall. Ian gasped and turned to look around the hallway for her but she was truly gone. He wouldn't have believed what had just happened if there hadn't been several new holes in the walls.

"Who was that girl?"

"That was the Witch Princess. Her name is Lilith and she has always wanted to rule Four Seasons Island. She will stop at nothing to ensure that her rule really will last forever."

Nanna went into her room and looked around distractedly. Ian stood in the hall in shock. He had never gotten an answer to one of his important questions like this before. Then he roused himself and walked towards her again.

"She said I was in the way. She said I was a prince!"

"That's because you are. Twelve years ago Lilith broke out of her enchanted prison. She swore vengeance upon the eight rulers of Four Seasons. Two of them were your parents. They worried that you were in danger living with them in the land of Winter so they sent you here. I came with you to keep you safe from Lilith," Nanna explained hurriedly.

"What!" Ian exclaimed angrily. "I'm the prince of the land of Winter and you never said anything! Is this some kind of joke? Why was Lilith in a prison in the first place? Where in Terramagus is Four Seasons?"

"I don't have time to answer your questions right now Ian. We need to move. I didn't realize that things were happening quite this fast."

"What?"

Not again. I was just starting to get some answers.

"Ian, I need you to listen to me. We need to go. This time will be different though. There are others that we need to go find. Go pack a bag, I'll explain everything on the way. Hurry up, Lilith could be back any minute." She thrust a bag towards Ian.

He stood there, gaping at her for a few seconds until she fixed him with a glare and shooed him off towards his room.

Stars, is this really happening? I can't believe this, I'm finally going to get some answers. She's going to finally tell me what's going on. It only took a creepy witch princess attempting to kill me apparently...

He dropped the backpack onto his bed and started rummaging around with his things.

What should I pack? Clothes. Warm or cold? Cold, duh, it's freezing outside. Cape, scarf; where did Nanna put it? Ah, here it is. Should I pack food or will Nanna? I don't have any food in my room anyways. Pocket knife. Is there room for my book? It's not very heavy. Flashlight definitely, where did I leave it? Right, Nanna borrowed it.

He picked up his backpack and walked back through the adjoining door into Nanna's room.

"Nanna, where did you put my flashlight?" he asked.

He found her in the small kitchenette. She looked up, and suddenly her gaze was riveted on something behind him. Her face went white, and he turned suddenly, expecting to see Lilith again. All he saw though was her small desk. Nanna walked over to the desk and picked up a small glass paperweight. It was a cube of clear glass that she had owned for as long as Ian could remember. Now however, Ian was startled to find that it was glowing bright red.

"Oh no." She said, sounding horrified.

She stood for a moment, looking torn. Then she turned to Ian.

"Alright, there's been a change in plans. I'm not going to be able to come with you right now." She rushed towards the closet and started digging around in it.

"What?!" Ian exclaimed.

"Ian, come here, I have something for you. You'll need it for your quest."

"You want me to go with you into your closet? What, do you have a magic portal in there?"

He knew he was acting childishly but for the moment he didn't care. He wanted answers and he was going to get them one way or another.

Nanna's voice drifted out of the closet. "Are you coming or not?"

Ian sighed and, abandoning his rebellious attitude, followed her into her closet. Inside Nana was digging around, throwing out an assortment of items behind her. Ian ducked and backed out of the closet. Forget staying in there if she was going to throw things at him! He waited safely to the side of the closet door watching the pile of objects steadily growing.

"Nanna, how much stuff do you have in your closet?" Ian asked as a sword, a book, a pen, a pillow, and a cloak were added to the mess.

"You have a sword in your closet!" he exclaimed.

"You never know what you may need." Nanna said in a slightly muffled voice from deep in the closet.

"Yes, but a sword?" Ian persisted.

Nanna ignored him and kept on digging through the mess in her closet.

How on Terramagus did that closet get so messy? We just moved to this hotel a week ago. At least now I know why she insists on having a magically expanded closet.

Finally she came out of the closet with a victorious look on her face and a large tatty bundle in her hand.

"Here it is! I was worried that I'd lost it."

Ian raised his eyebrow. In his opinion she had lost it.

"This is for you," she said handing him the old bundle.

"Thanks," Ian said sarcastically.

He stared at the old bundle.

I want answers and she gives me a tatty old bundle. Brilliant, just brilliant.

"It will help you to find the others. Now Ian, listen to me. I know that none of this makes sense, and I'm sorry. I wish I could stay and explain everything to you, but I have to go. There are others that are fighting against Lilith, and I've just received an urgent call for help from them. They know I'm protecting you, and they wouldn't call me if it weren't completely necessary. There's a letter in this bundle, it will explain some things. Start on your journey, go find the others, and then use the compass in there to find a safe house. I will either meet you there, or leave a message for you, alright? If I can't come myself, I'll send help."

The cube on the desk started to flash, the red light radiating out into the room like a small spotlight. She glanced at it worriedly. Then she stepped forward and hugged him fiercely. His head was whirling as she stepped back.

"You are a brave young man Ian. I'm very proud of you. I'll see you again soon alright? I love you." Tears welled in her eyes and she smiled at him.

He nodded, feeling a lump in his throat. "I love you too Nanna. I'll be ok."

She hesitated for a second longer, and then grabbed both her backpack and the flashing cube. A few seconds later she was gone.

Ian was completely alone, blinking rapidly, and he suddenly felt like the room was closing in on him. The silence and Nanna's absence left the room feeling oppressive and slightly ominous. Ian stood there, holding his large tattered bundle in one hand, his backpack dangling from the other, staring at the spot where Nanna had just been. He slowly sat down and set the bundle on his lap. He was actually completely alone for the first time in over a year. Nanna wasn't in the other room, or just down checking the mail, he was all on his own now. It made him jumpy and empty. He shook his head to distract himself from his own thoughts and the dread that seemed to have settled into his stomach.

Stop being such a baby, Ian.

He inspected the bundle and found that it was actually a small, old blue blanket with the corners tied together to make a sort of sack. He pulled out the knots that held the corners of the blanket together and spread the contents out on the floor in front of him. The first things that he noticed were the two letters sealed with blue wax. He picked one up and turned it over, looking for any names or labels. There was nothing. He picked up the second envelope and inspected it as well, but the results were the same: no words were written on the envelope. Looking back at the rest of the objects, he found a silver prince's crown; an inch thick circlet of metal with a snowflake pattern on it, and a round metal object that looked like a silver ball with a flat spot on one end so it could stand up. Ian picked up the silver ball and turned it around in his hands. There was a small gold button on the flat side of the ball; and as Ian rolled the ball around, he accidentally pressed lightly on it. With a pop the ball sprung open to reveal a strange compass inside. One half of the ball had a small silver quill and a small silver square in it. The other half just had a big arrow in it like a compass but instead of pointing north right now the arrow pointed straight up!

"Stars! That's weird." Ian exclaimed softly as he fingered the silver quill pen.

He then snapped it shut, set it down and picked up the circlet. A cold wind blew through the room. When he looked, however, the window was snapped shut. He told himself that it was coming from the holes in the hallway even though he knew instinctively it wasn't. Shivering slightly, Ian put the crown back on the floor and picked up one of the letters. He peeled the wax seal off and opened it up, trying to push away the feeling that he was spying. He also had a creeping suspicion that the letter contained things he really wasn't sure he wanted to know.

"Don't be ridiculous! Nanna said the letter was for you, didn't she?"

He hesitated for a moment longer and then pulled the crisp piece of paper out of the envelope, unfolded it, and started to read.

Dear Ian,

If you are reading this letter, then I had to leave you before your quest was completed. I'm sorry, but you must find help from others now. The silver ball is a compass. If you push the small button on the bottom it will pop open. You will find a quill inside it. Use the quill to write where you want to go on the small silver square. The arrow will point you in the right direction until you get there. Then it will reset itself and point up again. The next object is your crown. We can't have you running around trying to claim to be the long lost Prince of Winter without even wearing a crown! Just don't wear it unless you need to or unless you can hide it, because it will draw unwanted attention and danger. Now about your quest: you need to take back your parents' kingdom; because, unfortunately, it is now in the clutches of Lilith the Witch Princess. Also, before you start that part of your quest, you'll need to find each of the heirs of the three other lands of seasons. I have searched long and hard, and I finally figured out how to get the compass to take you to them. Just type in one of the words that you will find in the other envelope and it will lead you to one of them. You need to stop Lilith not only in your kingdom, but also in all the others; so you'll need the other heirs' help. Good luck Ian! Love, Nana.

What kind of joke is this? Nanna is sending me on a dangerous quest? Yesterday she wouldn't even let me go down the street. This is crazy. She thinks that I can just take back the kingdom-- that I didn't even know I had till today-- from a crazy witch princess who wants to kill me. How does that seem like a good idea? I'm only 15!

Ian snorted and opened up the other envelope and found a slip of paper with three words written on it. He noticed that they were all color words, one was red another was green and the last was yellow. He pulled out the silver ball and rather awkwardly wrote the word yellow on the square using the tiny silver quill. The arrow whizzed around in a circle for a minute before coming to rest in the direction of the doorway. He stared out the door.

So. I have a crazy quest now. Do I go on it? What else am I supposed to do? That witch princess will probably come after me again. I could try to hide. Really, though, I don't want to hide for the rest of my life. I'm not a coward. I could at least give it a try. If it seems too dangerous I can...I don't know...go hide off in the swamps I guess. I'm as crazy as Nanna. I can't believe I'm doing this.

He picked up the small silver circlet and put it on his head. It was way too small for him, and he guessed it had been his baby crown. The crown grew colder suddenly and then it stretched until it fit his head perfectly. He took it off and looked at it in surprise.

"This is so weird!"

Then he put the crown back on his head.

"I am Prince Ian of the Land of Winter!" he said pompously.

Then he started to laugh.

That sounded completely ridiculous. I'll just stick with Ian.

His face turned serious again as he studied the compass ball once more. He glanced at the letters then at the door. Then he nodded once, gathered the letters and compass together in the old blanket, tied it up again, and shoved the whole thing into his backpack. He stood up and walked over to the purse that was lying on the bedside table and picked it up. After he figured out how to open the complicated latch that held it shut, he poured the contents out on the bed. There were a total of one-hundred and seventy standard gold coins and a few strange silver coins. Ian picked one up in his hand and stared at the strange marks on it. One side had a large silver snowflake and the other had a strange symbol that looked like a sideways curly letter S. He shrugged and gathered the money up and added it to his backpack as well. He added some bread, apples, and a water bottle from the small kitchenette, and a few other items he thought he might need.

He walked out of the room, and then turned to look

back inside. It wasn't that their room here had been particularly wonderful, in fact it felt rather empty now that Nanna was gone. However, he knew that if he left his life would change forever, and he wasn't sure if that was good or not.

Everything's going to change whether I like it or not. If I leave now, then at least I'm not waiting for that crazy witch Lilith to come back and finish me off.

"That's right Ian: think those positive thoughts."

Besides, Nanna said she'd meet me. She trusts me. I can do this.

Chapter Two

He walked out of the hotel and onto the sidewalk. Then he turned to face a small building on the other side of the street. A sign with fancy gold script over the door read "Tracy's Transportation: Fastest Portals in All of Terramagus". Ian walked across the street and stepped inside. He had used portals before this when they were moving, so luckily he knew how to work them. He stepped up to one of the large empty metal hoops and put a few coins into the slot in the side. Ian watched as the magic swirled out of the machine and started to form a thin sheet of purple in the empty middle of the device. Teleportation could be a bit tricky if you weren't paying attention. Once, when he was little he had stopped repeating where he wanted to go in his mind, and he had popped out on the wrong station and gotten lost. Nanna had been so mad at him when she finally found him. After she had calmed down, Ian had

asked her how she had found him. That's when he had
found out that you didn't have to know the name of the
place, you just had to know where you wanted to end
up. Nanna had wanted to find Ian, so she had. He hoped
that it would work if he wanted to end up where the
compass was supposed to take him, but he wasn't quite
sure. He stepped into the portal and thought extremely
hard about where he wanted to be. When he stepped
out he saw that at least he had teleported. Now he just
had to find out if he had teleported to the right place. He
consulted the compass. It was pointing straight out the
door onto the street so he figured that the teleportation
had probably worked. Ian left Tracy's Transportation to
find whoever the compass was supposed to take him to.
After about 20 minutes of wandering around, he finally
stopped in front of a huge old mansion. To his dismay,
the arrow was pointing right at the gigantic front door.
This is crazy! There is no way I'm going to go knock on
their door just because this compass told me to. No
way! But Nanna said there's something I need to do,
something important... If I don't go in, what am I going
to do? Go wait for Nanna? No. But if I do go in, what
are those people going to think? They'll think I'm crazy.
How am I supposed to get this "yellow" person to come
with me anyways? No, I'm sure that someone in there
will know what I'm talking about. They might even know
more than me. It wouldn't be all that hard, I have no
idea what I'm doing.

"Well I've come this far," he told himself, and he started

forward.

He knocked on the door and waited for an answer from inside. A few moments later a tall man in a black suit opened the door. All of a sudden Ian didn't know what to say to this strange man. Nanna hadn't remembered to leave him any names, or tell him what he should say to these people.

I knew this was a bad idea!

"How may I help you?" the man said in a stuffy, bored tone.

Shoot! Uhh...

"My Grandmother, Marian Adair sent me. She said, umm, that I was supposed to find someone who, umm, goes by the name of yellow..." He trailed off, shifting from foot to foot a bit nervously.

I sound like I'm six. Great.

"Mmm, are you expected?"

"I don't know. I don't think so...but, maybe?" Ian said, internally cringing at himself.

"Yes, I'll go tell my lady that you're here. Follow me to the parlor, please."

He led Ian into a large room filled with sofas and chairs. There were also cabinets filled with things that looked quite expensive and very fragile. There was lace everywhere, and everything was painted in pastel shades of green and pink. It looked very manicured, and very feminine. Ian felt distinctly uncomfortable in the doll house looking room. He gingerly sat down on the corner of the plainest looking chair in the room as the man left. Ian glanced around uneasily.

Stars, what was I thinking? This was such a dumb idea! I'm going to make history as the most ridiculous prince Winter has ever had. Knocking on strangers' doors. Brilliant Ian just brilliant...

"Maybe I should just forget Four Seasons and go back home," Ian muttered to himself.

At that exact moment a tall blond woman came into the room. She looked startled for some reason and Ian hoped that she hadn't heard what he had just said. He fiddled with the edge of his hood self-consciously. He had decided to wear his crown, since he was announcing himself as the Prince of Winter, but not to reveal it until he was a little surer of what was going on and that he had found the right house. The last thing he needed was to be reported as some lunatic invading people's homes.

I think you aren't supposed to wear hoods in other people's houses...now she probably thinks I'm rude. Too late to do anything about it now.

The woman just stood there in the doorway staring at him. Finally she shook herself slightly and came a little closer.

"Who are you?" she asked in a wary voice.

"My name is Ian."

Why do I always sound like I'm six whenever I'm nervous?

"Ian? What is your last name Ian?"

"Umm, I'm not supposed to say that to strangers." he said a little hesitantly.

I'm pretty sure you're supposed to tell her if you're in her house though! Brilliant.

"Oh, yes...of course." She raised one eyebrow slightly. "Why are you here Ian?"

"Umm, well, it sounds a bit strange, but my Grandmother gave me a...magic ball, umm, that works as a compass and it kinda lead me here."

That was so pathetic. Why did I just say that? What was I thinking?

"What is the compass for?" she asked nervously.

"Well, she said it was supposed to lead me to umm.... Well, she said it was supposed to lead me to the, umm, the heirs of the seasons, I think."

Bad idea, really bad idea! I need to stop now and just run. There is no way she is going to believe me. I can't believe I did that! What happened to the, wait a bit and figure things out a bit more before announcing things, plan?

The lady turned very pale and looked extremely frightened.

"Who is your grandmother?" she asked.

"Marian Adair." He straightened slightly, glad to have a question that he could answer without second guessing himself.

"What does she look like?" she asked suspiciously.

Well I might as well tell her everything now. Great job Ian. You have officially botched your quest.

"Well she is old and plump with curly white hair and a long nose. She has blue eyes and she's very short."

"You don't work for Lilith do you?" she asked abruptly.

"No! She tried to…"

I'm in so much trouble. I don't even know if I can trust this woman. I just met her like five minutes ago. But Nanna sent me here so that's got to count for something.

"How do I know you're not one of her spies?"

Excuse me, what did she just say? Spy for that crazy evil witch woman? No! Are you crazy?

"I wouldn't spy on anyone for Lilith! She tried to kill me earlier today." He said slightly indignantly.

"Hmm, I'll have to check and make sure." she said, and before he could move, she had pointed at him and said "Reveal!"

There was a bright flash of yellow. Ian's hood fell off, and he was radiating a faint silvery blue light. The woman's hands flew to her mouth and she gasped. Ian reached up quickly to fix his hood but then stopped. He figured it didn't make a difference either way, now that she'd already seen his crown.

Great. I've made a real mess of this. Probably should have just tried a straight forward approach. Hi, I'm Ian, Prince of Winter. I'm supposed to find someone here to help me on my quest, are you from Spring, Summer, or Autumn?

"You must be Tira and Robert's son! What are you doing here?"

"I don't know who you're talking about," Ian said in confusion.

"Are you the Prince of Winter?" she asked abruptly.

Before he could answer, she had raised her hand to point at him again. She closed her eyes and Ian could tell she was concentrating. Nothing happened as far as he could tell, but a moment later she opened her eyes and smiled in a satisfied way.

"So you are Prince Ian then."

He nodded.

I was going to tell you anyways. What was that? Was it a spell? Is she psychic? I mean she could be. A lot of people have magical talents, that's just a bit of an unusual one. And a bit creepy...can she tell what I'm thinking?

"Oh my goodness is it time for us to come home? Has Lilith been defeated then?" she asked excitedly.

He explained quickly what had happened that day and what he had to do. The woman was a surprisingly good listener, only nodding encouragingly. However, as she listened she started to look more worried and much more conflicted. When he reached the part about Tracy's Teleportation, he was interrupted by a knock on the door.

"Mom, are you okay in there?"

"Oh dear. Chloe!" She whispered, looking pale and frightened.

The door swung open revealing a girl in the doorway. Ian guessed that she was about 14 with long golden blond hair and worried green eyes. She saw Ian and smiled at him warmly.

"Hello, I'm Chloe. Who are you?

"I'm Ian."

"Hi Ian, it's nice to meet you."

"Chloe, go back up to your room. I'll just be a few more minutes." She said, casting worriedly glances between Chloe and Ian.

Ian realized that this must be the person that he was supposed to be meeting. From the look of things though the woman did not want him to meet her.

"What's going on Mom?"

"It's nothing Chloe, just a son of an old friend. He needed some help."

"Is everything ok?" Chloe asked, turning to Ian with a concerned look.

Other than the fact that I was almost killed this morning, Nanna left, and your mom doesn't seem to want to help me on my crazy quest?

For the second time that day Ian explained the day's events and tried not to sound crazy. Chloe's mother stood, looking like she hadn't quite decided whether or not she would throw him out of the house or not.

"I followed the compass and it led me here."

"Does that mean we'll be going with him, Mom?"

"No!" her mother practically screeched.

"Why not?" Chloe said, looking hurt. "I am who he's looking for, aren't I?"

"Yes dear, but it's not safe. I told you why I left Four Seasons in the first place was to protect you. I'm not going to let you go gallivanting all over the country with a fifteen year old boy and a couple of other kids, trying to stop Lilith."

"But Mom, haven't you always told me that a ruler's duty is to her kingdom? Besides, he needs my help."

Ian stood still watching the argument in silence.

Why does she want to come with me so badly anyways? If some strange person came to my house and told me we were going to go save a kingdom, I'd slam the door in their face. Is she crazy? Maybe she's desperate for an adventure. She doesn't really seem the type though. Maybe I should just do this alone. It's my kingdom anyways so why do I need their help? I should just do it by myself with no one else to worry about or slow me down.

"I can just leave now."

"What? I thought you needed my help."

Chloe looked hurt, and Ian winced inwardly.

"It's not that I don't need, I mean want, your help it's

just your mom and..."

Suddenly it felt like an electric current coursed through him. He turned quickly and saw a rope made out of light was winding around the room. It was made out of four different colored strands; red, blue, yellow, and green. The rope formed a loop around him and then Chloe. Ian could see two other shadowy figures wrapped in the rope too. It formed a kind of circle with the four of them at intervals. Ian yelped and looked at Chloe in surprise.

What is this? Is this some kind of spell? What am I supposed to do? Chloe doesn't look worried. Is this normal for her?

The light and the shadowy figures faded away a few moments later.

"What was that?" Ian asked.

"Mom? Was that a vision? Like you used to have in Spring?" Chloe sounded excited.

"Yes." Her voice sounded tight. "Your future is woven together with the three other heirs of Four Seasons. I haven't had a vision so clear since the Seer's Staff was stolen. I cannot ignore it."

"Does that mean that I can go with him?"

Her mother nodded jerkily, and all of a sudden Ian realized that she was about to start crying. Chloe rushed forward and hugged her mom, and Ian went out into the hall quickly.

I think I'll wait out here. That looked private. And like they were going to start crying.

Chapter Three

The man in the suit came back and took Ian to the library to wait, so he just curled up on a soft pastel green armchair with a book. An hour later, Chloe appeared looking slightly red-eyed. Ian chose to pretend he hadn't noticed. He put his book down and Chloe sat on a chair next to him.

"Why do you want to come?" he said trying to make his voice sound curious rather than accusing.

He remembered how hurt she sounded when she thought he didn't want her to come earlier and didn't want her to start crying again.

It must have worked because the girl didn't seem to take offense or get suspicious of his question.

"Well, my mom doesn't say so, but I can tell that she

really misses Spring. It makes her really sad to be away but she stays to keep me safe. If I go and get back her kingdom, she and I can live there together, and my mom won't be so upset anymore. Besides, you need my help."

"Oh."

Okay that is a weird reason to go on a dangerous quest. I think her mom would probably be happier if she stayed home. But whatever floats her boat I guess...

Chloe's mom came into the library. She was carrying a large pale pink backpack with small golden flowers dotted all over it. Chloe grabbed it and put it on. Then her mother handed her a golden flower about the size of her palm on a chain. Chloe looked at it in awe.

"But Mom I can't take this. It's the power charm for Spring!"

"And you're the heir of Spring. Take it, you'll need it on your quest," her mother answered with tears in her eyes.

Chloe put the chain around her neck and tucked the charm underneath the collar of her shirt. Then she turned and gave her mother a big hug. Ian turned and carefully studied the door knob in front of him. He reached over and grabbed it with one hand and turned it, letting in a rush of cold air and then stepped out into the street and watched the snow falling. The wind rushed passed making the tiny flakes dance in swirls and lines. As Ian stared at them, the flakes rearranged themselves to become a picture of four children who were standing on the edge of a ravine looking at something in front of them in terror. Ian looked closer and saw that he sort of recognized two of the kids. One of them was a girl who was small and thin with long wavy hair and familiar flower printed backpack. It must be Chloe! The other one he sort of recognized was tall with sharp-cut cheek bones, piercing eyes and extremely messy hair. Ian realized with a start that he was staring at himself, only he looked older, like he had been through a lot. Not all of it was nice, judging by the cuts and scratches that covered the four kids. He figured that the other two were the two heirs that he was supposed to find. Then the picture rapidly changed to show a large castle with a large key in front of it. The vision was startling and a little alarming but before he could make sense of it the snowflakes broke apart and fell like regular snowflakes are supposed to fall.

"Wait! Don't go I haven't figured you out yet!" Ian hollered after the vanishing snowflakes.

At that moment Chloe came out of the house.

"Figured what out?" she asked cheerfully.

Her breath came out in little puffs and she pulled her fluffy jacket around her tightly.

"Oh umm nothing, are you ready to go yet?" Ian said guiltily.

I should probably tell her. I did see her after all. Still it's not like I know what it means. I could have imagined it though, today has been pretty long and crazy. I'll wait until we find the other heirs at least. Then I'll only have to explain it once. I've never seen something like that before. I wonder if it was me or leftover magic from that spell inside. It didn't feel like I was doing anything.

"Let's go then," she said looking at him funny.

He followed her out of the gate and onto the sidewalk. Then it was time for him to pull out the compass ball. He pulled it out and explained how it worked to Chloe, who stared at it in amazement.

"That's so cool! You have a seeker ball!"

"Oh is that what it's called? Well now we need to decide what color to enter next: red or green."

"Red, definitely red."

"Why?"

"I don't know I just think we should do red next."

He studied her for a minute and then shrugged. "Okay, then...red it is."

He wrote red into the ball and then followed the needle. To his surprise instead of leading them back to Tracy's Transportation the ball led them to a really small hotel. They guessed that since it was getting late the ball figured they needed rest, so they went inside. The room they were in was small with a counter at one end. Behind the counter was a short balding man with thin wisps of brown hair and a pale complexion. He looked at them both suspiciously as they entered. His gaze turned to Ian who had pulled his hood up again to hide his unusual hair when he had come in.

"Can I help you?" he asked Ian, looking him and Chloe up and down.

"My name is Ian, this is Chloe. We're umm, on a trip and we need two rooms." He said feeling very self-conscious.

"Where are your parents?"

He was saved from answering by the sound of a large crash followed by someone stomping down the stairs. The man closed his eyes briefly, and seemed to Ian to be summoning patience. A girl stormed into the room, muttering under her breath and gesturing angrily. She marched over to the man behind the desk.

"Dad. Coach put Veronica on short stop! How am I supposed to be pitcher with her as my backup? She's not even any good. I mean sure, I don't really need the back-up, but really? She's afraid of the ball. I mean seriously! Why is she even on the team anyways? Ugh!" She stomped her foot loudly on the last word.

Her father raised one eyebrow and pointed at Ian and Chloe, standing behind her. She turned, and Ian readied himself for another explosion. However the girl grinned at him, not seeming at all angry or even apologetic about her outburst. Ian studied her for a moment. She looked about as old as him, with short messy brown hair that hung just a little lower than her jawline and had a single streak of bright red on the left side. Her storm-colored eyes glittered with fierce energy. Ian suddenly had a feeling that the compass hadn't led them here for a hotel room. He hoped that she wasn't who they were looking for, because she screamed trouble. Trouble was the last thing he wanted right now, because plenty of it was finding him already. Unfortunately for him the compass ball that Chloe was holding pointed at the girl and then reset itself. Ian sighed. It looked like he would be traveling with trouble after all.

"Hi, I'm Alexa. Either of you play softball?" The girl asked.

Ian raised one eyebrow and shook his head slowly.

That's her first question?

"Hi, Alexa. I'm Chloe. No I don't play softball, I do ballet."

Alexa didn't look terribly impressed.

"So, you two here on vacation then? What's your name anyways?" she asked Ian, attempting to peer under his hood at him.

"My name's Ian." He said, stepping back so she wasn't invading his space quite so much.

He could feel Alexa's dad staring at him, and it seemed to be a bit of a calculating gaze, like he was trying to figure Ian out. Ian shifted a bit and glanced at him out of the corner of his eyes. He saw the man pull something out of his pocket slowly. Ian caught a glimpse of red-gold metal and something that looked like the tip of a maple leaf.

Must be Autumn then. I knew we were going to get stuck with her. Better do something before he does and this whole introduction thing gets messed up again.

Ian flicked his hood off, and turned to face the man.

"We're looking for the heir to Autumn." He glanced reluctantly at Alexa before returning his gaze to the man at the counter.

Ian explained everything all over again, for the third time that day.

If I have to repeat this story one more time, I'm going to go crazy.

Chloe chimed in wherever she could, trying to help validate his unusual story.

"It's true. My mom is the Queen of Spring and she recognized him," she would say or, "Look I even have the power charm of Spring."

The man was certainly convinced that they were who they said they were, but he looked like his daughter wasn't going anywhere. The girl looked excited to go and, yet again, Ian wondered why. It's not like they were going on a fun vacation to a tropical island or anything like that. Given the choice, he would have much rather stayed home than set off with a bunch of strange kids to save a season.

"But Dad, " the girl was saying, "It will be an adventure!"

"I said no Alexandra."

"Please!"

"No! You are not leaving this hotel. An adventure may sound exciting but it's a lot more dangerous than it seems, and you're all much too young for adventures."

They sat there and argued for a long time. At one point, is seemed that Alexandra had been winning her argument, but then it became apparent that if her dad had anything to do with it she would stay there forever. He tried reasonable explanations and, when that didn't seem to dampen her enthusiasm, he gave out plenty of warnings about what would happen if she argued about it anymore. In the end Alexa was shouting and stomping again, had lost two weeks of after school sports, and was grounded for a month. She stomped off to her room in utter frustration, slamming all the doors she could on her way.

"You can stay the night, but you have to leave first thing in the morning. I may not be able to stop you both from going on this quest, but I can certainly keep my daughter from it. What Marian and Marie were thinking, I have no idea." He said with a disapproving frown.

He showed them up to their rooms which were tiny, but clean, and had a window in each.

"We'll talk more about this in the morning." He told Ian.

Ian and Chloe stood in the hall for a few minutes feeling dejected. Didn't they need all the heirs of the seasons for their quest?

"Maybe it can work with only three." Chloe said hopefully

"Maybe." Ian said.

He went into his room and gazed out his window and thought about his snowflake vision earlier that afternoon.

The quest is supposed to have four. What would happen if we could only get three or even two? If we couldn't get Alexa would we even be able to get the fourth person to come with us?

He lay down on the bed and stared at the ceiling, unable to sleep. It had been a long stressful day for Ian and the next one wasn't promising to be better. Anxious thoughts chased around his brain until he finally fell asleep. Early the next morning Alexa's dad got them up and moving. It was six o'clock in the morning, and neither Ian nor Chloe felt like getting up yet, but they did. As the two of them ate a hurried breakfast, the man flew around them urging them to hurry. When they finally got out of the hotel he stood in the doorway looking at them for a moment. He looked like he was seeing something or someone else for a moment. Then he focused on them again.

"You should both go home. Wait till you're older. I don't know what you think you'll accomplish, but this is dangerous. Lilith isn't someone you should be messing with. It never ends well."

He shut the door, and they heard it lock on the other side. They trooped dejectedly over to a bench where they both sat silently. Ian grabbed the compass out and scribbled the word green on it and they both watched dismally as the compass got ready and then pointed down the street.

"Well let's go then."

They set off down the street. Suddenly there was a loud thump behind them and they both turned. On the sidewalk, there was now a large mattress just lying there. A second later a small figure jumped out of a second story window and landed on the mattress. The figure got up and ran down the street towards them. They both guessed who it was before they had even seen her up close. It was obviously Alexandra.

"Alexandra! That was an awful thing to do! Your poor father will be so worried about you when he finds you gone." Chloe exclaimed.

I cannot believe that someone would so blatantly disobey rules like that. Also the way she did it is just crazy! Who jumps out of a second story window, with a good chance of serious injury, to try and join a quest to practically certain death? How weird can you get?

"Did you get hurt when you jumped out of the window Alexandra?" Chloe continued.

"Nah, I do it all the time. And stop with the Alexandra thing. I feel like I'm in trouble. Just call me Alexa."

"You are in trouble! Think about your poor father." Chloe said, looking shocked.

"I left him a note."

Ian sighed, feeling very conflicted about this rather determined girl standing in front of him. She was a little too quick to bend or even break the rules for his tastes. Still, she was the heir of Autumn, so they only had one more person to find. Ian turned his attention from his thoughts to his two traveling companions. Chloe was still reprimanding Alexa, who looked like Chloe could be talking about unicorns for all she cared. In other words Alexa was paying more attention to Ian than to Chloe lecturing on apologies. She was staring unabashed at his pale skin and the white blond hair that barely showed under the edge of his hood. Pulling his hood down farther, he glared at her. She didn't seem to care. He sighed, thinking how long of a trip this was bound to be, and started walking down the street, following the directions of the magic silver ball in his hand.

"Are you two coming or would you prefer to stand around talking all day?" Ian asked over his shoulder.

Chloe turned and saw him walking away. Both girls ran to catch up with him.

"Where are we going?" Alexa asked.

"To go find the heir of Summer." Chloe explained.

Apparently Chloe had forgotten for the moment that Alexa should be back there apologizing to her father and not here on the adventure with them, because she had stopped looking at her like Alexa was evil or something.

"Hey, is that a compass ball thingy? Cool, where did you get one of those? Who's this kid we're supposed to be finding anyways?" Alexa asked, trying to peek at the compass over Ian's shoulder. Ian twisted around so she wasn't crowding him, again, and sighed.

"If we knew that we wouldn't have to follow this ball, because we could just go get him." Ian explained.

This is going to be a long trip isn't it.

"How do you know it's a him, then?"

"Just guessing."

Or because there had been two girls and two boys in my snowflake vision thing. I just don't want them to think I'm a crazy maniac and have them both go home.

Sadly, Alexa didn't seem to think that he was really just guessing. She was eying him suspiciously. He stared back at her until she had to look away. It seemed to annoy her that he had stared her down. It put her in a foul mood for the rest of the time it took the ball to guide them to Tracy's Transportation. Luckily it didn't really take them long to get there. Inside, Ian led the way to a portal all the way in the back. He started to count out the right amount of money into the machine, when suddenly the bell on the door jangled. Someone else had come into the store. Handing the rest of the money in his hand to Chloe, he turned to see who it was. There was no one in sight.

"Calm down Ian. It's a big store, so they could be anywhere. Or someone could have gone out."

"Who are you talking to?" Alexa asked.

You're just jumpy. Don't be such a big baby, you'll freak the girls out.

"Only crazy people talk to themselves you know." She teased.

He ignored her and continued to look around the store. It wouldn't normally bother him that someone else was in the store; but this particular someone was nowhere to be found, and that did bother him, a lot! Suddenly he felt a cold breeze threading its way through the portal stands. He suddenly shivered, not because it was cold, but because he could feel something tingling in the air when the wind had gone. The girls had felt it too. Chloe had stopped counting in the money, and Alexa had stopped badgering him about being crazy.

"Chloe fire up the teleporter, we're getting out of here now!"

There were a few beeps, rattles, and clunks; but no magic liquid came down to form the portal they so desperately wanted. Alexa started to bang on the portal loudly with her fists. Ian stared around the shop, thinking. He paced forward a few steps warily. There was no explanation for why they suddenly felt desperate to get out of Tracy's Transportation shop, but they were all getting scared silly because of it. He felt chills creep up his spine, and he turned slightly to the left. There, standing just four portals away, was Lilith, the Witch Princess.

Chapter Four

Ian's heart started to thump loudly, and his breathing quickened. He took a step back and then another as he realized that they were stuck in the back of a shop, all alone except for the one person they were trying to defeat: the evil Witch Princess who was probably going to kill them all. The other two hadn't noticed anyone there yet, because they were so preoccupied with the transportation device. Ian backed up one more step and ran straight into Alexa. She jumped and hit Chloe into the machine, which made it start to hum softly. The magical liquid started to flow out, but it was incredibly slow. Alexa turned to Ian rubbing her back.

"Why did you do that...?" She trailed off when she saw Lilith.

Chloe turned around with a big smile on her face.

"I've got the transporter working!"

Her face changed abruptly from happy, to confused, to scared.

"Who is that?"

"Remember that witch I told you about? You know: the one that wants to kill me?"

"Oh," Chloe said in an even smaller voice, and she seemed to shrink back into herself.

"Hello Ian. It's so wonderful to see you, alive. It's the last time I'm going to see you that way, after all."

Then she seemed to notice the girls for the first time. It might have had something to do with the fact that they were both hiding behind Ian. Well, strictly speaking, Chloe, was hiding behind him and trying to keep Alexa back there with her. Alexa had suddenly jerked out of Chloe's grip and came out from behind him, causing Chloe to lose her balance and fall sideways.

"Aww did you find yourself some traveling companions? No one special I presume?"

Ian stepped forward a bit so that he was in-between Lilith and Alexa.

"Nope. No one in particular; they just wanted to go traveling so I said they could come. That's all."

He must have said it too quickly, because she stared at

him with a knowing look in her eyes.

"So, you've found yourself a couple of new friends. That's all. I see," she said thoughtfully, with an evil smile on her face. "I think I'll say hello to these two friends personally."

She walked closer to the two girls, who backed up against the solid part of the teleporter. Out of the corner of his eye, Ian saw that it was finally almost full of the oozing purple liquid. He just hoped that it would hurry up because he wanted out of here! He attempted to step back in front of the girls again, but Lilith stared at him, and he felt momentarily frozen in place. As Lilith passed him, he caught a few mumbled words. Then he felt a small magical flare go off. It seemed to surround Lilith, and as Ian stared at her, he got a strange urge to run up to her and join her side. He shook his head quickly, fighting the ridiculous urge, and looked harder at her. If he really concentrated, he could see a practically invisible aura of blue and then, deeper, a strong aura of black that the blue was hiding.

"Hello girls," she said sweetly, "my name is Lillie. What are your names?"

Both girls said their names in sort of strange voices that didn't even really sound like them. They sounded almost robotic, and their eyes had glazed over. Even though he had only known them both for a little while, Ian felt infuriated that Lilith had put them both in a kind of hypnotized trance. Briefly he wondered why the spell hadn't affected him the same way. He walked steadily forward trying to think up a plan as he went. Then, as he passed the liquid part of the portal, he got an idea.

"Why are you here with Ian?" she asked, as if she were merely curious about it.

"He came to get us, because we are the heirs of Autumn and Spring," they said at the same time, in the same weird tone of voice.

"I thought so!"

Ian had been working his way around the back of Lilith and now was on the other side of the girls. Suddenly he caught another string of murmured words from the Witch Princess. He knew it was time to act, so with a yell, he ran toward the girls. He rammed into them at full speed, knocking them sideways just in time. A spell fired off behind them. Ian grabbed both girls' arms and pulled them after him, directly into the portal, which was now all the way filled up and ready to go. In the distance Ian heard a loud shrill voice.

"You can't run forever Prince. I'll catch up to you sooner or later!"

Her voice faded away and then, within a minute, they were out of her reach. Well, at least they were out of her reach for a little while. Ian was sure they'd see her again sooner or later. He seriously hoped it was later rather than sooner. He gripped both girls arms tightly, and focused on trying to get them wherever the compass was leading them, hoping that they didn't get lost since he was so distracted. With a loud pop, they were out of the portal in another Traveling Tracy's. This one, however, was very busy and happened to be evil witch-free. Ian let out his breath and sank down onto the floor. He opened his bag and pulled out an apple. He had just realized that he was starving, and rightly so. It was now about one o'clock in the afternoon. Both the girls seemed to be coming out of their trances and were confused about where they were.

"Where are we?"

"All I remember is that we were in Tracy's Transportation and then there was this beautiful girl. She was talking to us about something. I don't remember what it was though," Chloe said as she stared around as if looking for Lilith.

"Hey! I remember now! You shoved us into the portal!"

"Yah, to save you from Lilith, who had you both under trances; and, by the way, was trying to kill us all. You're welcome!"

In reality, he was glad that they were coming out of the spell, but he had expected maybe a 'thank you' at least. Plus he had really been very terrified for a while and his heart was still beating a mile a minute. The combination of the two made him extremely crabby. Alexa looked startled.

"You did?"

"Thank you very much Ian! We really are grateful; don't be angry."

Chloe then gave Alexa a look that said 'aren't we' Alexa as clearly as if she had spoken out loud.

"Yah thanks Ian," She said, not very gratefully.

He got the feeling that Alexa thought he was exaggerating the whole death thing. He wasn't, but he didn't want to upset Chloe by starting an argument. Besides, they didn't have time for one anyways. He stood up and brushed his pants off. Then he walked over and threw his apple core into the garbage can near the door. By this time, several people's attention had been drawn to the three of them because of the raised voices and arguing. Ian thought it would be a good idea for them to get out of there before someone started to ask questions. He motioned for the girls to join him at the door. Behind them a man started toward them. He lifted his hand to wave to Ian.

"Hey kid! Wait up a minute," the man said.

Ian pretended not to hear him and quickly darted out the door. Chloe followed him outside and then came Alexa. They looked through the window in the door and saw the strange man running toward them.

"Quick, run!" Ian yelled.

He took off running, and the girls darted after him. Ian glanced over his shoulder quickly and saw at a glance that both girls were behind him. Unfortunately, the strange man was running after them as well. The immense amount of snow wasn't helping them to get away. There were some people on the street, but apparently most people were inside because of the weather. As a result all three of the kids left deep footprints in the snow that were very visible. Ian glanced behind him again, and saw that the man was gaining on the two girls who were behind him.

"Hurry up girls! He's catching up to you!" Ian yelled.

Alexa put on a burst of speed and ran up ahead. Ian got ready to follow her; but then noticed that instead of speeding up, Chloe was slowing down. She wasn't as fast as they were, and she was getting tired. Ian knew he had to do something, but he couldn't think what. Then he suddenly got an idea. Turning around, he quickly ran back to Chloe, then he turned to the strange man.

"What do you want?" he yelled.

The man stopped. "Did you say Lilith was trying to kill you?" he asked.

"Oh, that was why you were following us?" Ian said in a forced light tone that he hoped was convincing. "We were only practicing for our school play that we're in. I was having some problems with my part, so my friends decided to help me by acting it out so I'd remember what to say. You just happened to hear one of my lines. Funny! We thought you were trying to kidnap us or something," Ian said laughing brightly.

The man said that he was sorry and then turned and left. He had a confused look on his face when he started back to Tracy's Transportation. When he had gone out of ear shot, Ian let out his breath and ran to catch up with Chloe and Alexa.

"That was way too close!" Ian said when he finally found them.

"What did he want? How did you get him to leave?" Alexa asked.

"I told him we were practicing for a play."

"So you lied to him!"

"Chloe, what else was I supposed to do? Tell him the truth?"

He got a weird cramping feeling in his stomach when he thought about the lie he had just told.

"Wow that was great thinking!" Alexa said a little jealously.

It sounded like she wished she had been able to help trick the strange man. Ian wished that she had been able to do it all by herself. Then maybe he wouldn't feel so oddly guilty. They sat on a bench in a park talking. Both girls were enjoying some of the food from Ian's pack while they sat. Ian noticed that while Alexa seemed completely excited and full of energy, Chloe seemed a little upset about something. She nibbled at her bread with a worried frown on her face.

"I think this might have gone on for long enough guys," Chloe finally said.

"What's gone on for long enough?" Alexa muttered through a big mouthful of bread.

"This whole adventure."

"Why? It's just starting to get exciting!" Alexa said with a big grin.

Ian could see why Chloe might want to go home, but he couldn't believe that after all this work his quest was going to fall apart.

"That's the point Alexa. This is way too dangerous for three kids to do on their own. Maybe we should go home and let adults deal with this."

"What!? But Ian said it's our quest. Grownups would probably just mess it all up anyways. Plus we have something that grownups don't have: powers!"

Chloe snorted.

"A lot of adults have powers. And do any of us know how to use these powers? I know I can't do anything really useful with mine." She said angrily.

Now Ian was really worried. He had known Chloe only two days, but in that time, through all the crazy things they had done, she had never lost her temper. She had not even really gotten annoyed, even at Alexa, who Ian thought was the most annoying person ever.

"I can...Well, okay so I can't do anything great either! Now are you happy?"

"Girls, calm down! Look, it's getting late so we'd better go find a place to spend the night. We can solve this thing in the morning."

"Fine!"

"Alright."

He grabbed the silver ball out of his tattered pack and pushed it open. Then taking the pen, he decided to see if the ball could take them anywhere he wrote. He scribbled the words 'safe place to stay'. The ball whirred to life and pointed down a small side street.

They walked along until nearly six o'clock searching for the place that the ball was leading them to. Finally they stopped in front of an old abandoned-looking house. The front yard was covered with snow that had dead branches and an assortment of odd shaped objects sticking out of it. It would be dangerous just getting up to the house. Then there was the house itself, which was even worse. It looked like it would fall over if anyone breathed on it. The paint was peeling and the windows were in pieces. The roof was caving in at places and nonexistent in others.

"This is safe?" Alexa asked skeptically.

"Well at least we know that Lilith won't kill us in here." Ian said.

"How do we know that she won't kill us in there?" Chloe asked worriedly.

"Because the roof will beat her to it." He said with a smirk.

"Oh thanks, that makes me feel so much better!" Alexa said, rolling her eyes.

"You're welcome!" Ian said pretending that he hadn't heard the sarcasm.

Alexa glared at him in response. Then she turned back to surveying the house. Suddenly there was a creaking noise, and the front door swung back on its one hinge. All three of them jumped back. Then Alexa stepped forward. A small man came out the door and stared at them in surprise. Ian recognized him as the same man who had chased after them at Tracy's Transportation earlier. For a while they just stood there staring at each other, and then the man smiled.

"Hello children. My name is Thaddeus Frost. What brings you here talking about the Witch Princess Lilith?" he asked.

"Oh did you hear Lilith? I said Lily. Like the flower. I'm going to grow some in my garden this year." Alexa said, apparently taking a page from Ian's book.

"No, I won't be fooled that easily again."

"Fooled by what?" she asked with very convincing sincerity.

"You're good little girl, but so are my ears. I heard you talking about how my house was going to finish you off before Lilith could get around to it."

Ian's heart was racing again, for about the fifth time that day. He was sure that it had to be bad for you to be this scared this often. He knew he had to do something, but he couldn't think of anything. Then it hit him. Well, actually, an icy breeze hit him, but it gave him an idea. He walked straight up to the man and stared intently at him. All he had to do was get a little closer so he was in range, and then he would hopefully be staring at a man incased in ice. His focus wandered for a moment when he started wondering what it felt like to be frozen. Then he snapped back to the real world in a second when he saw that the man was now coming towards him and riffling in his pocket for something. He took it out and pointed what Ian assumed was a weapon. He took a deep breath and pointed his finger at the man.

"Freeze!" Ian yelled, like he was a magic enforcer officer.

A streak of cold blue light flew from his finger and went for the strange man who pulled up the thing in his hands and muttered something. Ian watched in horror as the bolt of magic rebounded off of an invisible barrier surrounding the man. A split second later he was engulfed by a blinding blue light. He suddenly felt very cold and had a sudden thought that this was what it felt like to be frozen. Then his vision went black.

Chapter Five

an woke up feeling freezing cold. He wondered fuzzily if he had fallen asleep with his window open again. Normally Nanna would come in and shut it by morning. He opened his eyes a tiny bit to see if there was snow on top of him or something. It felt like it. His eyes flew open and he realized that he wasn't in his room at all. The room around him was blurry and out of focus, but he knew it wasn't his hotel room. His room hadn't been this big or had a fire in it. Then he saw a couple of moving blurs. They were standing a little off to the side of him and talking...sort of. He assumed that they were talking, but he couldn't understand what they were saying. He wondered briefly if he was dreaming and would soon wake up and find that he had left the window open and the cold was making him have strange dreams. However, the more he looked around the room, the clearer it became. Then suddenly the voices he had been hearing made sense. It was sort of like listening to a conversation that was going on at one end of a really long empty tunnel when you're on the opposite end of the tunnel.

"Is he going to be alright?" one worried voice asked.

"I don't know. Oh look I think he's waking up, I'll go get Mr. Frost." another one said.

"Ian? Ian are you okay?" the first voice asked.

The voices sounded strangely familiar to Ian, and he struggled to remember who they belonged to. Then the first voice called his name again, and when she did he suddenly thought the name Chloe. Ian sat there for a moment trying to think who Chloe was and why she was so upset about him when it hit him all at once. Lilith, the quest to find the heirs of seasons, meeting up with Chloe and Alexa, the portal and the man who came after them and finally the strange house and even stranger man. But how did he get so cold? He couldn't remember that part. He just remembered trying to freeze the stranger and then waking up here, now. He sat up and rubbed his arms, trying to warm them up. He felt extremely cold for some reason.

"Ian, you're okay!" Chloe exclaimed.

"Where are we?"

Now that the room wasn't fuzzy, he could see that

he was sitting in a large tub in front of a fireplace in someone's living room. The living room was painted a warm red color that made the room seem like it was a giant oven. Ian wished that he was in a giant oven! He was still so cold. Ian tried to move closer to the fireplace and discovered that, when he got up, he got extremely light-headed. He sank clumsily back into the tub with a thump and put his hand on his head.

"Ohh."

"Are you okay?"

"Yah I think so. I think I just got up too fast. Where are we? What happened? What's going on? And why am I inside a giant tub?"

"We're in Thaddeus Frost's house. There's nothing that you need to worry about right now. Why don't you just lay back down and rest for a little while, Ian."

Ian lay back down in the tub and tried to get comfortable but then realized that something Chloe had just said didn't sound right. He closed his eyes and ran through what Chloe had just said. Then he sat back up suddenly, causing him to get a sudden fierce wave of dizziness. He put his hand on edge of the tub to help support him.

"Ian, I really think that you should be lying down."

"You just said we're in Thaddeus Frost's house! He's the man who tried to kill us isn't he?" Ian asked, angry that he was being treated like he was going to fall apart.

"Look Ian, that was all just a misunderstanding. He wasn't trying to kill us. He's on our side!"

Ian looked at her in confusion for a few moments.

"Where's Alexa?" He finally asked.

"She went out to get Mr. Frost. He was getting some more hot water."

"Why do they want hot water?"

He suddenly realized that not only was he freezing cold, but he was all wet too. That explained the tub part of things at least.

"Well you remember how you tried to freeze Mr. Frost?" Chloe asked hesitantly.

"Yes."

"And you know that he pulled something out of his pocket?"

"Yes." Ian said, getting irritated.

"Well, he didn't mean to hurt you, and he felt really bad about it afterwards; so don't be mad at him. He's been helping ever so much since, and he truly does feel horrible."

"Chloe, tell me what happened!"

"Well the thing he pulled out was magic. He...he...Just remember that he really didn't mean to, Ian, he really didn't."

Just at that moment Alexa and Mr. Frost came back into the room.

"Ian! You're alright!"

"Is that water hot?"

"Yes, why?"

Ian stood up and grabbed the hot water from her. Then he dumped it over his head. It sloshed around his feet in the tub, bringing the water level up slightly.

"Excuse me may I have that one please?" he asked pointing to Mr. Frost's bucket.

"Certainly, young man," Mr. Frost said with a smile as he handed the bucket to Ian.

Ian poured it over himself again and then realized that he had almost stopped shivering and he wasn't light headed anymore. Then he balanced himself on the edge of the tub, since sitting inside what was basically a giant bathtub while talking to the others just felt wrong. He stared at the three of them.

"Now will someone please tell me what happened? Why am I so cold all of a sudden? And why does everyone think that I'm about ready to fall apart!"

"Well you see Ian, when you tried to hit me with that spell of yours, I blocked it with this." The man, Mr. Frost, paused and held up a small broken statue of a wolf. "It made your spell rebound and hit you, causing you to be frozen by your own spell. People aren't generally frozen, but when it does happen it's not a scraped knee sort of incident. Also, we had to factor in that you were hit by your own magic, which is never good for a magic user. It affects your mind, magic and body at the same time. Needless to say, we were very worried about you, and I am very sorry to have caused you so much trouble."

"That's okay. After being frozen for a while I can understand why you would want to deflect a spell that you know will freeze you. How long was I frozen anyways?"

"About five hours."

"Five hours!"

"We had to keep bringing in buckets of water to try and defrost you." Alexa said, gesturing excitedly, "Ian, how did you do that? I didn't know that you could freeze people. Why didn't you tell us?"

Ian sat there staring at the floor for a long time. He didn't want to admit that the real reason that he hadn't told them was because he didn't trust them. They had just saved his life, so that would seem really ungrateful. That didn't mean he wanted to lie to them either, so he settled for the only other option. Ignoring the second question he chose to answer the first one.

"I don't know why I can do it, I just can. I've never frozen a person before, just small objects. I guess I could only do it because I was really, umm, really concerned for our safety."

"You were scared! Admit it, Ice Boy you were scared."

"I was not scared! What did you call me?"

"Ice Boy!"

"Don't call me that, please. It makes me sound like a popsicle."

"Fine," she said and she rolled her eyes.

Ian realized that everyone seemed to have forgotten Alexa's other questions and he was eager to keep it that way.

"So where are we exactly?"

"You know that house we were in front of before?" Alexa asked.

"Yes!" Ian said, feeling like he had just been answering questions like this a few moments before.

"Well, we're in that house." Alexa finished.

"What! We can't be in that house! It was ready to fall down at any minute. That house was all old and broken down, and this room is so nice and warm and in one piece."

"It was an illusion Ian! Mr. Frost put it on the house to keep people away from it. He needed to hide from Lilith, so he put a bunch of protective spells around his house. One of them happened to be an illusion shield," Chloe said excitedly. "Now Lilith won't be able to find us."

"Well it's only temporary, but it will work to keep her off us for a little while longer at least." Mr. Frost warned.

Chloe's smile melted off her face at these words.

"But for now it's safe. I'm afraid I only have one extra room and you girls will need to share. Ian, staying on the couch by the fire may be the best way to get you dried off and keep you warm. You'll all need to be getting your rest."

He led the girls off to a room and left Ian to get comfortable on the couch. Ian lay down and closed his eyes. He tried to sleep, but he kept waking up because of nightmares about Lilith and being frozen every hour or so. It didn't help that the couch was partially wet from his clothes. Finally, the clock on the wall showed it was eight o'clock in the morning, so Ian got up. He had dried off somewhat during the night, but he was still damp. Sleeping on a wet couch didn't really help. Standing in front of the fire, he tried to get his clothes to dry before he started to get cold again. While his clothes slowly dried, he became aware that someone was watching him from the edge of the room. He whipped around with his hand outstretched, ready to fire off a freezing spell. Then he realized that it was only Mr. Frost. He sighed with relief and lowered his arm back to his side.

"I would be more careful with that freezing spell if I were you. I've heard that being frozen is rather unpleasant."

"You can say that again."

"Did you get a good night's sleep?"

"Not really. I kept waking up."

"Ah, nightmares?"

Ian shrugged noncommittally.

Mr. Frost smiled at him gently.

"How exactly were you able to freeze yourself last night, Ian?"

"I don't know. I just discovered that I could do it a few weeks ago. Before last night, I've only frozen small objects like feathers and socks. I don't really know how it works, I just know that if I really concentrate, I can sometimes freeze things. It takes a lot of energy to even freeze a sock, let alone a person. I've been wondering if I passed out from being frozen or just from using too much energy in that one spell."

"It was probably a combined effect of both."

"Yah probably." Ian agreed after a moment's thought. "Mr. Frost, if you don't mind me asking, why are you hiding from Lilith?"

"Well let's just say she's mad at me for something that I did that gets in the way of her keeping the kingdom she stole," Mr. Frost said with a strange twinkle in his eye.

"Oh."

He wondered what Mr. Frost could have done that would still get in the way of Lilith claiming the kingdom. Hadn't she already taken over Winter completely? Then it dawned on him that he didn't even know what kingdom Mr. Frost had secured, it might not even be Winter he was talking about.

Although with a name like Frost which kingdom do you think he's going to be from?

"Which kingdom did you keep her from getting?"

"The Kingdom of Winter."

"But Lilith said that the only thing in the way of that crown is..." Ian said trailing off as he realized he was talking out loud.

"Is what Ian?"

"Is, is...me."

"You?" Mr. Frost asked sounding curious rather than disbelieving.

Chapter Six

Ian was quiet for a moment before deciding that, now that he'd started, he might as well finish it and told Mr. Frost everything about the past few days. Mr. Frost looked thoughtful and then smiled.

"Well then, yes Ian, you are the only thing keeping Lilith from being secure in her place as Queen of Winter. I helped to smuggle you out of the Land of Winter on your parents' orders. It was a dark time when the prince was safer outside the kingdom than in. I got you and your grandmother out safely, but just barely. By the time I got back from the two-day trip, Lilith had taken over the palace. She heard about what I had done and tried to catch me to make me tell where I had taken you. She didn't catch me, but even if she had, I wouldn't have told her anything!"

Ian just stood there digesting this latest bit of

information. Mr. Frost had helped to save him, but when he had gotten back to Winter, it had fallen. A sudden thought hit him.

"You knew my grandmother? She said that she would leave a message for me at a safe house if she couldn't get back here. Have you heard from her at all?" Ian asked, hopefully.

Mr. Frost looked concerned. "No, I haven't heard from Marian in quite a while. I'm sorry Ian."

Ian felt dread settling in his stomach.

Why wouldn't Nanna leave a message? She said that she would meet us here, or at least leave us a message. Did something go wrong? Whatever she left to do was probably dangerous...but maybe it's just taking her longer than she thought. It's not like she's been gone all that long. Stars, has it only been three days? It feels like it's been much longer than that. Three days isn't that long. I'm sure she thought it would take me much longer to get to this point.

"It can sometimes be difficult to get messages through from Winter." Mr. Frost said reassuringly, although Ian could tell that he was still uneasy. "I can however try to answer any other questions you might have about your kingdom."

"What about my parents?"

"No one knows for certain. Everyone assumes that she killed them, but I don't believe that."

A strange feeling fluttered in Ian's chest when he heard that. It competed oddly with the heavy feeling left by the thought that something might be wrong with Nanna. He wondered if Mr. Frost was purposely trying to distract him, if so, it was working.

"Why don't you think that Lilith killed them?"

"The Island of Four Seasons is in a rather delicate balance amongst all four of the seasons that are on it. If you upset the balance of one of the kingdoms, it upsets the whole island. Then, with the island in complete chaos Lilith could take over. One of the things that would definitely throw the whole of Winter and the Island of Four Seasons out of order is if the wrong person is on the throne of Winter. If your parents are still alive, then that would make them still the rightful rulers even though Lilith is currently on the throne. The Island of Four Seasons is being thrown off of its natural balance. It's been happening slowly however, and my guess would be that it's because of that."

Ian hadn't really thought about his parents much before. We'll he had wondered about them a bit, especially after he had figured out that he could freeze things. The last few days had been so crazy that he hadn't really stopped to think about the fact that he was a prince trying to take back his kingdom, which meant that his parents were both royalty and possibly both dead. But now that there was a hope that he could see them, it filled his thoughts. He wondered if they both missed him as much as he just realized he missed them. Then he remembered the shock on Chloe's mom's face when she saw him. How she had said that he must be Tira and Robert's. Ian wondered if that meant he looked like them. If they had the same strangely pale complexion, white-blond hair, and shocking ice-blue eyes. He wondered if he had inherited his tall, thin build from his mother or his father. He was just deciding to ask Mr. Frost about his parents when a voice broke through his thoughts.

"Good morning Ian!"

Chloe stopped and frowned at the look on his face.

"Is everything alright?"

"Huh? Oh, yah everything is just fine Chloe."

"Um, okay then."

"Good morning. How about some breakfast?" Mr. Frost asked.

"Thanks."

Chloe and Mr. Frost both walked out of the room. Ian stood for a second longer, then followed them out the door. He would need all his strength if he was going to save his parents and his kingdom.

Two days later, the three of them stood on the sidewalk, waving to Mr. Frost who was standing on the porch of the old broken-down house. Ian picked up his pack, Mr. Frost's last words of help and instruction were ringing in his ears as he walked:

"You'll need to go get the heir of Summer next. His name is Tristan. Tell his guardian that Thaddeus Frost sent you along, and he should let Tristan go without too many problems. With the other three of you together he'll see that it's time. Then you'll need to head down to the docks to get a ship to the island. No one sails out there anymore, but my boat is still docked in slot number fifteen. If you can get to it, here are the keys. Just put the keys in and dump the contents of this bag down a small chute marked dust. It should take you straight to the Island of Four Seasons. Good luck and watch for houses with a sign like this. Those are safe houses that have supporters of your cause hiding in them. They should give you help." He held up a piece of paper with a small circle on it.

The circle was divided evenly into four parts. In the center of it was a smaller undivided circle.

As much as Ian liked Mr. Frost, he was glad they were

finally setting off. He had been ready to go since that first morning talk with Mr. Frost. He was full of nervous energy, and he needed to be doing something. Now that they were out of the safe house, that compass ball realized that they wanted to go to the place that was connected to the word green and so it spun back to life. Then there was a dreadfully disappointing walk through the city in the snow. They had all had high hopes for a speedy trip to the green place, where they would hopefully find the heir of Summer quickly, and then setting off for the harbor by the end of the day. However, this walk seemed to be proving them wrong. The ball seemed to be taking them to a bunch of different places, like it couldn't make up its mind as to where it was supposed to be taking them. Ian finally realized that green wasn't the place, it was actually the person, and they were probably following him around everywhere. Ian told this to the girls, and they both moaned.

"We'll be following him around until he goes home for the night!" Alexa said annoyed.

"I'm cold," Chloe simply stated.

Ian had been feeling extremely cold himself but hadn't wanted to mention it. He hadn't wanted to bring it to the attention of the other two. Now that Chloe had started it, Alexa started complaining about her cold sore feet. Then it was about her cold nose and fingers and pretty much every other body part that was exposed to the element of cold. Ian sighed and then turned back to his compass ball. It was pointing back the way they had just come from! He sighed again and turned around and walked back toward the beginning of the street.

"Not again!" Alexa said.

"We don't even know what he looks like, Ian. We could be passing him on the street and never even know it," Chloe said in an exhausted voice.

"That's it! We just passed him! Think about the people that just passed us on the sidewalk going towards the beginning of the street. There was a tall man, but we're looking for a kid," Ian said excitedly.

"There was a mom with her two kids, but I think the kids were too young to be the Tristan we're looking for," Chloe said with a giggle, seeming to perk back up at the idea that they were so close.

"Umm, there were two girls chatting with shopping bags and a boy on a bike." Alexa said.

"There was also a boy who passed us just a few seconds ago. He had bright red curly hair, that's why I remember him! That must be him come on!" Ian yelled.

He took off in the direction the boy had gone and both girls hared after him.

"Here, give me the ball. You look for the boy you saw and lead the way. I'll check that we're still following the ball's directions," Alexa said.

Ian tossed the ball to her and continued to run. Alexa caught it with a soft exclamation at how heavy it was and kept running. Ian turned around and saw that Chloe had grabbed her hand and was leading Alexa when she wasn't watching where she was going. He turned back, glad to know that Alexa wouldn't be running into a lamp post or something. They had reached the end of the street and Ian looked both ways trying to find which way the boy had gone. He saw someone with a red hat and a girl with red hair. Then he saw the boy they were looking for, just rounding a corner.

"Come on!" Ian yelled.

"The directions match!" Alexa told him as they turned.

"Great!" Ian called back.

As they ran after him the winds picked up and blew against them. Now they were running against the wind, but they still kept going forward. A light snow started to fall again and it began to cover up all the tracks and ice on the side walk. It made it a bit harder for Ian to run without slipping. Then he saw that they had gained on the boy, who was only walking, in the street ahead of them. Ian darted forward and yelled at him through the howling wind and the steadily increasing snow.

"Tristan?" Ian yelled.

"What?" the boy hollered back.

"Are you Tristan?!?" Ian screeched.

"Yes. Why?" Tristan yelled, stepping back a few paces and looking wary.

This is getting us nowhere, Ian thought, and so he tried suggesting a better spot for a meeting. He pointed at Tristan, himself, and the two girls who were now right behind him again. Then he pointed at a brightly lit window display. The boy seemed to get the message, because after hesitating for a moment, he plowed towards the store. Ian and his two companions followed suit. Once inside they huddled near a clothes rack and started talking in hushed whispers. Tristan was rather defensive at first, and Ian could tell that he was a bit freaked out by the three of them.

"How'd you know my name?" He asked, twitching nervously.

"We're looking for the Heir of Summer, a friend told us who to look for." Chloe explained soothingly.

Ian gave a brief summary of their adventure so far, with Alexa interrupting frequently. The more he explained, the more Tristan relaxed, switching from nervous fidgeting to excited bouncing. Tristan admitted that, like Ian, he was on his own although he didn't really volunteer any information about why his guardian had to leave. His guardian had told him that he was supposed to be finding these heirs of the seasons, but his guardian obviously hadn't been as prepared as Nanna had since

Tristan had no idea where he was supposed to have started. Ian was suddenly very grateful for Nanna's occasional paranoia since at least he had known some things and had a compass to help him figure other things out. When Ian and the others finally got him convinced that they really were the other three heirs of the seasons and were not just playing a practical joke on him, or working for Lilith, Tristan happily agreed to join their quest.

"As long as there's food!" he said happily.

At that moment, all three of the others' stomachs started to grumble.

"Oh." he said looking disappointed.

"Hey Tristan, do you know where we could get some food?" Alexa asked.

"Sure thing Lexie. There's a really good burger place just a little ways away," Tristan answered.

"What did you just call me?" Alexa asked angrily.

"Lexie. Cute isn't it?" Tristan asked.

"Augh!" Alexa yelled. "Don't call me that."

"What? Lexie?" Tristan asked innocently.

"Yes that!" Alexa seethed.

"Okey dokey Lexie," Tristan said cheerfully.

Ian could see that this was not going well.

"Hey, Tristan, will you please lead the way to the burger place?" he asked quickly.

"Sure thing, Ian," Tristan said, "oh and call me Trist."

"Fine, Trist will you please take us to the burger place?" Ian rephrased.

Trist led the way out of the warm store and out into the snow again. The contrast was so sudden, it took Ian's breath away. When he caught his breath, it came out in little clouds, barely visible through all the snow. They walked down the street and then turned down another. At the end of that street was a building with a flashing hamburger sign.

"I think we've found the hamburger place," Alexa said sarcastically.

"Yep it's right at the end of this street," Trist said obliviously.

"No duh."

Alexa is going to need some time to get used to having Trist on our team. In the meantime I'm going to have to keep them from killing each other. Actually more like keep Tristan from driving Alexa crazy enough to kill him. Great, just what I needed. More responsibilities. Why did I decide I needed more people on this trip?

Ian started walking down the sidewalk and then turned to look at them.

"Come on guys, let's go get some food."

Alexa sniffed at Trist and then turned and stalked toward Ian. She looked just like a tiger and every part as dangerous as one. Then Chloe and Tristan came up, and they walked toward the hamburger restaurant. Once inside, they placed their orders and paid. Then they sat down at a corner table to wait for their food to get done.

"What's next?" Tristan asked.

"Next we have to find the dock like Mr. Frost said," Alexa said in a 'no duh' kind of voice.

"No, actually what we need to do next is...Oh good the food is done. I'll be right back."

Chloe got up and walked over to the hamburger counter. She came back a few seconds later with a tray of food. She handed everyone their hamburgers and French fries. Then she passed out drink cups.

"The soda machine is over there in the corner. You can fill up your own because I didn't know what you wanted."

Ian grabbed his cup and walked over to fill up his cup with lemon-lime soda. Then he returned, wondering the whole time about what Chloe thought they should do next.

"So what do you think we should do next Chloe?"

"I think that we should go try and find a safe house to spend the night. It's getting late and I really don't feel like camping out in a hamburger place."

"That's a good idea." Ian agreed.

They all stopped talking so that they could finish their dinner faster. Then they got up and cleared the table. Throwing a last longing glance at the comfortable benches and the warm food-smelling building, they went out to brave the weather. Although it was night there were plenty of streetlights, so they could see fine. It had stopped snowing as well, which really helped. Although Ian really wished that the weather would just make up its mind since the constant shift from snow to just freezing was creating icy patches on the sidewalk. Alexa took the small silver ball out of her backpack and handed it to Ian. He again wrote, 'a safe place to stay' on the silver ball and then gave a short laugh.

"I just hope that this trip doesn't end with me frozen!"

"An Ian-cicle!" Tristan pointed out, having been told the story of Ian being frozen by a very enthusiastic Alexa.

They all started to laugh. Then Ian pointed down a side street.

"That's the way we're supposed to go."

"Okay."

They set off down the small side street, following the arrow on the ball. It was pointing directly at a small alley off the already-tiny street. With a wary glance, Ian led the way down into the pitch-black alley. He turned around suddenly at a noise from behind him, with his hand again outstretched. This time he was determined to see what was going on before he got himself frozen. The alley had been suddenly flooded with light. He relaxed as he saw that it had only been the two girls turning on flashlights from their bags.

"I knew I forgot something!" Ian said, remembering the flashlight he had meant to find before he left.

He leaned over to the side of the alley to give Alexa room to pass him. That way the person leading had a light. He kept close behind her, though. She had already admitted to not being able to do any really useful magic, and he wasn't sure if Tristan could either. Needless to say, he was alert and ready to cast a spell at a moment's notice.

"Ian! Stop staring at me that way! It makes me feel like I'm going to explode or something." Alexa snapped.

"Sorry."

As they walked farther on, they started to realize that the alley was extremely unlikely to lead to any houses. Just as this thought was occurring to them, the alley came to an abrupt dead end. The ball still pointed straight back at the brick wall at the end of the alley.

Alexa gave the compass ball a hard shake.

"I think the dumb thing is defective."

Ian got a strange prickling feeling on the back of his neck. He turned around quickly but didn't see anyone there. Chloe noticed and shot a nervous glance behind her. Tristan noticed too, but his reaction was completely different.

"You guys are scared of shadows?"

"Weren't you listening? We've been almost killed by Lilith before. We just don't want it to happen again. If you had been there, you'd be jumping at shadows in dark alleys at night too." Alexa said, bristling at the suggestion that she was scared of anything.

"Alright, alright, I was only teasing Lexie."

Alexa glared at him and then turned back toward the wall. She was rubbing her finger lightly down the bricks. Suddenly she gasped.

"Guys look at this."

They all crowded around and looked where Alexa was pointing. There was a design engraving in the brick that she had been touching. It was concealed very well, and moss had almost covered it up but it was still there: a small circle divided into four equal parts with a smaller circle in the center.

"Soo it's a safe brick wall. Lovely! We can spend the night here. Great find Lexie! I call that trash can!"

"Ha, ha very funny Tristan. I think it means that there is a safe house on the other side of this wall. And stop calling me that!"

"I read a book once, and the girl in the story had to get through a secret door. To open it, she had to find a certain spot and push on it. Maybe this wall is the same." Chloe offered.

Immediately, Ian and Alexa started to run their hands firmly over the wall, pushing on every brick. Ian was so preoccupied that he didn't even notice when something rustled behind them. Luckily, the second time it happened, Trist noticed it.

"Um guys, I think there's something behind us."

"Oh so we can't jump at shadows but you can? It's probably nothing." Alexa said dismissively.

Ian again felt the strange unpleasant prickling feeling on his neck. He was just about to tell Trist to go look and see if anyone else was in the alley, when he heard Chloe give a sharp cry. He and Alexa whipped around to find that someone else was in the alley with them. It was a tall hooded figure all in black, including a cloak, so it was hard for Ian to tell how big the person really was, and whether or not to try and freeze them. Unfortunately, he had to decide against it, because the person all in black had grabbed Chloe and now had a knife to her neck.

"What do you want?" Ian asked, trying to stay calm and not sound scared.

The someone laughed a cold malicious laugh.

"Yes, do you want money or food or what?" Alexa asked, crossing her arms and glaring at the cloaked figure.

"Let her go." Tristan said, looking actually serious for the first time since Ian had met him.

Chloe made a series of alarmed squeaks and wriggled in her captor's grasp.

"Hold still." a low voice said warningly.

The voice had tried to sound rough, but it hadn't been able to hide something from Ian. This person wasn't all that much older than he was, and he sounded reluctant to actually do anything to Chloe.

"Who are you?" he asked, bolder now that he knew this was a kid just like himself.

"I am the great Lilith's second in command?"

He meant it to be a statement but it ended up coming out a question. His hood was knocked back by the wind and it revealed a boy with shoulder length black hair and even blacker eyes. He was probably about the same age as Ian, and about his same height which was slightly impressive since Ian was rather tall. He would have looked sinister in the dark light if Ian hadn't noticed the eyes were filled with indecision. As soon as Ian saw him his confidence raised even more. Ian wasn't even sure if he was evil or not, but he did know that he could probably deal with the boy either way.

"Who wears their hair like that anymore?" Alexa asked giving him a 'you're weird' look.

"Alexa," Ian said warningly to her.

"What? I was just asking,"

She didn't seem to be aware of the danger that they were facing right now and only seemed interested in antagonizing this strange new person.

I knew that she would get us into trouble. Why does she like picking fights so much? Honesty Alexa, can't you be quiet for just a few minutes so I can figure out how to not get Chloe killed? Please?

Just as she was getting ready to ask another question, Ian sidled over and casually stepped on her foot, hard.

"Ouch! Ian, what did you do that for?"

"Oops sorry Alexa, I didn't know your foot was there."

"Oh sure you didn't," she said, glaring daggers at him.

She caught his drift, though, and remained silent; though still not really cautious as she was glaring at the strange boy and twirling one finger around her ear. Ian stood there trying to decide how best to get Chloe away from that weirdo and then all of them permanently away from him. An idea hit him as he saw Trist creeping behind the strange boy. Trist pointed at Ian then at the strange boy and then made a talking gesture with his hand. Ian got the point and started talking to the boy.

"What's your name?"

Behind his back he was pointing at Alexa and then the wall. She saw his hands and leaned back casually against the wall as Ian talked.

Huh, maybe she does get how serious this is. She picked up my hand signal pretty fast.

Then she started slowly running her hand along it. The boy had ignored his question so Ian decided to try a different one.

"Did Lilith send you here?"

The boy hesitated for a moment and then sighed.

"Yes. I'm her assassin," he said with a slightly guilty ring in his voice.

"Oh. Hey! Ow!"Ian yelped at a sudden sharp pain in his side. "Watch what you're doing."

Alexa had just elbowed him in the ribs.

"Oops sorry."

Alexa made a face at him and sort of pointed at the other boy with her eyes. Ian turned to look at him and discovered that he was going to turn around. Trist stood directly behind him and would be discovered as soon as he turned around. Trist's eyes were huge, and he was searching around for something to hide behind that would be large enough to hide all of him. There was nothing around him that was big enough and Ian could tell that Tristan was panicking.

"Um so what are you here for exactly?" Ian asked quickly, bringing the boy's attention back to him.

"Isn't it obvious if I'm her assassin? I'm here to, well, to..." he trailed off.

"To assassinate us?" Ian said with sarcastic helpfulness.

"Yes," the boy said, rather apologetically.

Ian noticed that he was slowly loosening his grip on Chloe, though.

"How did you get your assignment from Lilith?" he said, trying to make it sound curious rather than disgusted.

The other boy obviously took it as a question, because he didn't look insulted. Instead he just looked sheepish and a bit guilty.

"Well...I actually didn't get this assignment from her directly. It's just an assassin has to find a mission and well...complete it before he can be fully trained. If he doesn't by the end of the year...well let's just say they're never seen again. Right now I'm only just out of my basic training. I've only got a few weeks left so when I overheard Lilith talking to the captain of her guard the other day..."

Ian thought that he could definitely see why he was still in the training program. If he had been a real assassin they would all be dead by now, and he wouldn't stand there talking on and on to Ian. Plus he wouldn't be telling Ian this much personal information. Ian doubted the possibility of Lilith promoting this guy anytime soon. He didn't say any of this out loud, though, and instead decided to try the first question again.

"What's your name?"

"My name's Conner. By the way, that boy behind me is about as stealthy as a moose." He said, tipping his head back slightly to gesture at Tristan behind him. "I would appreciate it if you'd come over here where I can see you. I don't really want to get hit in the back of the head." He said, addressing Trist.

Tristan froze, and Ian felt a slight chill run down his spine. Slowly Trist edged around Conner and Chloe, back over to Ian and Alexa.

I guess he does sort of know what he's doing...

"Why do you work for Lilith?" He asked, figuring that he might as well try to keep the assassin distracted. At least until he could come up with a new plan.

He noticed that Chloe had gone very still and was slowly slipping downward. Ian knew he needed to keep Conner busy, so he wouldn't notice. The knife he had been holding had actually wavered just a little bit, so it was now held further from Chloe. Ian figured it was a sign that his distraction was working.

"It's a family job. My mom and dad were palace guards before Lilith came. She spared them when she took over the castle, and so she says that the whole family is indebted to her."

"And do you like working for Lilith?" Ian asked, watching as Chloe's head moved down another painfully-slow inch.

The boy looked like he had never been asked that question before. Ian figured that he probably hadn't, if he had been working for her his whole life. It looked like he didn't quite know what to say.

Finally he said, "I don't know. It's not like I really have a choice, do I?"

Ian gave that some thought.

"Do you want to be an assassin?"

There was no pause before Conner answered.

"No! That's why I've been talking to you this whole time.

You were just so friendly...I guess you weren't really being friendly though, just trying not to be killed."

Ian felt sorry for Conner. He didn't want to be involved in this crazy conflict either, but at least he wasn't stuck on Lilith's side of the war.

"Here," Conner said letting go of Chloe and dropping the knife completely. It clattered on the ground and he glanced at it, looking almost disgusted. "I don't think I would really have been able to do it anyways. I just thought that if I did it for Lilith, then she might let me go, I don't know. Seems like an awful reason to almost kill someone. I'm really sorry. " He addressed the last part to Chloe and then turned to go.

Chapter Seven

T hen the whole alley started to get freezing cold. There was a blinding flash of purple light, then Lilith was standing in the alley in front of them. She looked just as magnificent as before, but this time she looked positively furious.

"You! I made sure you heard me talking! I wanted you to come and finish them off. I gave you a chance to prove yourself and this is how you repay me? You are a positively ungrateful wretch! You horrid boy! Now you've sat here talking to Ian and his little friends and told them all sorts of things that they never needed to know! Now I'll have to kill five people tonight, instead of four!"

Ian doubted that she was bluffing. Conner seemed to agree with him. He now bore no resemblance to the fierce, chilling, evil boy that Ian had first thought he was. Right now he just looked petrified. Conner slowly backed up a few paces until he stood right next to Chloe. Then Lilith raised her hand. Without realizing it, Ian raised his hand to match hers. Then they both let spells blast out of their fingertips. Ian's spell was a cold frosty blue, and Lilith's spell was black shot with dark purple. They collided right in front of Conner and Chloe. Both of them ducked, and Chloe lost her balance and fell down on the ground as the spells collided and spread above their heads. Then, before Ian could gather his energy for another blast, there was a black and purple spell heading straight for Chloe! She screamed and covered her head with her hands. Conner looked up when she screamed and jumped in front of Chloe, spreading his arms out to shield her. Then the spell was there, and it hit him in the shoulder with a bang. He groaned dropped to the ground, curled up in a ball holding his shoulder tightly. There was a faint hum of magic in the air, and Ian could tell Lilith was readying another spell. She narrowed her eyes and shifted her aim to Ian. He concentrated and got ready to counter it when he heard something grating behind him. He almost turned but didn't, he didn't really want to be hit with a spell from behind.

"I've got the doorway open!" Alexa exclaimed.

"It took you long enough!" Ian growled.

Trist ran over to Chloe and pulled her up and then shoved her toward Ian and Alexa. She stumbled and then ran over joining Alexa in the passage beyond. Ian stepped forward and stood in front of the moaning

Conner. He heard Tristan behind him trying to help Conner into the tunnel. Just in front of him, a lot closer than he ever wanted her to be again, was Lilith. She looked even more dangerous up close.

"Why are you protecting this sorry excuse for an assassin? He just tried to kill you, and now you're ready to die to save him. I never have understood you heroic types. I'll get him right after you anyways." She said, looking at Ian like his efforts were pathetic.

Ian set his jaw and said nothing. He was readying for the biggest spell he had ever had to do.

This is probably the worst idea I have ever had. I have to try something, though. I hope Conner and Tristan got into the tunnel.

The spell hit the unsuspecting Lilith with a huge bang. Ian saw her face, shock and anger passing over it before the ice covered her completely. She was frozen solid for a split second, and then tiny cracks started forming all over the surface. Lilith was trying to break free and his spell wasn't strong enough to stop her. He turned and ran. Trist had just gotten Conner into the tunnel when Ian slid into it and started to pull the door shut. Trist and Alexa rushed to help him, and with the three of them, it started to scrape along faster. Just as Ian heard the ice shatter with a loud crashing noise, they shut the door and heard it lock with a loud click.

"That was way too close," Alexa said breaking the

silence. Then they heard someone pounding on the brick wall from the other side.

"Great going Alexa you jinxed us!" Trist said, obviously trying to lighten the mood a bit, even though his voice was still shaky with nerves.

Ian turned around to look for Chloe. She was kneeling over Conner and looking at his shoulder.

"This isn't an ordinary kind of wound but it looks really bad. It's glowing purple and is growing. I don't know what to do about it, though."

"How are you doing Conner?" Ian asked him as he sat down next to Chloe.

Conner didn't answer for a minute because he had suddenly started to violently shiver as the purple area spread a little farther down his arm. Then he shook his head miserably.

"He's going to need help soon," Tristan said with an uncharacteristically grim face, all attempts at humor forgotten.

"Let's see if we can find the safe house. Hopefully there's someone there. If there is, they might know how to undo what Lilith just did to Conner." Ian said.

"Alright."

"But how will we move him without making it worse?"

Alexa asked.

"I don't think moving him will make it worse. It's not an ordinary wound after all. Conner do you think you can walk if we help you or do you need us to carry you?"

"I can walk."

Conner pulled himself up until he was standing, then he swayed and almost fell over. He would have landed on his face if Ian and Tristan hadn't grabbed his arms just in time. Conner groaned when Ian touched his wounded arm, so he just walked right next to him and let Conner lean on him. Tristan kept him steady on the other side, and in that fashion they slowly moved down the passage. Alexa ran ahead to move anything that would be in the way and to warn them of any possible dangers she couldn't fix. Chloe walked behind them looking out for anyone following them. They had learned their lesson when Conner had snuck up on them earlier. It began to grow light as they slowly made their way towards what they hoped would be help.

This is so weird. He just tried to kill us, and now we are trying to save him. I don't think he's dangerous though. And he did decide to leave before we made him. He was just trapped on the wrong side. I wonder how many other people in Winter are like that? It's so strange to trust these people that I've only just met. I mean I've known Tristan, like, what? Two hours tops? And I've only known the girls for a few days really. I guess you can only go through so much with people before you trust them. I don't know about Conner yet, but at least I know he's not on Lilith's side anymore. Will he join our side or just stay as far away from this battle as he can? I wouldn't blame him if he did, but it might be nice to get to know him.

Ian was actually surprised by this last mental revelation, and he glanced down at Conner. He actually would like to get to know him better. Clearly there was more to him than met the eye, since he had sacrificed himself to save Chloe. By now the purple had spread all the way down both arms and his chest. The only non-purple parts left uncovered were his head and his legs. Ian was starting to really get worried, they hadn't gone very far because of their slow pace; but his watch told him that it had been almost 15 minutes, even though this wasn't a really long alley. He was starting to hope that Alexa would come running back any second to tell them they were almost there. Unfortunately she had been held up by all the odd pieces of lumber that had been left across the path and remained a tripping hazard for Conner. Ian really wasn't sure if he and Tristan could manage to carry Conner on their own so they needed him to be able to stay on his feet. He turned his head around and glanced back at Chloe. She sensed his gaze on her, and she turned to look at him. She shrugged at his questioning stare and shook her head. There was nothing. At least that was good news. He turned back to look at the path ahead of him.

"There's a building up here," Alexa's clear but distant call came floating back to them.

"Come on back Alexa."

"K."

A minute later Alexa came sprinting back and skidding to a halt just in front of Conner. She stopped just in time to keep from hitting him and backed up, panting, to stand beside Ian.

"How long do you think it'll take to get to the building?"

"Well at the rate that spell is spreading, too long."

They both turned to look at Conner. The purple glowing patches were growing more rapidly now and Ian realized she was right.

"Let's try to pick up the pace guys."

Trist and Ian sped up and practically carried Conner along at an almost-run. Ian could tell that four of them were getting tired. Chloe was still reasonably fresh but she was a bit petite to help carry anyone. Ten rather exhausting minutes later they arrived panting at the building that Alexa had seen. Trist was already knocking on the door and yelling to the person inside.

"Hello? Is anyone here? I have a friend out here who was just hurt and we need some help. Hello?"

Alexa ran up behind her and pushed the door open.

"It's unlocked!"

"Alexa that's someone's house." Ian pointed out, too tired and worried to really care.

Ian found that he wasn't really surprised, however, since it was Alexa. What he was actually surprised about was that she wasn't already inside. Then she stepped into the house pulling Trist in with her. Ian helped Conner up the stairs and into the house. They were in a living room almost like Mr. Frost's living room except a lot larger and covered in a thin layer of dust. Ian could hear Alexa was digging around in another room. He assumed it was the kitchen, because he could hear drawers and cupboard doors being opened and then slammed shut. Chloe was missing too but just as soon as Ian and Tristan had sunk into chairs after laying Conner down on the big couch, she reappeared. She was holding a blanket in her arms, and she sat down on the floor next to Conner's couch and pulled the blanket over him. He was violently shivering even with the blanket on, and a purple glow was seeping through. He was now completely covered in dark purple light except for his head.

"Conner, do you know what this spell does?" Chloe asked gently.

Conner shakily nodded his head. Ian could have kicked himself. Why hadn't he thought to ask Conner if he knew anything? After all he had worked for Lilith, so it would make sense that he would know at least a little bit about the spell that had hit him.

"What does it do?"

Conner opened his mouth and then suddenly he went rigid, his eyes blankly staring up at the ceiling.

"Conner?"

"What's going on?" Alexa asked popping her head back into the room. "Oh."

She had just noticed the three of them clustered around Conner's couch. She slowly walked over staring at the back of the couch. Ian turned his attention back to Conner. The spell was rapidly spreading over his head until it had reached the very tips of his long black hair. Then there was an almost visible pulse of magic that surrounded Conner. The rest of them jumped back as the magic tried to pull them into the spell. They stood back far enough to evade the spell's grasp, but still close enough to see what was happening. Then there was a flash, and the lights flickered and went out. All that could be seen was Conner's glowing purple figure, and then that, too, was suddenly gone. The room was suddenly enveloped in a pitch-black cloud of nothingness. There was no sound, no light, and no visible motion. It felt like it lasted for much longer than it probably did, and the four of them stood frozen in the blackness that felt too still. It was broken by the howl, the low mourning call of a wolf. The lights flickered back on just in time for them to see a long tail whip around the edge of the doorway into the kitchen. Conner's couch was empty and the tall boy was nowhere to be seen.

Chapter Eight

"Do you think that wolf got him?" Trist asked.

"Why would there be a wolf in this old house anyways?" Alexa demanded.

Ian had another idea entirely about Conner and the wolf, but he kept his ideas to himself. It didn't even seem remotely possible, and yet the thought wouldn't go away.

"Let's take a look around." Ian suggested.

It would give him a chance the see if his idea was true. They all walked slowly and carefully over to the kitchen door. It was open, and they each poked their heads cautiously through it into the room beyond.

"I don't see anything. Where does that hallway lead to?"

"I went down it just a little way earlier. It's a hallway with lots of rooms coming off of it. That's where I got the blanket from," Chloe said.

"Well let's split up," Ian said after a tense moment in which no one said anything. "Alexa you were in here earlier so you can search this room. You'll know most of the good places that someone could use to hide. Be careful, though. Tristan, Chloe, and I will split up and start searching the rooms that come off that hallway. Okay with everyone?"

They all nodded, although Alexa looked slightly indignant that he was in charge. She started to tiptoe loudly around the kitchen opening cupboards and drawers with bangs. Ian didn't see what the use of tiptoeing would be if she opened things that noisily, but he wisely remained silent. The three of them walked into the hall being as quiet as they could. Ian figured they could have stomped down the hallway, and the wolf wouldn't have heard them what with the racket coming from behind them. He took the first room off the hallway and silently swung the door open. He guessed that this was where Chloe had gotten her blanket, because although the bed had sheets, they were twisted around a little and there was no blanket. Ian looked under the bed and in the closet, but those were really the only hiding places this room offered to a wolf.

It is probably a really bad idea to go looking for distressed wolves trapped in houses.

He sighed and kept going anyway, firmly closing the door to show that he had searched it and to keep the wolf from getting into that room. Then he walked over slowly and searched another room. Chloe seemed to be the most timid, sticking close to Tristan who was actually looking nervous himself. The two of them were searching pretty slowly, and Ian sighed to himself.

At this rate, we'll never find anything. There's only 6 rooms, it's not like it should take too long to look in them.

A few minutes later, Alexa joined them, shutting the main door into the hallway behind her. Now they were trapped in a hallway with a wolf. Again it hit Ian how potentially dangerous this situation was, but he figured they had been in so much danger lately that a wolf wasn't really very high on the list of potentially threatening things. A few moments later Ian was on his last room. He opened the door, which was already partway opened, and stepped inside. There, lying on the bed was a shaggy black wolf. Then he jumped back out and slammed the door shut behind him, letting out a startled yelp. His cry had caught the attention of the other three who came over. From inside the room they heard the wolf let out another long mournful howl accompanied by a couple of whimpers. Chloe was immediately inclined to feel sorry for the "poor little wolf" as she called it.

"You probably scared it slamming the door like that." She

told him. "Animals have sensitive hearing."

"Me, scare it? I think it scared me more!"

She's probably right though.

He looked sideways at the door.

"Now what?" Tristan asked.

"Well I don't think we can do much of anything, unless one of us can speak wolf." Ian said.

It had been meant as a joke, but Chloe looked very scared.

"What is it Chloe?" He asked.

"I can try to talk to it."

"What?" He asked, startled.

"I don't know if it'll work. So far I've only tried to talk to small furry animals like hamsters and rabbits, sometimes my cat, but I can try."

"I'll come with you so I can freeze the wolf if you have any problems."

If Chloe was going to go in there and talk to the wolf, she would need back up in case anything did go wrong.

"Thanks Ian."

Ian hesitantly reached for the door handle. Then he

opened it a crack, and the two of them slipped inside. Ian closed the door, then turned quickly to look at the wolf. It was a young wolf, not fully grown but passed the pup stage, and plenty big enough to rip them apart limb from limb.

This is a very, very bad idea. But if I'm right...Conner was hit by a spell...But that's insane. And really the only logical explanation for the sudden appearance of a wolf...

Chloe slowly walked right up to the wolf who buried its face in its paws and let out another pitiful whimper. Chloe looked at it sadly and then hesitantly reached out her hand and then, to Ian's shocked amazement, placed it on the wolf's head, right in between its ears. Then she gently stroked it and whispered softly in its ear. Ian stared at her incredulously.

"Chloe what are you doing? I thought you were just going to talk to it. Like, from way back here, where it can't bite your hand off." Ian hissed.

She ignored him and continued to pet it gently. Then she whispered to it again. It barked once and then started into a rapid string of barks and yips. Then it seemed to realize that she couldn't understand it and another howl of anguish tore through the room. She rubbed its head and spoke softly to it. Then it started to bark. It was just one bark that sounded completely the same over and over, with a long pause in between each one. Chloe's face took on an expression of concentration as she listened in rapt attention to the barking wolf. Then she smiled.

"Ian the wolf keeps saying Conner over and over again. Do you think he knows where he is?"

"Maybe."

"Do you know where Conner is?" Chloe asked.

The wolf's ears drooped and it nodded.

"Where is he?" She prompted.

The wolf howled again and looked so miserable that Ian did feel sorry for it. As long as it howled on the bed and not on top of him or Chloe he was fine with feeling sorry for it.

"Can you show us where he is?"

The wolf suddenly jumped to the floor. Ian followed it with his finger ready to cast his spell as soon as the wolf made a wrong move. The wolf reared back until it was standing on his back legs. He balanced there for a minute before toppling over onto the floor and howling. Ian and Chloe stared at in in confusion. The wolf looked up at them hopefully, and then its ears and tail drooped when it saw their expressions. It stood up and did it all over again. Ian got the feeling that the wolf was trying to tell them something important. He took a deep breath and considered the question that had been nagging him the whole time they were searching for the wolf.

"Are you, are you...Conner?"

The wolf jumped up and before he even knew what was happening it was almost on him, barking excitedly and wagging its tail.

"You are?"

The wolf nodded and Ian gave it a shove.

'"That's great! Back up! Your tail hurts!"

"So that's what the spell does? It turns you into a wolf?" Chloe asked, looking confused.

Conner the wolf shook his head, and then pointed his nose at something in the corner and then at his paw.

"Huh?"

Conner barked sharply and turned to Chloe. Then he talked to her for a couple of seconds.

"What's he saying?"

"Something about shadows and wolves."

Ian sighed.

"Great a guessing game with a wolf. Did she turn you into a wolf without a shadow?" He asked.

Conner shook his head and pointed to his shadow,

very visible, next to him. He gave Ian a look, and Ian shrugged.

"Oh. How about a wolf the color of a shadow?" He tried.

"Or a wolf with a shadow?" Chloe offered.

Conner shook his big head at both and then sat down and glared at them both.

"Did she turn you into some kind of creature that actually exists?" Ian asked.

Conner nodded, giving him another pointed look.

"Ok, sorry. You're right, stupid question. Do you have magical abilities?"

Conner thought about that one. Then he nodded.

This is so weird playing a game of charades with a big black wolf thing.

"Let's get the others to help." Chloe suggested.

Ian opened the door to find that Alexa and Tristan had raided the kitchen. They both had huge butcher-type knives in their hands, and they both jumped into the air when they saw Ian.

"Did you freeze it?" Alexa asked.

"Where's Chloe?" Trist asked over the top of her.

"You can put those down guys. Everything's fine. Come

on in, and I'll explain."

They both jumped again when they saw Conner, but relaxed when Ian explained the situation to them.

"So now we play guessing games with a not-quite wolf? That'll be loads of fun!" Alexa said sarcastically.

"I like games too Lexie! Let's start!" Trist said, bouncing lightly on his feet.

Chloe had pulled a book out of her bag and was flipping through it. Then she stopped and looked at Conner.

"Are you from the Land of Winter?"

Conner nodded slowly with his head cocked to one side quizzically.

"No, the not-quite wolf thing that you are now. Is that from the Land of Winter?"

Conner straightened up and nodded his head. Chloe started to flip through the book on her lap again.

"Here's the Winter section!"

Ian looked over her shoulder at the page. It showed a big picture of a beautiful wood covered with deep snow. Ian sighed and felt a pull to go there.

"Where's that?"

"Ian, that's in the Land of Winter. It's the Winter Woods.

Conner does your animal live in the Winter Woods?"

Conner nodded, and Chloe started slowly flipping through pages. Then she looked up at Conner while she continued flipping pages absently.

"Stop!" Alexa shouted.

She was looking over Chloe's other shoulder and had noticed something. Ian and Chloe looked down at the book, which was open to a page describing something called a Tranquility which looked like an interesting white wisplike creature.

"Go back a few pages."

Chloe slowly flipped backward, and this time they all saw it.

"A Shadow Wolf!"

"Are you a shadow wolf?"

Conner stopped playing with Tristan and nodded vigorously.

Chloe read parts of the page out loud. "Shadow wolves live deep in the Winter Woods. Hmm, oh it says that they are fierce and loyal pack animals. It also says they're very wise."

"Hear that Conner? You're very wise now. Give me advice oh great one."

Conner growled playfully and bowled Trist over onto the bed.

"Oof. Get off, Conner, get off. You're squashing me!"

Ignoring the two boys Chloe read on. "They have telepathy, speed, invisibility at night, and shadow pulse. Hey it says they can sometimes talk to humans. Conner can you talk?"

Conner shook his head sadly.

"Can you use telepathy?"

He looked thoughtful. Then he tipped his head to one side and closed his eyes.

Then Ian heard a quiet buzzing sound in his head. It slowly cleared until he could hear very quiet words.

"Can anyone hear me?" the voice asked in barely a whisper.

"Sort of. You might want to try to be a little louder next time; I can barely hear you." He answered.

Conner howled and looked quite pleased with himself, and the other three stared at Ian.

"Well what did he say?" they asked almost simultaneously.

"He just asked if anyone could hear him. That's all." Ian told them.

"Can you talk to all of us at the same time and not just one person?" Alexa asked.

Again Ian listened for the little voice to come. This time it was a little louder, but he still had to listen carefully.

"Can you all hear me?" Conner asked.

"I can." Ian answered.

"No." Chloe said.

"I can sort of hear something. No wait, that was my stomach." Trist said.

"I don't hear anything." Alexa said, looking annoyed.

"Maybe I can hear him because I'm from Winter too." Ian suggested.

He didn't want them thinking he was a show-off or anything like that. He guessed that that really was the reason. That or maybe he just knew what to listen for, because he had heard it before.

"Hmm, probably," Alexa said with a contemplative look. "Yes, definitely, that must be it."

"Or maybe it's because he's wise just like Conner is now." Trist said, chuckling to himself.

Conner cuffed Trist over the head with his huge paw.

"Hey!" Trist exclaimed, exaggeratedly rubbing his head.

"Well now that we know what he is, how are we going to undo it?" Alexa asked.

Ian stared at Conner as he heard him talking again.

"You won't be able to undo it. No one has ever figured out how to before. I'll just be stuck a Shadow Wolf forever." Then he whimpered slightly.

"Come on Conner there has to be something that we can do." Ian insisted.

"What did he say?" Trist asked.

"He said that there's no way to undo the spell that Lilith just did to him. He says he's stuck as a wolf forever." Ian told them.

"That can't be true. What one person can do with magic another person should be able to undo with magic. Except killing. That gets into dark necromancy stuff, and you don't want to mess with that. My mom told me about it," Chloe said.

"Your mom told you about dark necromancy?" Alexa asked, sounding both intrigued and revolted.

"No! The magical law of spell reversal." Chloe said, sounding slightly offended.

"Oh, sorry."

"Can you undo it?" Ian interrupted.

"No, Lilith's too powerful. You'd have to have equal or greater magic in order to undo one of her spells. None of us have equal or greater magic than Lilith."

"Ah but we have a wise Shadow Wolf and a wise prince who can understand him. Plus Chloe, who is a master animal tamer, and Lexie, who could skewer Lilith with her butcher knife. Oh, and me, the incredibly talented and funny Prince of Summer. What more could we need?" Trist said, trying to inject some humor into the conversation.

Ian rolled his eyes and turned back to Chloe.

"So if we find someone that's more powerful than Lilith, that person should be able to undo her spell on Conner?"

"In theory."

"Great now to find someone who's more powerful than the Witch Princess. If that's all we have to do, then that should be easy." Alexa rolled her eyes.

"Not helpful," Ian warned her, noticing that Conner the wolf looked seriously upset.

"I can only think of one way to become more powerful than her." Conner said telepathically to Ian, looking defeated. "You'd have to take away some of her magic. When she stole the throne of Winter, she also stole the Winter power charm. With it she has control over all the magic in the Land of Winter. If you could get the power charm, then you would have stronger magic than Lilith. Plus it would put the Island of Four Seasons back in order to have the true heir of Winter in possession of the power charm. There's almost no chance that you could get it, though. She's too strong, and we aren't even in the Land of Winter. I'll need to go there soon but there's no reason for you to all put yourselves in danger for me."

"Why will you need to go to Winter soon?" Ian asked.

"Shadow wolves like cold, and now that I'm one, I feel the tug to go back to Winter even stronger than ever."

"Hey, what are you both talking about?" Alexa interrupted.

"Great. We can go together then." Ian said, choosing to temporarily ignore Alexa.

"No! I don't want you to come, because you'll be in horrible danger if you are in Lilith's territory." Conner insisted.

"We were going to go before we met you, and now we have an even better reason to go." Ian told him firmly.

"Are you sure?" Conner asked hopefully.

"Positive."

Ian explained to the others the new urgency to get to the Land of Winter and overthrow Lilith. They all agreed that they were going to stick with Conner.

"There's no way we're leaving you alone to be a Shadow Wolf forever. Even if it does make you wise." Trist said, shoving the shadow wolf's shoulder.

"Thanks guys! Oh, tell them thank you please Ian. Why though? Why are you doing this for me when I tried to kill you before?" Conner asked, almost hesitantly, like he was reluctant to remind them.

"You're our friend now Conner. Like it or not you're stuck with us!" Trist said after Ian had explained Conner's question to the others.

Chloe wrapped her arms around Conner. "Conner, you saved me. If you hadn't jumped in front of me, I would have gotten hit by Lilith's spell. We can't leave you alone stuck as a shadow wolf forever. Thank you."

Conner bared his teeth in a way that Ian guessed would have been a smile had he not been a wolf.

"You guys are great!" Conner grinned again.

Tristan proceeded to pounce on him, and Chloe jumped back quickly to avoid being tackled as well. Meanwhile, the other three talked about possible ways to get to the Island of Four Seasons while watching Trist chase Conner. Then Tristan's stomach growled, which made Conner jump into Chloe. From there it was a domino effect, ending with a very squished Ian on the bottom of the pile, while Tristan rolled around on the floor with laughter.

"Sorry. I thought he actually growled," Conner said sheepishly as he got off the stack of kids.

"That's okay. We should probably get something to eat before that happens again though," Ian said getting up and rubbing his back.

Chapter Nine

They all went laughing into the kitchen. Alexa pulled out some of the food she had found earlier and heated it up. They had tomato soup with crackers. Tristan pulled some steak out of the freezer and offered it to Conner.

"Tell him I may be a Shadow Wolf, but I refuse to eat raw meat. I want it cooked before I'll touch it," Conner said disgustedly to Ian.

That sent Ian off into a fit of laughter about the Shadow Wolf who wouldn't eat raw meat. Eventually he calmed down enough to tell Trist and then started laughing all over again at the look Trist gave Conner. When all the food was done, including Conner's steak, they sat down and ate hungrily. They hadn't realized how hungry they were, but it was now long past dinner and they hadn't eaten since the hamburgers earlier.

"This is good," Trist said through a mouth full of crackers.

"That's disgusting, close your mouth!" Alexa said.

Trist grinned and swallowed. Alexa shot him a disgusted look as she pushed her bowl away.

"I'm full. Good thing too, because after seeing that, I don't think I could eat any more even if I were starving!" Alexa said, glaring at Tristan.

Tristan laughed out loud at this. Luckily he didn't have any food in his mouth, because it would have only made Alexa more disgusted. As it was, she was mad enough at him and that might have led to serious trouble between the two.

"Sorry Lexie, I didn't know you don't like see-food," he said.

"What? I like seafood just fine. Why do you think I don't like seafood?" she said.

"Oh so you do like see-food. Would you like some right now?" Trist asked mischeviously.

Ian couldn't see where this was going. He didn't know why the topic of conversation had suddenly turned from Tristan's lack of manners to Alexa's taste in seafood.

"What kind of seafood?" Alexa asked cautiously.

"This kind!" Trist said.

He shoved several crackers into his mouth and then opened his mouth wide.

"Ahhhh," he said through the food in his mouth. "See food!"

Then he swallowed just in time to keep himself from choking on all his food as he started to laugh. Ian had to smile as he watched Alexa chase Trist around the kitchen. Trist ran ahead of her laughing and pleading with her.

"It was only a joke Lexie! Can't you take a joke?" He laughed and almost tripped on the chair in his path.

"You're a joke! That was just disgusting you horrible boy. You better hope I don't catch you!" Alexa hollered.

She dove for his legs and fell flat on her face when she missed. She got up slowly and hit her head on Trist's foot. He was levitating a foot over the ground.

"Ouch!" she said rubbing her head.

She reached up and jerked his foot back down to earth, dragging the rest of him with it.

"Guys, whoa slow down. I think we need to all sit down and talk for a minute!" Ian said. "First off, we really need to know what everyone can do magically. I can freeze things and apparently people too, sometimes."

"We all knew that. I can make leaves turn colors," Alexa

said quickly as her face turned pink.

"That's it! You can only make leaves turn colors? That's so funny!" Trist said.

Alexa crossed her arms in front of her chest defensively. "Oh yah? And what can you do?"

"I can levitate up to one foot off the ground," Trist said through his laughter.

"Oh like that's much better," Alexa said rolling her eyes.

"Please don't fight. I'm sure we'll all get better with practice. I can talk to small fluffy creatures. Sometimes I can understand bigger animals too, but not very well," Chloe said.

"Great. Now that we have that settled, let's move on to how we're going to get to the island," Ian said quickly before a serious argument could break out between Trist and Alexa.

Those two were like baking soda and vinegar. Tristan just kept pushing Alexa until she exploded all over him and everyone else.

"Well Mr. Frost said we have to get to the docks first. Then we'd have to find his ship. Do you remember which one it is?" Chloe said.

"He didn't say. He just said that it was in slot... um fourteen or fifteen. I can't remember which," Alexa said.

"Fifteen. He said fifteen, definitely. He also gave us some keys and some dust in a bag," Ian said.

"Do you still have them Chloe? I gave them to you because your bag has pockets," Alexa said.

"Yes they're in the small pouch inside the main pocket," Chloe said. "I thought they couldn't get lost if they were inside two different pockets."

"Well do any of you know how to get to the docks?" Tristan asked.

"No, I don't even know where it is. Is it in this city or another one I wonder? Do we have enough money left over for a portal to the docks?" Alexa asked Ian.

"I don't, do any of you have anything? Mine was all spent on three portal trips and the hamburgers last night," Ian said.

"I've got some. I have about enough left for one portal ride, provided that we don't get a speed portal, or a long distance one. Those are always more expensive than the regular ones," Trist said.

"I have some that I umm, borrowed... from my dad, but I couldn't find much. He keeps most of it locked away, and I have yet to figure out the combination to the safe," Alexa said.

"Alexa!" Chloe said, shocked.

"What's new?" Ian muttered.

"What?" She said defensively. "He said it was for emergencies, and I figured that this counted as an emergency. If you look at it the right way."

"I have some money that my mom gave me before I left. That should be enough for us to take a portal and get some supplies. Have any of you been camping before?" Chloe asked.

"Yah. All you need are a tent and some marshmallows," Trist said.

"No. I've been camping a lot and you need much more than that. You need sleeping bags, a tent, food other than marshmallows, canteens, and all sorts of other things. How about you, Ian, have you been?" Alexa listed off each item on her fingers.

"No. Nanna always said camping was too dangerous," Ian said regretfully.

"Well I've only been once and I was little, so I think we should let Alexa be in charge of making a list of everything we'll need," Chloe said.

"Alright, but keep it light, Alexa, we'll have to pack everything with us. Also keep in mind the constant freezing temperatures," Ian said.

"Will do Captain," Alexa said with a mock salute.

"Ha, ha, ha very funny Alexa," Ian said sarcastically with a grin.

They talked for a little while about what things they would need and what things would be nice, but that they didn't have quite enough money for. Then Chloe broke off mid-sentence with a yawn. Ian glanced at the kitchen clock and saw that it was already ten o'clock.

"Guys, we'd better get some sleep. There's a lot to do tomorrow," Ian suggested.

"Good I'm tired," Trist said with a huge yawn.

They were all tired, so they were all eager to crawl into the soft beds and go to sleep. Each of them went into a different room and shut the door. Ian lay down in his bed and listened to the other four creak around in their rooms. He heard a brief scuffling sound from the mattresses, and then silence; all except for the occasional snore. Ian figured it was Trist, because he hadn't heard either of the girls snore before, and he would have noticed those snores. They were so loud that he figured he could have heard them across the entire house. Then he heard a different noise. There was a soft creak in the hallway, and then a scratching sound at his door. He slipped out of the bed and went to open the door. It looked like no one was there and he rubbed his eyes in confusion, trying to wake back up.

"Ian are you asleep yet?" Conner's whispered voice crept into his head.

"Where are you?" Ian answered aloud.

"I'm right here, by the door. Can't you see me?" Conner asked.

"No," Ian answered, after he had searched all around the doorway for a few minutes.

"Oh no! Now I'm going to be stuck as an invisible Shadow Wolf forever!" Conner's silent call was accompanied by a soft howl-like moan.

"Wait, that's right: you turn invisible at night now, remember the book?" Ian asked.

"Oh," Conner sighed in relief, sounding a bit abashed.

"What did you come in here for in the first place?" Ian prompted.

"Oh, to ask you how wolves are supposed to sleep. I wasn't quite sure," he said hesitantly.

This was so funny that Ian laughed silently for a while before he could answer.

"Was it something I said?" Conner asked in a slightly hurt voice.

"No Conner. I don't think it matters how you sleep because you're a wolf now so anyway you decide to sleep is the way you, the wolf, is going to sleep," Ian explained after thinking about it for a moment.

"Oh, okay," Conner said, and Ian heard him pad out of the room.

Ian laughed softly to himself as he fell asleep.

He woke the next morning to someone shaking him. He had just been having another dream that Lilith had sent another assassin after them, so what he did next was perfectly reasonable: he sat straight up in bed and threw his pillow at the person standing next to him. Then he jumped out of bed, firing off a spell as he went. It missed the person and hit the pillow instead flinging the now-frozen pillow back at the person's face.

"Oof," the person said.

Ian realized that it was Tristan as soon as he heard the 'oof'.

Oh stars I need to be more careful! What if I had hit him?

"Sorry!" Ian apologized guiltily.

Tristan caught his breath and rubbed his face vigorously and said, "I'll get you for that Ian!" He laughed and Ian relaxed a bit. Clearly Trist didn't mind the accidental almost freezing too much. Still, he would have to be more careful in the future.

Ian grinned at him and shrugged. He figured Trist wouldn't remember he was out to get him for very long. Soon he'd be busy needling Alexa.

"Hey! Why are you in my room anyways?" Ian asked.

"Oh Lexie said to tell you that it's time for breakfast, then she wants to go shopping for all our supplies," Trist answered.

"Great, shopping." Ian said grumpily.

"Yah shopping isn't my favorite either, but just think how much fun it will be with a giant wolf as our 'pet'! People are going to be freaking out big time!" Trist said with a laugh.

Ian pictured a busy camping store filled with people and them walking in with Conner. People would be screaming and running everywhere. Tristan might think that was funny, but to Ian, it was just an instant headache. He groaned.

"Alright I'll be right out," Ian told Trist as the younger boy left the room.

"See you out there," Trist said with a mischievous smile.

Ian silently told himself to remember to check for booby traps before leaving the room or entering the kitchen. Who knew to what lengths the boy would go to get back at Ian for hitting him with a frozen pillow before he forgot? The wake up hadn't been pleasant, and the rest of the day wasn't shaping up that entirely well either. The last thing he needed was to stumble into a trap from Tristan.

He joined the other four in the kitchen after successfully maneuvering the trip line that had been set up by his door. Trist jumped when he saw a perfectly dry, yawning Ian entering the kitchen.

"Rats!" Trist said.

"You'll have to try harder than that," Ian said with another muffled yawn. "Although I am impressed you managed to set something up that quickly. How'd you manage that?"

"That's my secret. Never underestimate the Prince of Pranks!" Tristan said, cackling.

Ian hadn't hung out with kids his age for a long time; in fact he never really had. He was always a bit of a loner, and people tended to treat him like a bit of an oddity due to his overall pale looks and his hovering overprotective grandmother. He hadn't realized how much fun it could be to hang out with kids his own age, even though they were arguing half the time, and one of them was temporarily a wolf and they were all under the shadow of death threats. Although he really wished that he didn't have to deal with the death threats and the whole transformed Conner problem. His mood darkened when he saw Alexa fretting over a list and writing things down on it. He glanced at it over her shoulder and saw that several items had been crossed out and then written again later. It looked like a rather chaotic version of several different shopping lists that had been shredded up and then smashed together in one big puzzle-like master list. He wondered briefly how she could read it. He felt it wisest not to ask her however, because she obviously wasn't having a great day either.

"We have at least three different shops to go to today. There is a lot for us to get and so little time to get it in," she said testily.

"I think we should try to find a portal and get to the docks by night fall." Ian added helpfully.

"Great! Now we have a deadline," Alexa muttered.

It was like she was a little black rain cloud trying to rain on everyone. Ian strongly suspected that she hadn't gotten very much sleep. She had woken him up pacing her room or running around searching for things at various times in the middle of the night, so he didn't blame her for being grumpy. He just hoped that she got a good night's sleep tonight. Otherwise he might be tempted to give her a sleeping potion and make her take a nap. Regular Alexa was like a bear, sleep deprived Alexa was like a hungry bear that you had just woken up by poking it really hard with a hot poker. Plus, he figured by the end of the day, she would be ten times worse, courtesy of Trist. He just had that effect on her. Ian wondered if he caused that effect on purpose or if it just happened. He suspected it was caused and not natural. As he thought about the mysteries that surround people in general, Ian munched on the slightly freezer burned toast with bacon that Chloe had made for breakfast. When the five of them had finished, Alexa stood quickly and pulled on her shoes.

"Let's go," she said.

"Wait! Alexa we can't leave someone's kitchen dirty like this after barging into their home! That would be so mean to make them do our dishes," Chloe admonished.

She started to clear the table and empty the dishes in to the sink.

"Ian and Tristan please make yourselves useful by washing the dishes," Chloe said sweetly.

Conner lay down and gave them his wolfish grin again.

"Wolves can't do dishes," he said happily in Ian's mind.

Ian shot him an evil look as he dried the dishes and put them away in the cupboard. Then he got a brilliant idea.

"Chloe, I bet that Conner would like you to find something for him to help with. He just looks so bored and I could swear I just heard him sigh," Ian said.

In truth, Conner had just sighed, but it was more a contented sigh then a bored sigh. Conner's smile disappeared, and now he glared at Ian. If you've ever been glared at by a wolf before, you'll know that wolves can really glare. They have the whole menacing appearance that goes with the glare, and everyone knows that they have the strength to do something about whatever they were glaring at you for. Ian felt chills rush down his spine. He decided that Conner the wolf was actually quite intimidating if he wanted to be, and to try and avoid being glared at by him in the future, if at all possible.

After the dishes were done and Conner's job of eating all the scrap bacon was done, they pulled on their shoes and got ready to leave. Ian still thought it was unfair that Conner got to eat the extra bacon while he and Trist had to do the dishes, but Chloe had said that Conner had been through enough recently without adding chores onto his plate. They walked out the door, and then Ian thought of something.

"Conner," he said, "do you mind if I put a leash on you? Otherwise people might call the M.C.C. on us."

"What's the M.C.C?" Conner asked.

"It's the Magical Creature Control," Ian explained.

"Oh. Alright, but don't tug just because your jealous about the bacon job." Conner told him with another quick glare.

"Okay," Ian said.

He pulled a length of rope out of his pack and carefully tied a large loop in the end. He fit the loop over Conner's head and made sure it didn't pull on his neck. Then he grabbed the other end and made a smaller loop for his wrist to slip through.

"Okay I'm done. Don't go too fast or you'll rip my arm off," he warned.

Conner nodded in reply and then set off. Ian had to run to keep up with him. He almost tripped, and gave the leash a sharp tug and hollered at Conner to slow down. Conner growled softly but slowed down, so that Ian could move at a more comfortable pace. The others ran up behind him. At least the sidewalks had been cleared off sometime early in the morning and it was showing no signs of snowing anytime soon. In fact if was even a bit sunny out, although still freezing cold. Still, they wouldn't have to trudge through the snow today.

"Well at least you understand the need to hurry," Alexa said with a frown at the pace they were taking. "The faster we get this done the faster we can be done and on our way and all, but the rest of us are jogging to keep up with you, Ian."

"Really? I thought I was going kind of slow, because I'm still tired," Ian said.

"Ha ha ha. Now slow down," Alexa said.

"No really, I don't know what you're talking about," Ian told her with a confused frown.

Alexa looked him up and down and must have finally

decided he really didn't know what she was talking about.

"Well just slow down okay? We don't want to get separated," Alexa finally said.

Ian slowed down until he felt they were barely moving, but the others caught up with him, slightly out of breath. He chafed at the slow pace they kept up but soon they were out on the streets and shopping. Tristan had been right: people scattered left and right when they saw Conner. This only seemed to make him more depressed however, so Ian went to sit on a sheltered bench in the park while the other three picked up their needed supplies.

Conner sighed quietly and flopped down onto the snow by the bench. He had been looking slightly depressed all morning, since Ian had put the rope leash on him before they left. It had gotten worse when people had screamed at the sight of him.

"What's wrong Conner?" Ian asked.

"Nothing," Conner said with another sigh.

"You're sure?" Ian tried again.

"Yes," he answered flatly.

"Alright then," Ian said hesitantly.

He'd wait until they met up with the others. Chloe would

know what to say to make Conner feel better. She was much better at the feelings stuff than he was anyways. He still felt bad for the older boy, but didn't know how he could help if Conner wouldn't let him, so he left it at that. The rest of the afternoon was spent trying to keep from dying of boredom in the park. By about three o'clock in the afternoon, they were both thoroughly bored enough to try playing games. They played tag and hide-and-go-seek. Ian insisted that Conner was cheating by using his nose to smell Ian out rather than searching for him. Conner deflected by saying that, if Ian wanted to find him easier then he should just follow the giant wolf tracks in the snow.

"It's not my fault that you're choosing to ignore your resources." He said, with one of his wolfish grins.

By five they were both bored and worried. They decided that if the others didn't show up by six, they would go searching for them. Luckily the other three arrived a half hour later, laden with bags.

"Alexa, how are we going to be able to carry those bags with us everywhere?" Ian asked.

"We'll have to manage, because we really do need it all," Alexa said.

"I hope you plan on carrying a lot of that yourself Lexie," Trist added.

Ian concluded that Trist did indeed aggravate Alexa on

purpose, otherwise he couldn't be nearly so good at it.

"Did you find a portal while you were out?" Ian asked.

"Yes, and we know just how to get Conner in without it being too much of a problem. Are any of you allergic to skunk?" she asked sweetly.

"Uh oh," Conner said softly.

Twenty minutes later, they stood in the alley beside the Tracy's Transportation back door, minus Alexa. She had just slipped in the store holding a vial of skunk-scented perfume she had found in a joke shop. A few seconds later, they heard a crash and all the people inside the shop ran out, holding their noses. The scent wafted out, and the three kids in the alley tied cloth over their noses to keep out the smell. Then they quickly entered the shop by the back entrance. Once inside, they found that Alexa already had the portal up and running. They jumped into it without a second thought, just as the bad smell evaporated and the more adventurous people came slowly back in. A few moments later they found themselves standing on the docks right by slot fifteen.

Chapter Ten

"**N**ow that's impressive!" Trist said with a whistle.

"What, the transportation or the boat?" Ian asked doubtfully.

"The transportation of course. I've never taken a direct portal before. There's nothing that impressive about the boat that I can see, other than the fact that it's small," Trist said. "It is impressively small though."

He was right, it was a small boat. It was painted blue with silver trim, and it wasn't a sail boat or a motor boat but seemed shaped more like a tug boat almost. Ian wasn't quite sure, since he didn't really know much about boats.

"That's what we are supposed to cross an ocean in?" Alexa asked, looking at the boat critically.

Ian doubtfully stepped on board. He realized as he ran his hand along the deck that the boat was covered in dust, but seemed to be in good condition.

"Come on, I think it's fine," Ian said, and he jumped just to make sure it was solid.

He made a loud hollow thump as he landed, but other than that, the boat didn't even make a creak. Carefully the other four got on the little boat as Ian set off to explore it. He found that there was a hold, which explained the echo when he had jumped, and promptly dropped his heavy bag down into it. Then he went over to explore the cabin. It seemed to be where the controls were. He found the slot marked dust, and poured the small bag into it. The boat gave a slight lurch, then it sped off in a pre-set direction.

"Hey! What was that! Ian what did you do?" a chorus of voices asked him from the other side of the door.

"I just started the boat, that's all," Ian said reassuringly.

"Hmph. You should have told us first. What if one of us had still been on the dock? What if we had forgotten one of the bags on the dock?" Alexa asked.

"Yes but we didn't, so there's no harm done," Chloe said.

"I didn't know it would shoot off like that, Alexa. I thought it would just start the ship or something like that. If I'd known that we'd go shooting off from the dock like that, I wouldn't have started it until I knew for sure that we were all ready to go," Ian explained, annoyed that she thought him so irresponsible.

"Hmph,"Alexa snorted disbelievingly.

The sun sank over the edge of the ocean leaving a blood red trail in the water.

"It looks so pretty," Chloe said.

Ian thought it looked more ominous than pretty, but he figured it was that 'glass half empty or half full' thing. He didn't want to rain on her pretty sunset with his more ominous outlook of things. A little while later, they were sitting on the deck eating sandwiches and looking at their camping stuff.

"I got us each a sleeping bag, except you Conner. I figured that you have thick enough fur and a sleeping bag would only overheat you. We can each carry our own stuff so that means we each get a sleeping bag to carry. They are all thermal sleeping bags that can withstand subzero temperatures, so we should be warm even without tents," Alexa said.

"Wait a moment! Without tents!" Ian said.

"Yes we didn't have enough money for supplies that we really needed plus tents, so I had to prioritize," Alexa explained.

Trist grumbled something about how they needed

marshmallows too, but they didn't get any. Ian laughed. Trist had been talking about marshmallows all morning, and now it looked like he wouldn't get any until this whole adventure was over. But when would that be? How long was this quest going to take? Only a few months or a few years? Ian seriously hoped a few months, because they didn't have enough supplies for a few years' worth of camping.

"What else did you get?" Ian asked.

"We each have a utility belt with a couple of necessities in it. Here they are. Keep track of them, because our survival could depend on you not losing what's inside them," Alexa said, handing out belts with pouches on them to each person.

Ian grabbed his and started to look in each one of the pouches to discover what would be found inside them. He discovered some rope, a compass, a mini first aid kit, a tiny sewing kit, complete with travel scissors, and a canteen hanging from a belt loop.

"Think we have enough stuff?" He joked, tucking everything back away in its proper place.

Alexa glared at him. He tied the belt around his waist and gave it an experimental tug.

"Let's put this stuff away for now and go to sleep. The boat seems to know where it's going, so I don't think we need to steer it or anything. We can deal with the rest of this stuff tomorrow," Ian suggested.

"Alright. We'll need a good night's sleep for tomorrow," Alexa agreed.

Chloe yawned to seal it. They all laughed and then pulled out their new sleeping bags. The girls took theirs into the cabin and the boys slept out on the deck. Conner seemed perfectly warm and content, except his ears, and the other two boys felt a little cold on their noses, but other than that they had a better night's sleep on that boat than they had had in days.

The next morning Ian woke up with the dawn light. It was just starting to get bright, and the sky was a rosy pink color with hints of light orange peeping through. Ian thought it looked like the sky was a giant thing of his favorite kind of sherbet. He wished it was too. He was hungry, but Conner had fallen asleep on the trap door that led to the hold. There was no way Ian would be able to move Conner, even if there were three of him. Conner was a big wolf! He settled for trying to wake him up.

"Will you please wake up Conner? You're on the trapdoor to the hold and all the food's down there," Ian pleaded.

Conner just growled and rolled over. He was now half off the trap door, but Ian still wouldn't be able to get him off, and even if he could, the risk of being trapped down there was too great. Ian might shove Conner all the way off, go down and have him roll back over the trap door so he'd be stuck. No, he really just needed to wake Conner all the way up before going into the hold for food. He tried to wake him one more time, but it didn't work. He settled down for a long wait. About three hours later, when Ian was now extremely hungry and extremely bored at the same time, the door opened to the cabin and Alexa and Chloe walked out. They joined Ian at the railing of the boat, and all stood there silently while the two girls finished waking up. Alexa broke the silence first.

"I'm hungry. Do you have any food out here?" she asked.

"No, I'm starving, but Conner's blocking the trap door down to the hold where we put all our stuff last night," Ian explained ruefully.

"Let's get him up then," Alexa said.

"I tried already," Ian explained.

"It can't hurt to try again," Alexa coaxed.

"Alright you try then," Ian said.

"Guys leave him alone. He's been through enough lately without you guys bugging him. He's probably having nightmares," Chloe said sympathetically.

That reminded Ian of his nightmares and how when he got woken up he had hit Trist with a pillow. What would a wolf do if he thought he was being attacked by his worst enemy?

"On second thought Chloe is right. We should leave him be," Ian said.

"She is? Why?" Alexa asked. "Aren't you hungry?"

"Yes, but if we wake him up, and he's startled enough to think he wasn't dreaming and he was having nightmares...think what Conner the wolf would do if he thought we were Lilith," Ian explained.

"Hmm, good point. I've got an idea to get around that though," Alexa said with a smile.

She took a deep breath and started to sing annoying little kids songs at the top of her lungs. Ian and Chloe covered their ears and shouted at her to stop, but she just kept on singing. She was purposely singing in a very loud and obnoxious voice that was loud enough to wake the dead. Sure enough, soon Tristan and Conner were stirring and muttering. Conner let out an earsplitting howl and covered his ears with his paws. Tristan moaned something about noisy neighbors and rolled back over in his sleep. Alexa started a new song about row boats or something. She added some extra volume and motioned to Ian and Chloe to sing along. Ian didn't know about Chloe, but they wouldn't catch him dead doing something as ridiculously silly as singing nursery songs at the top of his lungs on a boat, even if it was in the middle of the ocean. People would probably think he was crazy or was drunk or something. No, there was no way Alexa was getting him to help her with that. Chloe tugged on Alexa's shirt and yelled something about people needing sleep. Alexa ignored her and sang until her face turned red, and then she stopped suddenly, panting and grabbing her sides. Chloe must have decided that she wasn't that hungry, because she disappeared back into the cabin with one final plea for them to leave the sleeping boys alone. Ian fully intended to leave them alone. He still had his tool belt, and so he went into a corner to practice tying knots into his rope. He glanced up just in time to see Alexa sneak up right behind Tristan. She was grinning wickedly and holding something in her hands. As she turned it slightly Ian saw it was her canteen full of water!

"Alexa wait!" He yelled but it was too late.

Alexa turned her canteen upside down and emptied the contents all over Tristan's head. Some of it got in both his mouth and nose. He woke up spluttering.

"Help I'm drowning! The ship sank and I'm drowning!" he called out.

Alexa burst into laughter and clutched her sides. Tristan shook his head and stared around him in surprise. Then he noticed the empty canteen in Alexa's hand.

"Alexa!" He said menacingly.

"Yes," She said sweetly and innocently.

"I'll get you for that!"

Tristan stood up quickly and dove for Alexa. She laughed and ran. Ian sat there watching an almost-repeat of yesterday morning around the breakfast table. This time, however, they were running around on the deck. Ian just hoped they wouldn't trip and fall out of the boat. The circles came abruptly to an end when Trist tried to take a shortcut and tripped over the sleeping Conner. Conner woke with a start and gave a yelp as Trist landed on his tail.

"Sorry, Conner, sorry," Trist said.

Conner looked around wildly until he saw Trist. Then he snorted grumpily and lay back down with is eyes shut.

"Wait! Conner could you move over there because we need to get our supplies out of the hold, and you're on the trap door," Alexa asked quickly before Conner could go back to sleep.

Conner grunted and stood up. He came over and lay down next to Ian and sighed.

"What's wrong Conner?" Ian asked quietly.

"The only thing I'm good for is tripping over and blocking trap doors," Conner moped.

"That's not true!" Ian said.

"Than what am I good for?" Conner almost growled at Ian.

"Conner you're a good friend, and you're a hero." Ian said.

"A hero?" Conner asked skeptically.

"Yes. If you hadn't saved Chloe, she might have been turned into a wolf instead of you. You wouldn't want Chloe to be a Shadow Wolf would you?" Ian asked.

"No," Conner said. "That still doesn't mean I'm helpful though."

"Of course you are. Plus when we get to the island, we're going to need a guide and protection from wild animals. You could talk to any other Shadow Wolves we meet and get them to, you know, not eat us," Ian said helpfully.

"Hmm," Conner said thoughtfully. He fell silent but Ian could tell he was a little less upset.

Ian continued tying knots in his long rope. Then Alexa called him. He looked up at her.

"Yes?" he asked.

"Now that we're all up, let's finish going through the camping stuff," Alexa said.

"Alright, Alexa. I'll be right over," he said with a sigh.

They spent the rest of the morning going through camping things while they ate their breakfast. By the time they were finished, all their bags were stuffed to the bursting point, and Ian felt like his weighed a ton.

Alexa inspected each of their bags carefully.

"It won't be long before you'll be wishing these bags were heavier. The food makes most of the weight, and we'll be eating it all before long. Then you'll wish that the bags were this heavy again," Alexa predicted.

I doubt it. Maybe I'll wish for more food, but I doubt I'll want the bag to be heavier, especially if I'm hungry and tired. If this bag was any heavier it would weigh as much as this ship.

Alexa continued to check the bags many pockets and pouches to make sure everything was there. Ian checked the empty grocery sacks lying on the deck to make sure they had been emptied of everything inside them. All of their money had been spent on these supplies, and they were all necessary for their survival in the frigid weather of Winter. After he was sure they were all empty, they each settled down in various places on the boat to spend the rest of their afternoon. Ian went back to his corner and resumed trying to figure out how to tie all the knots. He had read a survival guide once, and it had had a bunch of diagrams and pictures of how to tie various knots. He remembered some of them from the pictures, but others he had tried on the sheets in his hotel room. That had messed up both the bed and the knots. The knots didn't want to tie into the bed sheets, so he had ended up in trouble and with a big knotted bed sheet to untie for company. Nanna had been annoyed, and told him to just ask for a rope next time he wanted to try tying things. Now that he had a rope though, he was able to tie and untie the various knots that he remembered from the handbook. Alexa was sitting in a weird position. flopped upside down over the edge of a bench bolted to the deck. She sighed and sat up.

"How long do you think it'll take to get there?" she asked with another particularly exasperated sigh.

"I have no idea. Didn't Mr. Frost say something about how long it took?" Ian answered.

"I don't remember anything about that. I thought we'd be doing things. Not sitting on a boat. I'm bored," Alexa moaned.

"Ask Chloe," Ian said testily.

Alexa sighed again and got up. Chloe was in the cabin, and Alexa disappeared into it. He heard Alexa's voice and assumed that she was asking her question. Chloe's voice was way too quiet to hear, but Ian knew she must have answered because he heard Alexa sigh loudly. Then Ian's thoughts were interrupted by a loud noise. Someone was snoring, loudly. Then there was another snore. Tristan had fallen asleep on top of Conner. Conner growled softly and tried to gently shove Trist off onto the deck. He succeeded just in time to have Tristan roll over back on top of him. Conner let out a long wolfish sigh and stared at Ian as if to say, "help me!" Ian laughed aloud and walked over to him.

"Are you having some trouble Conner?" he tried to ask seriously.

"This isn't funny. He's heavy and loud and smells funny, like garlic and dirty socks!" Conner growled.

Ian laughed.

"He does!" Conner complained.

That just made Ian laugh harder. Conner frowned with a hurt expression on his face.

Ian gave Tristan a shove while Conner rolled away from them both. Then Ian let go of Trist, and he and Conner ran to the other end of the ship. As soon as they got to the other end of the ship Tristan sat up and yawned.

"I'm hungry." He said.

Conner and Ian just sighed. Alexa came back out with Chloe behind her.

"Chloe doesn't remember anything about that either," Alexa said.

"I remember now. He said it took him two days round-trip. How long have we been on this boat so far?" Ian said.

"Too long," Alexa complained.

"Umm, almost half a day," Chloe said.

"Well then we should be there in a couple of hours," Ian told her.

"Good, because I'm getting bored," Trist sighed.

"I've been bored for a long time now!" Alexa complained loudly.

"I'm still hungry too," Tristan said, and his stomach growled to prove his point.

Alexa rolled her eyes and went over to the cabin to get the food they had put aside for lunch. A few hours later, they had dinner. By this time it was extremely foggy, and they couldn't see from one end of the tiny ship to the other. Alexa was leaning over the railing and staring out into the fog. She was obviously tired of sitting around on the boat but there was nothing they could do until they arrived at the Island of Four Seasons.

"Hey!" Alexa said.

There was a big bump as their boat hit something. Then there was a scream and a splash. Ian had fallen to the floor when the boat had shaken. He wondered what had made that splash. Then he remembered Alexa leaning over the railing and ran over to where she had stood just a few seconds ago. There was no sign of her anywhere along the railing. Then Ian heard a few splashes coming from the water below. Alexa's wet bedraggled head broke the surface, and she took a gasping breath. Then she saw Ian.

"Help!" she called, teeth chattering. Ian got ready to jump in after her when he remembered the rope in his belt. He started to retrieve it.

"Just a minute Alexa," he told her.

"Hurry up! This water is freezing," she called. "I think there's something in the water!"

Then Ian heard another splash. He looked over and saw Conner swimming through the water to Alexa. She grabbed onto his back, and he swam toward the thing that the boat had hit. The water swirled dangerously around the boat, and Ian rushed up to the front to see what was going on, with Chloe and Trist right behind him. From the front of the ship, Ian could see that they had hit some sort of rocky peninsula that jutted out of the mainland. He could barely see beyond it.

"Come on!" he said.

The boat had started to slowly retreat away from the rocks, and Ian knew they had to get off now, or they would lose their friends. Ian shouldered his pack and grabbed Alexa's pack with both hands. Now he felt like he was dragging a baby elephant. There was no way he would be able to jump with those things on. He dropped both packs, glanced at the shore that was slowly slipping out of view, and jumped. He landed firmly and quickly turned back to the boat.

"Toss me the bags now!" he yelled.

"Alright here they come," Trist replied. He threw the first bag over to Ian. It almost squished him as it thudded right on top of him.

"Oof," he grunted and pushed the bag safely in between some rocks nearby.

Then he came back just in time to grab another bag as it came flying through the fog to meet him. They safely got all the bags but one across in this manner. Then the last bag came soaring through the air. It almost didn't make it to land safely, but Ian leaned out and grabbed it with one hand. The other was firmly grasping a big pointy rock behind him. Throwing the bag towards the others he turned back to the water. The boat was too far into the fog to see but he knew it must be pretty far if this bag had almost hit the water.

"Come on and jump!" Ian called.

He heard a shout that he recognized as Chloe. Then she landed on top of him with a crunch of gravel.

"Ouch!" he yelped.

Then he heard Tristan calling from the boat.

"I don't think I'll make it all the way over!" he said.

"You have to! The only other option is too swim like Alexa did," Ian shouted back.

"I can't swim!" Trist said, his voice high-pitched and

panicky.

"Well I can, and if you fall in I'll come and save you, now hurry up and jump!" Ian said.

"I can't! I won't make it all the way there. I'll drown!" Trist panicked.

"Jump now!" Ian shouted sharply.

Ian suddenly saw him fly through the fog towards them. He wasn't quite going to make it and he knew it. He was yelling and flapping his arms like he was trying to fly.

"Chloe grab that rock!" Ian commanded. "Grab my arm and don't let go no matter what!" Ian said.

He leapt onto a small rock away from the land and leaned out precariously towards Trist, feeling Chloe's weight anchoring him. He grabbed Trist's hand and then gave a sharp tug. They both fell back, Ian onto Chloe and Tristan onto Ian's rock.

"Thanks," Trist said panting.

"Next time tell me you can't swim sooner. I would have had you jump over first and catch the bags," Ian said.

"Yah I just didn't think it would be a problem," Tristan said sheepishly.

They sat there for a little while and caught their breaths. Then a sound drifted towards them from the mainland. It was an eerily echoing wolf's howl. The fog made it sound strange, so they couldn't tell where exactly it was coming from, but they picked a general direction and went towards what they hoped would be Conner and Alexa, not a just random hungry wolf that was looking for its dinner.

"Conner, Alexa, where are you?" Chloe called.

Chapter Eleven

The wolf howled again. This time it was definitely closer than before, and they ran carefully toward the sound. Well actually, they kind of jogged, what with their heavy bags plus dragging Alexa's behind them.

"Next time Lexie wants to jump off a boat, she better take her bag with her. I'm tired of dragging it already!" Tristan complained.

"If that is a regular wolf instead of Conner, I hope it eats you first. That way my last few moments can be spent in happy silence," Ian muttered.

Of course he didn't really want a wolf to eat Tristan, but it felt nice saying it. Tristan really was getting on his nerves. He kept complaining about the fog and the cold and Alexa's bag. Then he'd make some strange and not very funny joke and start laughing so hard, Ian had to drag him along plus the extra bag! Needless to say Ian was not in a very good mood when Tristan made his last mistake.

"Ian are we lost? It feels like we've been going in circles. Did you lose us in the fog?" Tristan asked.

Ian tried to ignore him, but Trist kept repeating the question. Up to this point he had only really tried to annoy Alexa, so Ian hadn't realized how obnoxious he could be. Tristan kept blithely asking his questions over and over and over again, thinking he was so funny. Ian felt himself getting more and more annoyed. The more his annoyance grew the more his anger grew, until he was about ready to explode.

Deep breaths Ian. Just ignore him. Focus on getting to Alexa. Ignore the small obnoxious redhead. Why did I decide to bring other people with me again? I could be looking for Lilith in peace and quiet instead of tracking down a daredevil and a wolf with an irritating kid asking me about 90 billion questions!

"Tristan I think you should leave Ian alone," Chloe said hesitantly.

It was too late however, Tristan made his final blow.

"Ian, where are you Ian? I can't see you in all this fog. You blend in too well. Are you sure you know where we are going Ian?" Trist teased.

Ian knew in the back of his mind that Tristan wasn't trying to be mean, but he was a bit sensitive about his white hair and pale complexion. Ordinarily it wouldn't have bothered him, but he was already stressed enough without Tristan's attempt at humor. He lost the small amount of control he'd been keeping over his temper and erupted.

"Would you please be quiet? You are so annoying, it's no wonder Alexa wants to kill you! I don't know if we're lost, but I doubt you could do much better in this fog. I know I'm not invisible because I'm wearing a black backpack, but if you keep badgering me I'll take it off and then I will be invisible. None of you will be able to find me, and I won't have to deal with your infuriating questions and bubbly happy attitude all the time!" Ian burst.

He turned and stalked off into the mist toward the still-howling wolf.

"Ian, don't be mad. I was just teasing. I didn't know it would bother you, really! I'm sorry ok?"

Ian turned slightly and looked at Tristan. He really did look guilty and sorry staring at Ian with his wide innocent eyes.

Great, now I feel awful.

"It's fine Tristan."

He was still slightly mad though, when they found Alexa and Conner five minutes later. They were sheltering in a pine hollow. The ground was covered in thick glistening snow and it really looked quite beautiful; minus the freezing girl and wolf huddled under a tree. Just as they walked up Conner gave another dejected howl. Alexa lay on the ground in an uncontrollably shivering ball beside him. Her skin was pale and her lips were slightly blue. Chloe rushed over to her. She turned back to look at the two boys.

"Tristan go get fire wood and start a fire right here. Ian you can get into Alexa's bag and pull out the warm winter clothes she has. They're in the big pocket."

Each of the boys rushed off to do as they were told. When it came to sick and injured people, Chloe was definitely in charge. Ian grabbed out the clothes just as Tristan came back with a load of fire wood. It was all pretty dry stuff he had pulled out from underneath bushes.

"We'll need some heavier stuff later but this will do for now," he said, dropping it in the snow.

Both boys cleared the snow away in a small circle. Then they started to build the fire. Ian pulled out flint and steel and handed them over to Trist. He struck them a couple of times, struggling a bit and finally coaxed the little sparks to catch a twig on fire. From there, the fire spread rapidly to other little twigs, causing the boys to go running off into the woods for more brush to keep their small fire alive. When they got back with arm loads of wood, Alexa was sitting on her bag in front of the tiny fire. She had gotten changed while the two boys were gone. They saw Conner in some bushes and Ian figured she had just finished.

"You can come out now Conner," Chloe called.

Conner withdrew his head from the bush with a lot of snow and leaves attached to it. He shook his head and sneezed. Then he sneezed again and came closer to the fire. He lay down on one side while Trist stoked the fire up with some of the branches they had found. Alexa was still shivering violently and Chloe was watching her anxiously. Ian walked over to her.

"How is she?" He whispered.

"I don't know. I don't think she's caught anything serious, but I can't be sure. She was sitting here dripping wet in the cold for about 20 minutes before we found her. She's going to have a cold minimum, hopefully not anything worse though. We'll just have to wait and see. I don't really know that much about hypothermia," Chloe said with a worried frown.

She hadn't taken her eyes off Alexa for one minute while they were talking.

"I think I'd better get her to lay down by the fire," she said, and she bustled off.

Conner was wet too, but Ian hoped that wolves didn't get sick as easily as people do. Just to make sure, he walked over and sat next to Conner.

"How are you?" he asked.

"Fine. I just wish I could have started that fire for Alexa when we got out of the water. I tried to keep her warm, but I was cold and wet too so I'm not sure if I helped or just made it worse," Conner said dejectedly.

Ian knew what that meant. Conner had been wishing he were a boy again, because he felt useless.

"Conner. You jumped in and saved Alexa when no one else could without risking their life. I told you before you're a hero, and now this just proves it," Ian said.

"Great, so I'm a better wolf than I was a person," Conner said.

Ian sighed and rolled his eyes. He wished Chloe could understand Conner instead of only him. She was much better at this kind of stuff.

"You won't be a wolf forever," Ian reassured him.

Conner just sighed and turned to look at the fire.

Fine stare into the fire and mope.

By now it was getting dark, and Ian was worried about the attention a fire would bring to them. They couldn't put it out though. Alexa still needed it, and so did Conner whether he would admit it or not. Ian had changed into his winter clothes about an hour ago, and was now sitting in his sleeping bag trying to stay awake.

"We need someone to keep watch," Ian muttered sleepily.

"I can," Conner said.

He sounded wide awake, and Ian looked at him in surprise. He looked awake too. Ian nodded and lay down.

"Let us know when you get tired Conner," Chloe murmured.

Tristan snored loudly, and Ian almost couldn't fall asleep because of it. He was too tired to stay awake for long though and soon fell asleep to the sound of Tristan's snores and Alexa's tossing and turning.

He awoke the next morning and sat up. He saw Tristan snoring next to Conner, who was asleep, and Chloe, wide awake leaning over Alexa who was muttering something. He crawled out of his sleeping bag and stood up, enjoying the frosty morning air. It had snowed during the night, but they were only dusted with a light covering of it. The trees had kept most of it from falling down on top of them.

"Good morning," Chloe said without looking up. "May I use your sleeping bag?"

"Sure," Ian said, and he drug it around the sleepers to her.

"Thanks," she said, and pushed it over the top of Alexa, who was already covered with Chloe's. She was still shivering violently however, and Chloe looked worried.

"Worse than a cold huh?"

"Definitely," she answered tersely.

"Great. Do you know what it is, Chloe?"

"No, and if she doesn't get a lot better by the time Conner wakes up, I'm going to send both of you for help."

"Is that safe?" Ian asked.

"I don't know, but I do know that whatever Alexa has isn't," Chloe answered.

Ian looked down at Alexa and had to agree. Something had to be done about this.

"Should I wake up Conner so we can go now?" he asked.

"No, he was up keeping watch all night last night and he needs his sleep. I sent him to bed when I got up at sunrise to check on her," she answered.

"Why didn't he wake one of us up?" Ian wondered aloud.

"I don't know, and if you'll excuse me, Ian, I need to get back to Alexa."

The only time Chloe wasn't sweet and innocent-looking was when she was doctoring a person. Then she looked tough as a drill sergeant and acted like it too. Especially if you got in her way. Ian decided that it wasn't worth trying to talk to her anymore and sat down with his back against a tree.

Chapter Twelve

Almost an hour later Conner woke up, because Alexa got worse, drastically worse. She had sort of woken up, but she had a horrible fever. She couldn't recognize anyone or anything. She thrashed around a lot and muttered in her sleep. Then she screamed. It was a blood curdling shriek of terror. The only person around her was Chloe though, and she hadn't even been touching her. Chloe and Ian tried to wake her up, but she was in a world all her own and wouldn't wake up. At the scream Conner sat bolt upright, his ears pinned back and his teeth bared. He looked around for the thing that had caused the scream but didn't see anything. Tristan went over and explained it to him, even though he couldn't understand Conner. Conner could still understand Trist though. He ran up to Ian and started to talk really fast.

"What season is Alexa from?" Conner asked in a rush.

"What? Why does it matter?"

"Just tell me which season she's from."

"Alright, alright. She's from Autumn."

"Thank goodness!" Conner sighed.

Ian looked at his friend like he'd gone crazy.

"If she were from Summer, she'd be toast. As it is she still stands a chance. Well a better chance than the warmer seasons at least. She has the frozen fever. We'll need to head into the nearest village to get the cure. She has to have it soon too," Conner explained looking worried.

"Alright where do we need to go?"

"Go where?" Chloe asked.

Ian quickly explained that Alexa had frozen fever. He told her that he and Conner were going to the nearest village to find the cure.

"Hurry quickly," Chloe said with a glance at Alexa. "And be safe!"

Ian nodded to show he had heard her and walked back over to the edge of the clearing. Conner padded after him.

"Alright Conner lead the way."

Conner led the way out of the clearing and into the forest. He sped up until he was running through the trees far faster that Ian could run.

"Conner wait!" Ian panted after him.

"Sorry. I'm a lot faster now that I'm a wolf," Conner said backtracking. "We're almost there anyways."

Five minutes later, Ian stopped at the edge of a clearing staring out at a small village. There were several houses, some small shops, and a couple of other buildings he didn't recognize right away. The biggest buildings were arranged in a circle that seemed to be in the center of the village. All the other buildings spread from the middle in a slightly random fashion. A faint breeze carried an awful smell over to the tree line where Ian and Conner hid. Somehow it smelled dark. The two of them looked at each other hesitantly before Ian stepped out. He nervously flexed his hands, readying himself for a spell.

Something is seriously wrong here. I can't quite put my finger on it, but I'm not sure I want to go in there. Alexa needs that medicine though. I can't let her die because of some stupid paranoia. Everything's fine, I'm just a little nervous, that's all.

"Ok Conner let's go. Be on your guard, though."

"I don't like this Ian." He growled a little. "It smells wrong."

"I know, neither do I, but we don't really have a choice."

Conner nodded and stepped out to join him. The two of them walked towards the village. The closer they got, the more they could see the details of the village. There were several holes blasted through the walls of the buildings closest to the center, and the snow was seriously scuffed up. The smell was getting worse as well. It smelled burnt and slightly rotten. Ian gagged softly and Conner growled.

"Ian it's too quiet. Where is everyone?"

He's right. It's too quiet. Where is that horrid smell coming from?

They had reached the outer buildings now. Conner growled suddenly.

"It's blood. I smell blood."

"What?"

Ian looked around quickly and saw a few dark patches on the snow. Walking closer he saw that it was the reddish brown color of old blood. Feeling slightly panicked now, he turned and examined the village again. Now that he knew what to look for, he saw more blood patches and some smears on the snow.

"What happened here? The blood and the holes. No one's here at all. It's too quiet." Ian said, his thoughts whirling.

Conner had wandered a little ways off sniffing the air while Ian had been talking.

What is going on here? We need to find out if anyone is hurt. If anyone is still alive... Oh stars this is bad. Wait, where is Conner?

"Conner!"

Suddenly Conner howled. It was a loud mournful sound that echoed eerily through the quiet of the village. Ian ran towards the sound, almost panicked now.

It sounded like it came from that house. What happened to him? I should have kept track of him. We shouldn't split up in a situation like this.

He burst through the open doorway and skidded to a halt. Conner was staring straight at a body lying awkwardly on the floor. It was a woman lying face down in a crumpled heap. She had reddish brown slash marks on her back. Ian looked closer and realized it was blood. This woman was dead. He lurched back, suddenly feeling like he was going to be sick.

"What happened here?" Conner's voice was filled with horror as he looked around the abandoned house. Ian backed up quickly until he was outside the house again.

The smell, the blood on the snow, the holes in the buildings. She's d-dead. The rest of the villagers... Where is everyone? What happened here? Oh stars, we need to get out of here.

Conner joined him outside and growled loudly. His eyes were wild, and his fur raised in alarm.

"Come on. We need to get the medicine for Alexa," Conner said.

"Right. Alexa."

"We should see if their healer is still here. They normally live near the center of town so people can find them easily."

Ian didn't voice what he was thinking, that if anyone was still left in this town they would have done something about the woman.

The two of them walked quickly towards the center of town.

"Shouldn't we do something though?" Ian asked hesitantly.

"We'll need to look for someone first to see if there is anyo...anyway we can help."

He was about to say anyone. There might not be anyone left. They might all be...no. There are people still here. They are just hiding. That's it.

Ian couldn't shake the feeling of dread, though. They stayed out of the rest of the houses and skirted around all of the blood patches on the snow.

"It had to have happened recently or the snow would have covered these," Conner said, angling his nose at the blood stains.

"Why though? What happened to this village?"

"Lilith."

Silence fell as Ian glanced around the ruins again. They were now at the center of the village. It was still deathly quiet. Ian's fear turned slowly to anger.

Lilith destroyed this whole town? Why? I know she wants to kill me but I didn't know she would kill all these innocent people. I have to stop her.

"Ian. I think I found the healer's house."

"Right. Let's go."

We need to get that medicine for Alexa. I can't get distracted now. I'll deal with Lilith later. Besides...it's too late to help anyone here...

Conner walked over to a large building and nudged the door open with his nose. Ian followed him through the door quickly. The room he found himself in was full of dried herbs and bottles full of different colored liquids and pills. There was a large counter at the far end and two doors on the other walls. There was no one in the room, and Ian wasn't sure if he was more disappointed or relieved. Conner started snuffling around the herbs in one corner while Ian walked over to the door on the left wall. He hesitated before opening it.

Do I really want to open this door? I don't know what's on the other side. What if I find another...body...But what if there is some clue about what happened here? What if there is someone alive on the other side?

He steeled himself and opened the door. A quick glance showed him that no one was in this room either. He rolled his eyes at himself and stepped through the door. This room looked like it was someone's living space. There was a fireplace, a few comfy chairs, and a desk. Someone had been in there recently and messed everything up though. The chairs had slashes on them, and there were papers everywhere, probably from the desk. Ian bent down and picked one up. It had a few lines written on it about some herbs sold to a Mrs. Stone. He dropped it and picked up another. A few minutes later he concluded that the papers were all just about the healer's business.

It feels like there is something important here though. Maybe over by the fire?

He strode over and stared hard at the fireplace. He couldn't shake the feeling that he needed to do something here. There was something important that he needed to find. He flexed his fingers slightly and touched the fireplace. A thin layer of frost spread out from his fingertips and covered the mantle. Ian realized that in the middle of the fireplace there was a small design in the frost. It was the same design that had been on the safe houses: a circle divided into four equal parts with a smaller circle in the center. He ran his fingers over it and felt it move. The brick that had the circle design on it became loose. Ian reached his fingers into it and jiggled the brick out. Behind it was a small hole filled with papers. He pulled out the papers and spread them out on the desk.

"Ian, where are you?" Conner asked worriedly.

"I'm in here. I found something."

"I found the medicine for Alexa but I can't reach it. What did you find?"

"One sec."

He glanced quickly through the papers, not really sure what he was looking for. Most of them seemed to be notes on supplies or lists of names and dates. The last page in the pile caught Ian's eye though. It was about half a page written in much messier handwriting than all the other sheets, and the date on the top was from just a few days ago. Ian read through it quickly.

> This is an account of the last and most
> desperate act of the Sixth Branch of the
> Winter Rebellion. As the year has progressed,
> the people have been getting restless. When
> Lady Marian Adair contacted us about
> helping the young Prince, we all agreed.

We were to stage a raid on the castle. It
was to be a distraction so that Lilith would
be delayed in her search for the Prince.
However, something went wrong and our
people were tracked back to the village. Lilith
sent a small army after us. We do not stand
a chance. Many people have escaped into
the woods, but many more have perished.
Marian appeared halfway through the battle.
Lilith had already found the Prince. He has
escaped and is starting his quest. I can only
hope that he will succeed and save the
kingdom from Lilith. I fear that it is too late
for my village. – Elliot Dellik

Ian heard something behind him and he instinctively
shoved the paper into his pocket with a gasp. He turned
and almost ran right into Conner who had come up
behind him while he was reading.

"Ian, we need that medicine for Alexa and I...are you
okay?"

"Yes. Where is the medicine?" Ian said shakily, his head
spinning.

Conner gave him a searching look and then led the way
back to the main room. He pointed up to a top shelf.

"The small blue glass jar. Yes that one. Don't drop it!"

"I've got it. Come on. Let's get out of here."

He wanted to get out of that village as soon as possible. It was bad enough that the whole village was dead, but it was even worse that they had all died because of him. Then there was the little voice in the back of his head that reminded him what Nanna's name actually was.

Nanna's name is Marian Adair. It can't be her. She can't be dead. Elliot Dellik didn't say she died, maybe she escaped. Maybe there was another Marian Adair. She can't be gone. It's all my fault. Oh stars...I can't...

He felt like he was suffocating under the heavy guilt crushing him, and the sickly scent of blood seemed to grow stronger. His eyes were stinging, and he gripped the blue bottle tightly.

I will not cry. I will not cry. I will not cry.

Conner looked sideways up at him. "Are you sure you're alright Ian? What did you find in that other room?"

"Nothing. I'm fine. I'll tell you later."

He didn't want to stay in that village any longer. Suddenly he was running across the snow back towards the tree line. Conner easily loped along beside him, nudging him in the right direction when he got off track. The light of their campfire glowed in the distance between a few trees, and a few seconds later they skidded to a halt in the clearing.

"What's wrong? Why were you running?" Chloe asked.

"Here." Ian handed the blue bottle of medicine over to Chloe.

"Tell her to give Alexa a tablespoon." Conner said.

Ian relayed the instructions, then retreated to a tree about ten feet away from the others. He climbed up onto the first branch but didn't go any higher, since he was afraid of heights and didn't really want to fall.

He leaned back against the trunk and closed his eyes, determined not to think about what he had just learned. No matter what he tried though all he could think about was that village, the woman lying dead on her floor, and the letter which felt very heavy in his pocket. He covered his face with his hands and let out a long ragged breath. He was only in his tree for about five minutes before he heard Chloe below him.

"Ian. What are you doing up there?"

Trying to have some privacy and not cry in front of everyone...

"I'm sitting in a tree." He answered, shortly.

"I gave Alexa the medicine, now she's sleeping better. Conner went to sleep too. I think he's tired after staying up all night."

"Ok."

"Trist is asleep too."

"Ok."

"Are you sure nothing's wrong? You look upset."

"Chloe, I'm fine." He said.

Please go away Chloe, please just go away.

He closed his eyes again and a few moments later heard Chloe walking away. He sighed quietly. A few hours later he was brought out of his gloomy thoughts by a tap on the foot.

"Ian are you awake? You shouldn't sleep in trees, it's dangerous."

"I'm awake Chloe."

Like I can sleep when all I can see is blood.

He stifled a rather desperate bark of laughter, which was threatening to come out.

"Can you wake up Conner for me? I made some dinner, but I don't want to wake him up."

"Why don't you just let him sleep then?"

Star's how can he sleep?

"Because he needs to eat. We all need to eat."

"Alright."

With a conscious effort he focused on Chloe.

I can't do this right now. Alexa is still sick, we're still in Winter. There's no time for me to be having a break down. I'll be helping those people by focusing on getting rid of Lilith. Nanna will be fine, and I'll find her later. Nanna is fine. Focus on your quest Ian, the others need you.

Chapter Thirteen

He looked down at the ground below him. It wasn't too far so he perched on the edge of the branch.

Note to self, do not climb up trees...Okay that's not too far. You are going to jump on three. One, two, three, jump!

He landed on the ground with a light thump and walked over to Conner. He was lying on his side with his mouth wide open, displaying his sharp white teeth.

I don't blame her for not wanting to wake him up. Please just let him be having great dreams about pillows or something soft and not attackable.

"Conner! Conner, get up!" Ian said, poking him with a large stick.

The stick did absolutely nothing to wake up the sleeping

wolf, so Ian took a deep breath and knelt down on the ground next to him. He hesitated a moment and then shook Conner hard by the shoulder.

"Conner!" he yelled.

Conner jumped up and whipped around toward Ian, growling. Ian jumped up too and grabbed for the stick he had dropped. Then Conner saw it was Ian and relaxed.

"Don't do that! I nearly ripped you apart," Conner growled.

"Stars! I don't plan on doing that ever again." Ian said, feeling his heart race.

They walked over to where Chloe and Tristan were sitting by the fire. Ian grabbed a bowl of soup, and Chloe put a bowl down in the snow in front of Conner.

"Ask Chloe how Alexa is doing." Conner requested.

"How's Alexa?"

"I think the medicine is working. She stopped shivering and she isn't talking anymore. I think her fever broke."

"Good. When do you think she'll wake up?" Ian asked.

He glanced over at Alexa's still form. It was unnerving how quiet and still she was. Normally she was such a loud energetic person.

"I don't know. I've never heard of frozen fever, so I don't know how long it takes to recover."

"Normally not long once you have taken the medicine. It depends though," Conner informed him.

Ian relayed the message and Chloe nodded.

Throughout the rest of the evening, Alexa got steadily better. She still hadn't woken up, but she wasn't tossing, turning, muttering or screaming anymore. Suddenly Conner flicked his ears forward. His hackles rose, his fur stood on end and he growled a long low warning growl.

"Something's coming!" he warned.

Then a big shadow wolf rushed into their clearing, growling. Conner stared at it and howled. The larger wolf growled in reply. Conner raised one paw and sent a pulse of dark purple magic toward the other wolf. The other wolf jumped at the last second, and the magic missed, hitting a tree instead. The tree shook, sending a shower of snow and branches down to hit the other wolf on the head. Conner jumped to meet the other wolf and he landed on him. Soon they were a snarling, biting ball rolling around the clearing.

I need to do something. That wolf is a lot bigger than Conner, he doesn't stand a chance. What can I do though? I don't have a weapon. I could try freezing him. I might hit Conner though. If I don't try, Conner is going to get ripped to shreds. If I focus, could I focus my spell only on the other wolf? Now seems like a bad time to experiment. I have to do something though.

Trying to clear his mind he pictured the strange wolf, a frozen statue but Conner just fine. He took a deep breath, closed his eyes, and shot magic toward the two wolves. Then he opened his eyes. Chloe and Tristan gasped. Ian turned to look. He saw that he had frozen the other wolf solid but hadn't hit Conner, who was standing next to the wolf on the side closest to Ian. It really was amazing. The wolf was frozen in every detail, not just a rough chunk of ice with a wolf in the middle like the other things Ian had frozen in the past. It really did look like someone had just pushed the pause button on that wolf and painted him with a light see-through bluish white color. Ian walked over and ran his hand lightly over the wolf statue feeling the icy fur sticking up in all directions. It felt sharp like a thousand tiny needles. There was a spot on his leg that had frozen blood on it, and that reminded Ian that Conner had been fighting this wolf. He turned around and saw that Chloe was already looking at a bite on Conner's shoulder. There was another on his front leg but neither looked extremely bad. Then out of the corner of his eye, he saw something that drew his attention back to the other wolf. It had a small silver snowflake charm on a light blue string around its neck. It looked just like the snowflake that Lilith had tried to use on Ian, only smaller. It was made to look like the power charm of Winter that she had stolen from his parents.

"Conner, this shadow wolf works for Lilith!" he said surprised.

"Almost all of them do. She has them under a spell. Only the strongest succeeded in evading her spell and remaining free from her power. The others had no choice in the matter. They used to work for your parents, but when Lilith came, they didn't have the strength to withstand the spells she cast on them with her new magical strength," Conner explained tiredly.

"Is that why she turned you into a shadow wolf instead of just killing you?" Ian asked, dreading the answer.

Conner just nodded.

"But then you must be strong enough not to be effected, right? You've been acting just fine recently. You even saved Alexa from drowning," Ian told him reassuringly.

"For now yes, but I can feel it trying to work at me. She's doubling the magic she put into the spell in an effort to get not only me, but every last free shadow wolf in the whole forest. I don't think I can stand it much longer." His tail and ears drooped sadly.

"You can't give in to Lilith!" Ian said fiercely.

Conner just sighed and dropped his head onto his paws. Ian explained what Conner had just told him to the other two. Trist and Ian sat there staring at the fire, and Chloe gave Conner a big hug.

"You'll be fine Conner. I know you can do it," she said encouragingly.

"How much longer?" Ian simply said.

"I don't know. At least a few more days I think," Conner answered sadly. "I'll have to leave and go find some other shadow wolves to stay with. I don't want to put you in danger just because I'm not strong enough to hold out against Lilith's spells."

"Don't be silly. You're staying here with us until the end. We'll tie you down to a tree if we have to, but we're not letting Lilith have you," Ian said sharply.

Conner stayed silent, but he looked a little happier. Ian was glad Conner wasn't insisting, because they would have a hard time keeping him with them if he really didn't want to stay. It was strange that, even though their first meeting had been sort of unusual and definitely not trust-inspiring, Conner was now a full part of the team, and Ian would miss him if he left. He remembered his first and second opinions of Conner. The first, that he was a cold blooded assassin and the second that he was a not-so-bright follower of Lilith. Now that he knew him however, he realized that both of those impressions had been wrong. Now he knew the real Conner, and he didn't want to lose him just because of some spell of Lilith's. How would they keep the spell from affecting him and causing him to go over to Lilith's side though? At the very least, when Lilith's spell finally got to Conner they would need some way to keep him from doing something that he'd regret. His gaze traveled from Conner to the frozen wolf and back again. He knew it wasn't pleasant to be frozen, but he also knew that they could unfreeze him later and he'd be fine, hopefully. Could he actually do it though? Would he be able to freeze Conner? With these thoughts in mind, he settled down to take the first watch while everyone else slept. His watch passed uneventfully, but he felt wary just the same. He couldn't help remembering the shadow wolf bursting into camp and the fact that shadow wolves are invisible at night. Finally, when he was just about to fall asleep right there under the tree, he woke up Trist and headed to bed. On the way, he tripped over the invisible Conner who had fallen asleep right next to his sleeping bag.

"Oof," Ian grunted as he fell with a soft thump onto his sleeping bag.

"Hey!" Conner yelped.

"Sorry Conner it's only me," Ian said.

"Ow," Conner said plaintively.

"I said sorry," Ian said.

"That still doesn't make it hurt less though." He complained.

"Do you want me to kiss it and make it better?" Ian

asked sweetly remembering what Nanna used to do when he would fall and scrape his knee.

That thought gave him a pang of sadness but he mentally shook himself.

Not right now. Focus Ian.

"No! I've made a miraculous recovery, and I'm fine now thanks," Conner said in pretend horror.

Ian smirked, rolled his eyes, and got into bed. He fell asleep and dreamed about shadow wolves all night long.

The next morning he woke up to another scream. He tried to sit up, but his sleeping bag had caught around him, making him fall on his face when he tried to wiggle into a sitting position. Squirming out of his sleeping bag, he looked up and tried to find out who had screamed. It had been a girl's scream, but Chloe was still fast asleep. Actually the only other person he saw at first was Trist, who was on guard still. He was bending over the lump that Ian realized was Alexa and talking to her.

"Lexie, you can come out now. Ian froze the wolf yesterday. Lexie? Are you okay Lexie?" Trist said coaxingly.

"Stop calling me that," Alexa muttered angrily when she poked her head out of the sleeping bag.

In the middle of the night, she had rolled over until she lay right next to the frozen wolf. When she had woken up, it had been to find a huge wolf standing over her looking like it was just getting ready to tear her apart. When she saw Ian looking at them she blushed and got up quickly.

"I knew that," she said.

"No you didn't," Ian said quietly.

Alexa turned to look at Ian.

"Did you say something?" she asked suspiciously.

"No," Ian replied innocently.

"Whatever," she said, rolling her eyes and shrugging slightly at the same time.

Ian bent over to pick up his bag and pulled out his breakfast. "How are you feeling this morning?" He asked cautiously.

"Fine, why?" Alexa asked in genuine confusion.

"Well you were, you know..." Ian trailed off at the look of bafflement on Alexa's face.

"You were unconscious for two days," Trist said brightly.

"What!" Alexa said.

"You fell in the water remember? Then Conner jumped in and saved you. When we got off the boat and finally found you two, you were already unconscious. Conner said you had the frozen fever. Ian and Conner went to a village to get some medicine. Then Ian froze the wolf. Wait, no, then he climbed a tree. It was later on when he froze the wolf, after we ate dinner," Trist explained happily.

Alexa sat down on her sleeping bag and slowly nodded her head.

"I remember falling in and trying to swim out, but I can't remember much else. And Tristan, you are horrible at telling stories. I'm better now though, right?"

"She should be fine, but she might have awful nightmares for the next few days still."

Ian passed on Conner's message.

"Great..." Alexa muttered.

Ian opened his backpack and pulled out some bread. He began to eat it slowly while looking around the clearing.

"We've already stayed here too long. If that wolf was working for Lilith, that means she knows we're here. She'll send something else before long, and not just a scout like I suspect that wolf was," Ian said to Trist.

"Wait that wolf worked for Lilith? What's going on?" Alexa asked crossing her arms and demanding an explanation. "You'd better fill me in now."

So Trist started a long explanation of the many things

that had happened while Alexa had been sick. He greatly exaggerated his parts and didn't tell her anything about his fear of water and the problems it caused, or how annoying he had been. Ian sighed and interrupted the bouncing younger boy.

"Maybe I should tell the story," Ian suggested.

"Yes!" Alexa said.

"No I want to tell it!" Trist said at the same time.

"I'll start over at the beginning. Trist here left out a few major details that I think you'd like to know," Ian said with a smirk.

"No! Don't tell her please!" Trist begged but it was too late.

That's what you get for teasing everyone else Trist!

Ian started his tale. He told how they had gotten everything and everyone off the boat. Including Trist's water issue and the problems it caused them getting him off the ship. He told about finding her and Conner and how they needed to go get the medicine. Then he paused for a moment.

"We went to the village and brought back some medicine," he said finally.

Chloe gave him a curious look but didn't say anything.

Ian continued his story and told about the shadow

wolf spell and what it meant for Conner. Then he had reached the end of his tale and ended it by simply stating that then she had woken up. Alexa stared at him in amazement.

"I missed out on all the fun stuff! A shadow wolf attacked and I was sleeping. Just my luck!" she exclaimed. "Isn't there anything we can do about Conner though?" She asked with a glance at the sleeping wolf.

He twitched in his sleep and whimpered quietly, then curled up into a tight ball.

"I don't know. Not at least until we can get the power charm back from Lilith. Then we should be able to do something about it. Until then, I think he's just got to keep fighting it," Ian said with a sigh.

He suspected that Conner was fighting it right now in his sleep but wasn't sure how long the boy would last. Lilith was a powerful witch, and he wasn't sure how long a boy could hold out against her full strength or even against a part of her strength that was focused fully on him. Conner suddenly yelped and then howled loudly. Ian ran over to him and shook him.

"Conner get up. Conner wake up now!" he said loudly.

Conner shook his head and curled up even tighter, whimpering the whole time.

"Conner, you need to wake up now! Conner this is Ian

and you need to get up now!" Ian hollered in his ear.

Conner yelped and jumped up. He growled at Ian, swiped a paw at his head and then shook his head. Ian ducked under the paw and rolled away from Conner, readying himself for a freezing spell. Then Conner realized it was Ian and sat hunching his shoulders and hanging his head miserably.

"Sorry," he said.

"It's fine Conner. I'm sorry to have to wake you up but you were doing weird things in your sleep. Were you having a nightmare?" Ian asked.

"Sort of," Conner said evasively.

He offered no more, and Ian didn't ask. He figured Conner just didn't want to talk about it. He hadn't pressed Ian the other day in the village, so Ian decided to give him his space. He shrugged and turned back to Trist and Alexa.

"As soon as Chloe gets up we should pack up camp and get heading. Can you carry your bag Alexa?" Ian said to them.

"Of course!" Alexa said, looking insulted.

"Sorry," Ian said hastily. He had thought it was a perfectly reasonable question to ask but apparently Alexa had chosen to take it as an insult to her strength. She could think whatever she wanted though; as long as she carried her own bag Ian didn't care.

Let her take offence at every little thing. See if I care when she collapses underneath her bag. Although I'm glad she's feeling better, even if it does mean she's a bit cranky.

Conner padded up to Alexa and sniffed her experimentally.

"She's better," he said approvingly.

"Good," Ian replied.

Alexa pat the wolf on the head.

"Thanks Conner," she said quietly.

Conner looked at Ian.

"He says you're welcome."

He hadn't really said anything, but Ian had known what he meant anyway. Alexa smiled at him and then picked up her sleeping bag. The four of them ate and took down camp. Ian tried to hide the other wolf by pushing it into some bushes.

"He's heavy," he grunted.

He got Trist and Conner to come help him, and the three of them managed to get the frozen wolf into the thick bushes nearby. Then the frozen wolf fell over with a loud crashing noise. Ian peered into the bushes afraid of what he might see. The wolf was still frozen solid though, just lying on its side.

"Hopefully they won't find him and defreeze him in there," Trist said.

With our current luck they'll not only find him but send him after us again before long.

Chapter Fourteen

By now it was about lunch time, so they unpacked just enough to fix some quick sandwiches and then went off, being careful to brush their foot prints away in the snow behind them. Ian led the way out of the clearing. He hoped it would snow soon to clear away the evidence of the freshly shifted snow. Once they were pretty far away from the clearing, Trist, whose job had been snow-shifting stopped and dropped the large branch he had been using.

"Aren't we far enough away for me to stop brushing snow now? I'm tired, and I doubt they'll look for our prints way out here," Trist said in a complaining tone.

"Probably," Ian said hesitantly.

"Good!" Trist said, and he picked up the branch and threw it off into the woods. A few birds flew toward the sky from the place it had landed. They complained with loud calls and a few dropped pebbles on their heads.

"Hey! Birds aren't supposed to throw rocks! That's just weird!" Alexa exclaimed as a pebble bounced off her head.

Ian rubbed his head and silently agreed. These birds were certainly unusual. Then he noticed that Conner was shaking silently. At first he was alarmed, but then he realized that he was laughing at them.

"What's so funny?" Ian snapped.

"Those are mocking birds. They're supposed to do that to people. They're mocking you!" Conner said with another silent laugh.

"Mocking birds? I thought they just sang like normal birds. Why are they throwing rocks at us?" Ian asked.

He became more annoyed when Conner just laughed harder. The mocking birds were now perched in trees around them, and the really weird thing was that they seemed like they were laughing at Ian and his friends too!

"Conner what is up with those birds? Are they laughing at us?" Ian asked incredulously.

"Of course they are. They're mocking birds that's what they do."

"Not normal mocking birds!"

"These aren't mocking birds like from the main land. These mocking birds are enchanted mocking birds from the Winter Woods. You can't find them anywhere else. We're privileged to see them at all. Most of them went into hiding when Lilith took command," Conner said with a wolfish grin.

"I feel so honored." Ian said sarcastically.

The other three had been listening to this half-conversation with puzzled frowns.

"Well? Is there something wrong with these mocking birds or not?" Alexa asked impatiently.

"According to Conner these are just normal mocking birds for the Winter Woods. He also says that people don't see them very often anymore so we should feel privileged to see some," Ian informed them.

"I definitely don't feel honored or privileged to get pebbles dropped on my head by some crazy birds!" Alexa said.

"I think they're beautiful," Chloe said softly.

"Can you talk to birds?" Ian asked Chloe.

"I can try."

She started making a strange humming noise. Ian heard words in it and felt the magic laced behind those words.

Somehow he knew that the birds would understand Chloe. The birds whistled and sang loudly for a few seconds, then they stopped and listened again. Finally Chloe turned to look at the others. Her face was very pale and she leaned on to a tree for support.

"They said they'll leave us alone now if the stick boy apologizes for waking them up," she informed them.

"Sorry birds," Trist said rubbing his head.

"Are you okay?" Ian asked, remembering how tired he used to be when he did magic.

"I'm okay. It was even harder to use my magic here than back home though."

"Maybe Spring magic doesn't work as well in Winter," Ian suggested.

"Probably," Alexa said after a moment's thought.

"I could try mine and see if it's just Chloe's, or if every one's magic doesn't work as well here," Trist said.

Before anyone could comment on his idea, he was already starting the spell. Ian felt a different feeling of magic swell around Trist as his feet lifted slowly off the ground. He made it about an inch before Ian felt the magic falter. Then with a sudden vacuum-like sensation it sucked back to where ever it had come from, and Trist dropped to the ground. Even though it had only been about a 4 inch fall, Trist still landed on his back instead of his feet.

"I'm not entirely sure how you managed to land like that Trist." Ian commented.

"Ouch!" he said, standing up unsteadily. "Wow I'm really dizzy." He said, laughing.

"Oh, are you hurt?" Chloe asked worriedly.

"I'm fine Chloe. Stop laughing Lexie!"

He laughed and weaved unsteadily around in a circle before falling back down, laughing the whole time. Alexa and Ian each held him down with a firm hand on his shoulders.

"You're staying down there until your world stops spinning. That was a dumb thing to do," Alexa said, and she punched him in the shoulder.

"Aw I didn't know you cared so much Lexie," Trist said sweetly.

"I just don't want to carry you and your bag if you pass out."

Ian rolled his eyes as Trist pretended to pout.

"Ian, make her be nice. Chloe, make her say sorry. She hurt my feeling."

"Your feeling?" Alexa asked. "Don't you mean your feelings?"

"No you already broke my other ones!" Trist said with a fake sob.

The other four burst out laughing at this. Trist stuck out his lip in a really good imitation of a pout. The only thing that gave it away was the fact that he couldn't hold it for more than a few seconds before he started grinning, which ruined the whole pouting effect.

"I'm terribly sorry I hurt your last remaining feeling," Alexa said solemnly.

"You are?" Trist said in evident surprise.

"Not really," Alexa said with a grin.

"Oh well, I accept you're not-quite apology anyways. Do you want to know how my other feelings broke?"

"No, but I'm sure you'll tell us anyways." Alexa said with a sigh.

Ian, Chloe and Conner were laughing too hard to answer.

"Someone wouldn't get me marshmallows. I think it's because they don't like me!"

Trist buried his head in his arms and emitted a loud bawling noise that sounded suspiciously like laughter. Alexa rolled her eyes at him, but she smiled while she did it.

"We all like you Tristan," Chloe told him with a smile.

"Really!" Trist said. He was succeeding in looking very distraught, all except the twinkle that wouldn't quite leave his eyes.

"Yes really."

"Oh this is so wonderful!"

He got up and skipped around the clearing, evidently feeling much better after his brief rest. The others got up too and started walking again. Ian rolled his eyes and they all followed the skipping Tristan out of the clearing. The whole rest of the walk that day, Trist was happily chattering about whatever happened to come to mind. Ian wondered where he came up with all his ideas as he listened detachedly to Trist's rambling conversation with himself. If he hadn't known better he'd have sworn Trist was mad. Guessing from the annoyed look on Alexa's face though, Trist had a definite method to his madness. Without realizing, he said as much out loud.

"Or he just has a madness to his method!" Alexa said with exaggerated grumpiness.

Really she didn't seem to mind his crazy antics today. It helped to distract all of them from the heavy bags they all had to carry. Ian was definitely grateful for the younger boy's distracting chatter. Although Alexa was right, not that he would ever tell her so; the bags were already getting too light. Ian made a mental note to bring up tighter rations at dinner, he had no idea how much longer they would be out here.

I don't have any idea what I'm doing. I don't even have a plan. We're going to end up wandering around in Winter Forest forever unless I think of something. Preferably before one of us almost dies again. Stars what am I going to do?

Eventually it got dark enough to where they couldn't see and kept tripping over roots and bushes. Still, they were uneasy about using their flashlights to alert anything that might be nearby. When Chloe nearly ran straight into a tree stump, they decided to stop and make camp for the night. After setting up camp they fell asleep, forgetting their growling bellies in their sudden wave of sleepiness. Conner, the only one who could see in the dark was on watch duty. Ian pushed aside a slight feeling of unease at this arrangement.

What if Lilith's spell were to suddenly start working and they woke to find that soldiers had been led to find them? Or what if they just didn't wake up at all? Augh. Stop thinking like that. You trust Conner. He would never do that. Now go to sleep.

Chapter Fifteen

He woke abruptly early the next morning. He hadn't gotten much sleep, because he had been having horrible nightmares. He shook his head to try and rid himself of the remnants, flashes of blood and shadow wolves and someone screaming. He sat up and discovered that it had snowed. A thin layer of snow fell off his head and chest as he sat up. They hadn't found a really good place to camp out last night. They had been so tired they hadn't even cared. Plus none of them could see. They would have to start stopping when it was still light, otherwise they would have to use the flashlights. All except Conner, who being a shadow wolf, saw perfectly fine in the dark. They couldn't keep traveling like they had last night though. Ian had so many bruises that he felt he would be blue all over if he went through one more night like that.

What if I was blue all over and I just march up to Lilith and demand my throne? She might die of laughter. Then again, she might just punch me. Then I would be in so much pain I would have to be carried in a ball to the dungeons. Where am I getting this idea from? Oh stars, I think Tristan is rubbing off on me.

"Yah that's not such a good idea after all," he said softly to himself.

"What's not a good idea?" Conner asked sleepily.

"Marching up to Lilith's palace covered in bruises so that I turn blue and shock her into giving up. Then I figured that if I was covered in bruises and she so much as tapped me, she would win because I'd be in so much pain I wouldn't be able to do anything about it. I think Tristan's craziness is contagious."

"Oh," Conner said with a loud yawn that showed all of his long sharp teeth.

"You should get some rest. I'm awake now, so I'll keep watch till everyone else wakes up. You really should start waking us up to help keep watch. You're going to exhaust yourself."

"Alright."

He lay down on Ian's abandoned sleeping bag and curled up. Soon it was obvious that he had fallen asleep by the little grunting almost-snores he made.

Ian got up and walked around brushing the snow off of his friends' faces. Alexa was shivering again, and Ian figured that being covered in snow made her feel like she had the frozen fever again. She started muttering something about giant wolves. Then she started talking quietly to someone else that Ian assumed was in her dream. He couldn't quite hear what she said, but then suddenly she started to scream.

"No! No don't do it!" she shrieked.

Ian frowned worriedly. This trip seemed to be full of haunting dreams for everyone. Everyone that is, except Trist, who seemed to sleep like a log, if logs could snore like lions. Ian shook Alexa awake after another round of loud shrieking cries of terror.

"Alexa, wake up!" Ian called softly, trying not to wake up anyone else.

Although, if they could sleep through Alexa screaming, anything he did probably wouldn't do anything to wake them up. He shook her again, and she woke up with a gasp.

"Don't!" She called wildly.

"Don't do what? Alexa will you please be quiet before you wake up everyone from here to Summer?" It was starting to get on his nerves how often he had to wake people up from their nightmares. Plus Alexa had tried to hit him with a stick that he hadn't noticed her holding.

He definitely noticed it now as it passed inches away from his nose.

"Stop that!" he snapped, taking the stick from her sleepy hand.

"Give that back to me now! I need that."

"And why do you need a tiny stick?" he asked grumpily, getting ready to throw it into the bushes.

Alexa seemed to finally realize where she was.

"Ian why are you holding a stick?"

"Because you just...oh never mind," he sighed. He threw the stick down.

He got up and went back to leaning against the tree from which Conner had been keeping watch.

"That's the last time I wake you up when you're having nightmares," he muttered. After several hours they all got up and started walking again. The rest of the day passed by uneventfully until mid afternoon.

"Hungry, hungry, hungry..." Trist chanted, whacking snow encrusted bushes with a short stick he had picked up about an hour ago.

Ian took a deep breath, and told himself he was not allowed to whack Tristan on the head with the stick.

"We'll need to find a place to have lunch soon." Ian said.

"Yes! I'm."

"Hungry, yes, we know." Alexa muttered. She eyed Trist's stick meditatively and Ian got the feeling that she would have no qualms about knocking Trist on the head with it.

"We can't stop here. This is right in the middle of the Frostling territory."

"What's a Frostling?" Alexa asked when Ian had relayed Conner's message.

"They're nasty little creatures that are very territorial. They wouldn't like to find us in their territory at all, much less stopping for a picnic in it. If they do catch us, they might try to freeze us."

"Oh that's okay then. I'll just freeze them before they come close to us."

"That would be great, except you can't freeze a Frostling. They are too cold already. They eat ice and drink practically frozen water. They are basically ice themselves. No, you can't freeze a Frostling Ian."

"Why would they freeze us? What if I told them who we are and what we're trying to do? Then would they let us through?"

"They would be fine with you and they'd put up with Alexa and maybe me because we're with you and we're from cold lands. There's nothing they detest so much as heat though. It melts them into puddles. If we got caught by Frostlings, Chloe and Tristan would be in serious danger."

"Oh I never thought about that before. Don't people from the seasons get along well with each other?"

"The royals get along very well in most cases, but generally not everyone else. They think the people from other lands are weird. The ones they get along with best are the ones most like them, so really Trist is in more danger here than anyone else."

"Oh," Ian said, glancing warily at the trees around them.

He told the other three about what Conner had just told him. When Trist heard, he paled slightly. His abundant freckles stood out even more than usual when this happened. If the situation hadn't been so grim, Ian would have been tempted to laugh. Trist looked rather taken aback by this news. He was used to keeping a kind of floating happy attitude, but it's kind of hard to when you've just been told that certain people would be a little less than happy if they found you in their part of the land.

"We're not going to get caught by them though so I don't need to worry about that right?" Trist asked, clutching his stick like a weapon.

"Of course not. Besides, Ian won't let them hurt you, will you Ian?" Chloe reassured.

"Not much anyways." Ian said reassuringly.

"He'll probably just let them torture you a little bit. Don't worry Trist." Alexa told him, laughing.

"Ha, ha very funny guys." Trist said. He was looking a little less tense though.

"They'll love that red hair of yours especially." Alexa taunted.

"Well they'll just adore yours. They'll wonder if it caught on fire with that red streak in the front." Trist retorted.

"Hey! I like my hair." Alexa said.

The whole time they had been arguing, they had been walking deeper and deeper into the forest. Then they heard a loud snapping noise from behind them. A chill wind started blowing, and they all heard lots of loud crinkling noises that sounded a lot like ice cracking all coming from the woods behind them. Ian looked behind them and saw bushes rattling right where they had just been a moment before.

"Run!" Ian yelled.

They all sprinted forward as quickly as they could. Crashing through the bushes, they left the small path in an effort to shake the things following them. From behind them, the noises got louder and closer. They ran on through the trees crashing through the bushes that they could get through and dodging around the ones that were too big. They ran deeper and deeper into the woods until they were all completely lost.

"I think we're almost out of Frostling territory, but I'm not sure," Conner panted to Ian.

"Alright. How will we know when we're out of it?"

"Look for a line of small white rocks that glow. The Frostlings put them there to warn the Shadow wolves away."

Ian told the others to look for a line of glowing white rocks. Alexa clearly thought that he was crazy, but Trist and Chloe only nodded. They were too tired to really take in how strange a request this was. After what felt like forever, but was probably only a few minutes, they saw a thin line of white light far ahead of them in the forest. The bushes started to thin the closer they got to the rocks until they were able to run in a straight line toward the rock line. They were almost there when Ian hazarded a glance behind them. Following them were the strangest little creatures that Ian had ever seen. They were short little people that looked a lot like puppets made out of ice. They weren't very good puppets either, because their arms were way too long and their heads were kind of pointy at the top. They also didn't have any hair and were completely see-through blue, except for their clothes that looked like they were made out of frozen cloth. On their faces were looks of hatred that were all focused on Tristan. Ian noticed with alarm that the younger boy was falling behind the others. Going against all his instincts, Ian turned and ran toward him. That also meant running straight at the Frostlings. This seemed to take them by surprise, and a lot of them stopped to look at him in astonishment.

"What are you doing?" Trist panted.

What am I doing exactly? I'm pretty sure this is the worst idea I have ever had.

"Saving you. Come on hurry up. It's you they are really after, not me. If they catch me, I can get out of it alright; but if they catch you you're toast."

 He glanced back and saw that one of the little creatures was making a strange motion in the air. A second later he was holding a lasso made out of pure ice. He started to swing it around his head and threw it toward Ian. Ian, without really knowing what he was doing, waved his hand at it. A sudden wind sprang up and pushed the lasso straight into a tree in the direction he had waved. Startled, Ian faltered and almost stopped before continuing on toward the line of rock. He gave Trist a hard shove from behind, causing him to lurch forward. But no matter what he did the little Frostlings kept coming closer and closer. One reached up and tried to grab Ian from behind. Ian pulled out his pocket knife in one fluid motion and pointed it at the strange long-fingered hand.

"Don't even think about it." He snarled.

"You wouldn't dare," said the creature. It spoke in a cold crackling voice that sounded a lot like ice cubes rubbing together.

Hoping to distract the creature, he flipped back his hood with one hand, still holding the knife with the other. He had been wearing the crown off and on since they entered Winter. Now the lack of hood revealed the silver circlet on his head. The Frostling gasped and bowed quickly. So did the Frostlings close enough to see the crown. That took care of ten of them, but ten were still running toward the group. Ian turned and started running again. Now Trist was almost across the border. Ian ran faster and was almost across the border, when he felt a small hand grab his arm from behind. At the same time, his arm felt like it was being stabbed by thousands of dry ice needles. He yelled loudly. His arm felt freezing cold, and when he tried to pull it away, he found that he was unable to move his arm beneath the elbow. Slowly, the cold frozen feeling slipped up his arm until it had frozen all the way up to his shoulder. He gritted his teeth and leaned forward with all his strength. Then with the forward momentum, he stumbled forward a few paces until he was across the border.

He turned and saw, rather than felt, that the small hand let go of his wrist as soon as he had crossed the border completely. He tried in vain to wiggle his fingers or move his arm. When nothing happened, he looked more closely and saw that his arm was covered with a lace-like net of blue. It stretched tightly over his arm. He reached out and touched it with his free hand. It sent a shock of cold furious magic up his good arm. Shock waves from the spell traveled up and down his whole body. He figured that was how they kept people from undoing the spell if it only hit them part way like him. They had a built-in magic protective system, anything that touched it got the magic shockwave treatment.

He knew instinctively that the way to undo the lace-like spell was to undo the magic knot that tied it together. He looked and saw that the knot had formed right where the Frostling had first touched him. It was about the size of a marble and looked almost impossible to untie. Ian took a deep breath and slowly reached his hand out again. He tapped the knot gently and received a lighter magic pulse than the first. Then he reached out and loosely pinched the knot between two fingers. That was not a good idea. The shock wave that came this time was the worst Ian had gotten yet. He sat down with a thump and rubbed his head with his good hand. His vision was swimming, and he vaguely realized that someone was calling his name.

"Ian, Ian, are you okay?" the voice sounded strange and echoey.

Ian couldn't decide whose voice it was because it had been distorted and sounded loud and then quiet again. He opened his mouth to answer and then closed it again. His vision went black and he realized in a strange detached sort of way that he was going to faint. He slumped down on the ground and the voices that were calling him faded until he couldn't hear them anymore.

He woke up to cold water being splashed on his face. He shook his head and spat out water. Then he sat up rubbing his head and shaking it slowly to clear it of all the fuzziness that seemed to cling to his brain and vision. His vision cleared, and he saw that Tristan was standing over him with an empty canteen in his hand.

"Tristan what did you do that for? You could make him sick. You could have gotten water in his mouth."

I'd like to dump a canteen of cold water on you when you're sleeping Trist. Obnoxious imp.

He tried to get up, but when he tried to lift his left arm to push against the ground, he found that he couldn't. He suddenly remembered why Trist must have poured cold water over his head. That didn't make him any less upset with him, but it was nice to at least figure out why he had done it. He was thoroughly frustrated with the fact that he had now fainted twice thanks to magic. It made him seem like a wimp or something.

"I saw someone do it on a movie once. It worked then, so I figured it would work now. Besides, you were getting worried."

"Yes except you just got poor Ian soaking wet and wasted all the water that was left in your canteen,"

"Well it worked didn't it? He's awake now aren't you Ian?"

"Hmm yes thanks a lot Trist." Ian said.

He rolled over awkwardly and stood up.

He looked ruefully down at his useless arm. "I'm going to have to do something about this arm."

He reached hesitantly out to touch the knot again and Alexa slapped his hand away. "If you knock yourself out again I'll go get the water for Trist to dump on your head myself."

"I'll be careful."

He reached down and carefully prodded the knot with one finger. Tiny shock waves flowed up and down his arm like little waves of water.

Well, if water was extremely painful.

He grabbed a twig off of the ground and gently stuck it under one of the ropes that formed the knot. He felt a tiny shockwave but the twig absorbed most of it. He pushed harder until the end of the stick was poking out of the other end of the knot. Then he grasped both ends and gently teased the rope out of the first part of the large knot. As it came loose, Ian felt the net around his arm grow slack. He tried to bend his arm and was still unable to, but it didn't feel nearly so stiff and lifeless. The only problem with this was now he felt the freezing cold of the spell, whereas before he hadn't felt anything. His teeth chattered as he slowly undid the knot. Seven minutes later he flicked the last bit of magic off his arm with his twig. Then he watched as the last of the spell slowly evaporated into thin air. He let out the breath that he didn't know how long he'd been holding and slowly flexed his fingers. He lifted his arm and pinched Tristan experimentally.

"Ouch!"

"Oh good, my fingers are working again," Ian said, ignoring Trist's complaints.

He looked across the border at the Frostlings' territory. Then he turned and stared at the small warm fire that someone must have started while he was still passed out. How long had that been anyways? When he asked Alexa she shrugged.

"Only about 15 minutes I think. Chloe thought warming you up would help so Trist started a fire."

"Since there is already a fire started, maybe we should just stay here and set up camp, we can leave early tomorrow." Chloe said. "We're all hungry and tired, and this place seems safe enough."

"Yeah, plus Ian looks like he might fall over if I tap him." Alexa said with a smirk.

"I would not..." Ian muttered.

He still felt a lingering cold on his forearm, but ignoring it, he pulled out his sleeping bag and laid it out on the ground. Then he turned to see what he could do to help with lunch before Tristan recovered enough from his scare to start chanting again.

After a very late lunch, or early dinner depending on how you looked at it, Ian found himself roped into some sort of card game with Alexa and Trist while Chloe wrote in a journal.

"How did card's make the essentials list when we almost didn't get flashlights?" Ian groused.

"Trist already had the cards with him. Besides, you're just upset because I'm winning." Alexa bragged.

Ian glared at her, but she ignored him. 5 minutes later though she was just as grumpy as Ian, as Trist jumped up and down in a victory dance.

"Ha! Take that Lexie!" He shouted triumphantly.

"That was just luck," Alexa grumbled. "I want a rematch!"

Four and a half card games later Alexa was extraordinarily crabby, Ian was incredulous, and Tristan was rolling on the ground laughing. He was winning, again.

"It's not fair. Ian is messing with my strategy." Alexa said.

"Hey! I don't even know how to play!" Ian said defensively.

"Exactly..." Alexa muttered.

Chloe, who had come over to watch several games ago, stifled her laughter and patted Alexa on the shoulder consolingly. "It's actually getting late, so I'm going to go to bed. You probably should too after this game."

"Alright," Ian agreed. "Hey, where's Conner?"

"Already asleep I think. Remember he's invisible at night?" Chloe pointed out.

"Right."

Chloe padded over to her sleeping bag. A little while later Trist won his fifth game in a row. Alexa was declaring both how unfair it was, and that the deck of cards must be rigged. She insisted on inspecting it. Ian laughed as he walked over to his sleeping bag. Then he slipped inside it and yawned.

"Whoever is on first watch can wake me up for the second watch but right now I need to sleep."

Chapter Sixteen

A few hours later Tristan woke Ian up to take his watch.

"See anything?" Ian asked with a huge yawn and a stretch.

"Nope," Trist reported sleepily. "Lexie's got next watch after you."

"K thanks."

He watched carefully on all sides of the small clearing they were in. He watched the Frostling side especially hard though. Once, at about one in the morning, he thought he saw a small band of the horrible little creatures sneaking slowly around their borders. He hoped that they were just making sure they stayed on their own side of the border. What he really hoped was that the Frostlings would stay on their side. He could assure them that he wasn't crossing that border for a long time. He didn't really fancy freezing up again. Plus next time he might not be lucky enough to get away before they froze him entirely. Ian preferred his own method of freezing things. That way it happened all at once and you didn't really feel a thing.

I wonder if Frostlings would be so eager to freeze people if they had been frozen by their own spell. Conner said that was impossible though. I hope there aren't a bunch of frozen blue-laced people standing around their camp. Do you turn solid blue when you're all the way frozen, or would you just stay blue-laced? I guess I'll never know. Well, unless I want to be a frozen statue forever.

At about four, he woke Alexa for her watch. Then he went back to bed. He was still rather uneasy, because he felt that someone was watching them from the Frostling side of the border. He turned over so that he could stare at it and fell asleep staring deep into that side of the forest. He woke the next morning, feeling like someone was still staring at him. He narrowed his eyes and stared off through the slowly falling snow. Whoever it was, they weren't somewhere Ian could see them. He got up and walked over to Alexa, who was leaning up against a big tree.

"Anything?"

"Nope, it was all quiet for my watch. Kinda creepy being

so close to the border though. Sometimes it felt like something was watching me."

"It still feels like something is watching me. You're sure you didn't see any Frostlings?"

"I'm positive. Besides, even if I didn't see them I would still hear them. They aren't exactly quiet. Did you see anything on your watch?"

"Just a patrol of Frostlings that were checking the border. The feeling was from before that though, and it lasted until past the end of my watch."

"Yah I'm still feeling it."

"I wonder what it's from."

"I don't know. It could be a Frostling or a shadow wolf. It could even be something else entirely. Maybe it's one of those mocking bird things. Or maybe it's a person. That thought is kind of creepy though. If it's a person I hope they go away and leave us alone," Alexa said, raising her voice an octave when she said the last line.

Ian still felt the stare, although he couldn't figure out where it came from. Then he remembered what he had done last night. He raised his hand and waved it at the forest beyond like he was pushing something away with the back of his hand. The wind came rustling though the tree tops, and Ian pointed at the Frostling side of the forest in a wide sweeping arc. The wind blew the snow and bushes aside for a moment and the two of them saw a small dark shadow wolf in the bushes. Ian glanced around in surprise and realized that Conner wasn't in the clearing. He stared harder at the wolf across the border and noticed that it was a young wolf, and that it was lying down. He noticed a faint blue light coming from it.

"Great. Did any of you see Conner last night after the Frostling attack?"

"No I don't think so, but he's invisible at night isn't he?"

Ian took a deep breath and walked slowly across the border and over towards the bushes where he had seen the wolf. When he had gotten a little closer, he called up another icy wind that parted the bushes again. He looked intently at the wolf and saw that it was indeed laced with blue. But because of the blue strings of magic everywhere, it was impossible to see if it really was Conner or some other wolf. He shook his head. It had to be Conner. Where else would Conner be? He didn't let himself think of the other possibility of Conner's location. He walked forward until he stood right next to the wolf.

"Conner?" he said hesitantly.

He wasn't quite sure if Conner could hear him or not but after a moment with no answer he continued. "I'm going to get you out of there soon Conner."

He set to work finding the magic knot. It wasn't very

hard. It looked like one of the Frostlings had grabbed him by the tail, because that's where the huge knot was situated. He picked up a sturdy stick and poked at the knot experimentally. This time it was easier, because he wasn't doing it on himself and he had both arms to work with. Last time his poor fingers had been doing seemingly impossible stunts as they performed the splits and twisted at awkward angles to try to hold the stick and pull it right.

Why didn't I just get someone to help? I guess I'm just used to doing everything by myself. I'm not used to having this many people around all the time. Plus they might have messed it up and made it harder.

This time it barely took five minutes to get the knot undone, and this knot was bigger. He pulled the last of the knot out and pushed the threads of magic off of Conner's thick fur with a twiggy branch. Then he ducked as Conner shook himself, sending the last magic threads flying off into the snow.

"Thanks."

"You're welcome. Sorry we didn't notice you were missing sooner."

"It's fine."

"Let's get over the border before any Frostlings come along. They give me the creeps," Ian said. They both started to walk over toward the border, but ran when they heard a small crack behind them. When they were over the border they turned and saw that it had just been a small white squirrel that had followed them across. It looked up at Ian hopefully, and then cleared its throat.

"Do you happen to have any nuts Your Majesty?" the little squirrel asked Ian politely.

"I think so, give me a moment please," Ian said, not even registering the fact that a talking squirrel had just called him Your Majesty and asked for nuts.

He was too relived to find that it wasn't a Frostling to notice until he had gotten the zipper on his bag undone. Then he turned slowly to Conner.

"Did that squirrel just talk?" he turned to the squirrel next. "Excuse me but did you just talk?"

"Yes I did. I don't mean to be rude Your Majesty, but I really would like some nuts. My favorites are the big blue kind."

"The big blue kind of nut, a talking squirrel? Help!" Ian said to Conner.

"Just give him some of the nuts from your pack. They aren't frost nuts like he'll be used to, but who knows? He may like them. The squirrel can talk the same way that I can talk to you."

"That is a very wise Shadow wolf friend. He says give the

squirrel nuts, and he's right. I'm hungry!"

"Sorry." Ian dug around until he found some walnuts in his bag and pulled them out. Handing them gingerly to the squirrel, he tried to think of something to say to it.

"Here you go. What's your name squirrel?"

"My name is Pepper. And I'm a she not an it."

"Oh sorry umm Pepper."

He felt a little strange talking to a squirrel that communicated to him by telepathy. If anyone saw him they would think he was crazy. Then he heard someone come up from behind him.

"Did you just apologize to the squirrel?" Alexa asked. "Oh good. You found Conner."

Ian explained about untying Conner and then finding the squirrel. Then he explained about the telepathy.

"Oh that makes sense. That way the creatures could bring their problems to you without having to have anyone who could speak animal around to translate. I wonder if there's anything like that in Autumn for me and the creatures there? That would make life a whole lot easier."

"I wonder why I couldn't understand the mocking birds."

"Maybe they didn't want you to. Maybe you can only do it when either you or they want to. I wonder if you can talk back to them using telepathy."

"Mmm. Conner can you hear me?" Ian tried asking silently.

To his surprise Conner answered back quickly. "Yes! I think your powers are getting stronger Ian."

"Stars, that was cool!"

Silently he talked to the squirrel next. "Pepper can you hear me?

"Yes," the squirrel answered in its squeaky voice.

"Oh cool."

He reported the results of his silent conversations with both of the creatures to Alexa, who listened in rapt silence.

"That is so cool!" Alexa said a little jealously.

"I wonder...will all of you be able to do this? Otherwise how would you be able to talk to all your subjects? I guess they could all just speak English and that would work just as well." Ian mused.

"Yes but it's way cooler to talk with telepathy than to talk regularly."

"True."

He could also think of several advantages to that as well,

such as completely silent conversations that no one else could hear. You could tell someone to do something silently without anyone else knowing what they were going to do. They wouldn't even know that anyone was going to do anything at all.

"I wonder when the others are going to get up?" Alexa asked a few hours later.

"I have no idea. We should probably wake them up soon though. Otherwise we're never going to get to the castle."

"Hey Ian, what do you think is going to happen when we get to the castle?"

"I don't really know, actually."

"So you're just going to walk up and demand your castle back? That'll work great!"

She's right. Augh. Why does she have to be right? What am I going to do? I should have come up with a plan before now. It better be a good plan too if I want to get in to Lilith's castle. Well technically it's my castle. But still. I was just so focused on getting up there, and worried about Conner. This is bad. Stars Ian what were you thinking!? I don't even know what it looks like though. I'll have to scout around the castle first. When

I get in, I'll sneak around and try to locate the power charm. Lilith will probably carry it with her, but I'll need to check. Avoid direct contact. Maybe steal it at night? Then, once I have my power charm, I can confront her and make her pay for everything she did. Or I could just lock her in a dungeon or something. She's done so much though. She tried to kill me, temporarily brainwashed the girls, she killed that entire village. And Nanna. No, she might still be alive. Don't focus on that right now Ian. Think about your plan. Plan for getting into the castle and defeating Lilith.

There was a rustling sound in the bushes behind them that caused all of them to jump. They turned around to find a large shadow wolf standing in front of them. Ian glanced down at Conner to make sure he was still there. Then he looked back at the other wolf. Alexa's eyes grew big, and she looked at Ian. Ian nudged Conner, who was resting near him, and silently told him to wake the others and get ready to leave. Then he turned his full attention to the other wolf.

Chapter Seventeen

"Welcome Ian James Weylyn, Prince of Winter," the wolf said with a slight bow.

The wolf didn't sound hostile, and there was no sign of a small snowflake around his neck. You could never be sure though. Also, it was very unnerving that the wolf had known his full name like that.

"Hey I heard him that time. Do you think I picked up on this telepathy stuff?"

"No he's just talking regularly. Remember the book said shadow wolves can sometimes do that."

"Rats."

"What brings you here into the shadow wolves' territory?"

"We are just passing through on our journey." Ian said.

He didn't know who this wolf was, but he figured that it was probably a good idea to treat anyone as big as him with respect. He was nearly twice the size of Conner and looked like he probably had twice as much magic. The wolf's paws were as big as Trist's head. There was no way he was going to take any chances on making the wolf mad. Right now he seemed to be merely curious though.

"Where are you journeying to that takes you through our lands, young prince?"

"We are...umm... journeying to the palace?"

"What business do you have with Lilith that would bring you to the palace?" the wolf asked disapprovingly.

"We are on a noble quest to rescue the Island of Four Seasons."

"And who are you, young wolf pup? You are not really all that you first appear."

"I'm Conner."

"Are you a shadow wolf Conner?" the wolf asked, looking like he really already knew the answer to that question.

"No, yes, sort of. It's complicated," Conner said with drooping tail and ears.

"I see. And you are helping the young prince and his friends on their quest?" he asked suspiciously.

"Yes."

"There aren't many wolves strong enough to withstand the newly strengthened spell that the witch princess has in place, young wolf. Especially not many young wolf pups like yourself," he said in an extremely suspicious voice.

"I will not betray my friends," Conner said, his hackles rising as he let out a low growl.

"See that you do not."

Conner glared at him and turned back to Chloe. Trist sat up and stared around him in surprise.

"Oh hello Conner. Wait...that's not Conner, so who is it?"

"No, that one is Conner and the other is, well...he's another shadow wolf. I don't know his name yet. Excuse me but who are you?" Ian said.

"My name is Thunder Growl. I am the Alpha wolf of this pack. My pack salutes Ian, Prince of Winter and the friends who help him," He added with a pointed look at Conner.

"Is there something you want?"

"My pack will help you on your journey. We will help you get to the edge of our territory in safety, but then it will be up to you to save Winter."

He tipped his head up to the sky and howled a long howl. It echoed around the forest. Ian figured they could hear that all the way in the farthest corner of the forest. He heard the Frostlings chattering angrily behind them. They obviously didn't like the Shadow wolves. No wonder they had frozen Conner and just left him there. They were probably too scared of him to move him, but they disliked him too much to unfreeze him.

"Do the Frostlings not like you for some reason?"

"The Frostlings dislike anyone that isn't from their tribe, even if it is another Frostling from a neighboring tribe. They are very territorial. But yes, they have a particular dislike of the Shadow wolves. We fought against them many years ago when they tried to rebel against the crown. They have never forgiven us for that," Thunder Growl said.

Then through the forest came an answering howl, a chorus of other howls followed. Crashing through the trees came about ten large shadow wolves. Some of them were black, some gray, and some a dark almost-black but not quite. At the head of them was a slender gray she-wolf with a black-tipped ear. She walked up to Thunder Growl.

"Who are these strangers?" she asked in a low, growling sort of voice.

"This is the young Prince Ian and his companions on a quest to save the kingdom. We will help them get to the edge of our forest. Then we will watch their journey in the seeing pool. If they need help in the rest of their journey, we will try to send it to them wherever they may be. We owe him our alliance as the crown prince."

The she-wolf bowed, and so did the other wolves behind her. "My name is Lightning Paws. I am the Alpha female in this pack. We are at your service."

"Thanks."

A couple of the wolves were youngish, but most were as old as Thunder Growl and Lighting Paws. Ian hoped that they didn't all introduce themselves, because their names were too long to say comfortably in a normal sentence. One of the female wolves was about Conner's age, but she was the youngest. Ian noticed that she was giving a lot of attention to Conner who didn't even notice her in the slightest. He was much too busy glaring at Thunder Growl to notice her. Ian figured that she didn't see many wolf boys her age. He wondered how she would react if she knew he wasn't really a wolf at all. Thunder Growl and Lightning Paws had been having a short conference with each other. Now they turned to Ian.

"Our swiftest paws will carry you to the edge of the forest," he said. As he said this four wolves stepped forward.

"We will only need three. Conner will carry Alexa," Ian said aloud. Silently he asked Conner, "Is that okay? I'm afraid she'll insult one of the other wolves and get us in trouble."

"Yes I can carry Alexa."

"Thanks."

One of the wolves stepped back into the rest of the pack. Now there were only three wolves standing in front of them. Alexa went and got on Conner once she had picked up her bag. Chloe and Trist each picked their wolves, leaving Ian with the young female wolf that had been eyeing Conner earlier.

Of course she would be one of the fastest.

He rolled his eyes and walked over to her. She didn't even notice him, she was too busy staring at Conner.

"Run swiftly and be back to camp by sundown," Lighting Paws instructed them.

With a howl they were off. Conner took off like a black arrow. Ian hadn't realized how fast he could run, because he'd always been restricted to the pace of the rest of the group. Now he joyously raced past with a whooping Alexa on his back.

"Faster Conner, faster! Whooohoooo!"

Ian laughed, and the female wolf he was riding sighed

dreamily.

"Isn't he fast?"

"Yes very fast."

"And he's so handsome. What's his name?"

"Conner."

He was too busy watching everything going on around him to pay much attention to the moony-eyed wolf.

"How did you meet him?"

"Oh, poor Conner has an extremely sad story. He was bewitched by Lilith." Ian said with emphasized fake sadness, finally paying attention to her.

"Bewitched? Why?"

"He was her assassin, but he disobeyed her orders to kill us by helping us escape instead. As punishment, he was bewitched."

"Bewitched how? He looks just fine to me?"

"Well isn't it obvious? He was bewitched into a shadow wolf. Normally he's a boy like me."

"I knew there was something not quite right about him from the first time I saw him. I knew he couldn't really be a shadow wolf. I'm too smart to let that spell fool me."

Ian stared at her and saw her blush. He grinned. A

blushing wolf was a strange sight to see.

"You do believe I wasn't fooled don't you?"

Ian just laughed. Five minutes later, they arrived at the border. A very sheepish wolf let him off with a little frown.

"You won't tell him will you? Please don't tell him Your Majesty. Please!"

"I won't tell him." Ian walked chuckling over to his friends who were standing at the edge of the trees.

"What's so funny?" Trist asked curiously.

"Nothing," Ian said innocently.

"Uh huh. Only Trist is crazy enough to laugh at nothing, so tell us Ian." Alexa said.

"I can't. I promised her I wouldn't," Ian told them with another suppressed laugh.

He shot a glance over his shoulder. As soon as the wolves left, he burst into laughter. The others just stared at him like he'd gone mad.

"Fine don't tell us then."

"Alexa be nice, he's just keeping his promises." Chloe said.

"Hmph."

"Come on the path is this way." Conner pointed.

He led the way over to a long winding path that led up the side of a mountain. Near the top of the mountain was a small building. The path was a bit rough and steep in places but Conner had explained that this path was less used than the main road. However, they wouldn't be as likely to be seen if they used it. As they walked up the winding path, the building became larger and clearer until they were certain that they were staring at an enormous castle. Ian swallowed hard.

Lilith can have that castle. It's really creeping me out. When I become king, I'll probably live out in the Winter Woods or anywhere that I can't see that thing. It's giving me goose bumps just staring at it, let alone living in it.

"I hear it looked very nice before Lilith came to power," Conner said uncertainly.

He was staring up at the castle, and it was becoming clearer as he dragged his paws that he really didn't want to go up the mountain.

"I can't do it! I'm sorry but I just can't go up there again." Conner exploded he sat down and drooped his head sadly. "I know you're trying to help me, along with all of Winter, but I just can't go back up there."

Ian thought for a moment. He actually thought it would be a good idea for Conner to stay as far away from Lilith as he could. He was barely managing to withstand her long distance magical attacks on him. How would he be able to stand up against her face to face? They couldn't risk him turning on them, even if it was against his will.

"Conner if you stay how do we know you won't be forced to follow us?" Ian asked him telepathically.

"Freeze me." He looked like he didn't really relish the idea of being frozen.

"What?"

"Freeze me. Then I can't follow you, and Lilith can't use me to hurt any of you."

"It's not a pleasant feeling Conner. Are you sure? I don't want to freeze you." His thoughts raced, trying to think of another way to insure Conner couldn't follow them. He knew Conner was right though, and he felt dread and desperation and guilt mix heavily in his stomach.

"Do it now before I lose my nerve."

"Conner, I don't know if I can."

"Please." Conner said, sitting down and closing his eyes. The tip of his tail twitched slightly, but other than that he held perfectly still, bracing himself.

Ian looked away from Conner and cast his spell. He heard a sharp yelp and someone gasp. Then he looked back at Conner and saw that his spell had worked. Conner was frozen solid.

"Conner?" Ian tried to talk to him telepathically.

There was no answer and Ian felt horrible.

"Ian what did you just do? How could you do that?" Chloe asked.

"You just froze Conner!" Alexa accused.

"He told me to. I would never have done it if he hadn't insisted on it." He said guiltily, feeling defensive even though it was what Conner had asked for.

"What? He asked to be frozen!" Tristan exclaimed.

Ian explained about Conner's request. "I'll unfreeze him after we defeat Lilith." He shot one last guilty glance at the frozen wolf and turned back toward the castle.

I'll be back for you Conner.

"Let's go." He said, turning to start walking up the steep winding path up to the castle. A few moments later he heard the others follow.

Chapter Eighteen

The rest of the afternoon was spent silently, with each wrapped up in his or her own thoughts as they walked up the path towards the castle. Ian was thinking about Conner, his parents, and Nanna, but mostly he was thinking about Lilith. How he would soon come face to face with her in a battle where his companions couldn't help him without passing out. He was dreading finally getting up to the castle, but eventually, around evening time, they made it to the top. He studied the castle, trying to figure out how he was going to get himself inside.

"There it is," Alexa said slowly.

"How are we ever going to get in there?" Chloe asked in despair.

Conner had never told them about the castle before.

None of them had ever thought to ask about it. Now that he was staring at it, the problem looked practically unsolvable to Ian, and he wished that he had thought to ask Conner about it more. The castle had a huge moat surrounding it that was actually more like a giant gulf. Across this gulf, and the only way to get to the castle, was a thin strip of land like a bridge, spanning a massive river. It had no guard rails and falling would mean certain death. Then there was the castle itself. It was massive, built out of thick solid gray stone. There were shadow wolves everywhere. Right now Ian and his friends were safe hiding behind a big rock, but the moment they moved, the shadow wolves on patrol would see them and set off the alarm. They would be caught and thrown in the dungeon or worse before any of them could move. Past the shadow wolves on patrol was a large frost giant that was chained to the castle wall. It looked meanly down at everything and was blocking the door into the castle with its massive bulk. Then there was actually getting through the solid oak doors that looked like they would take fifty Ians to push open.

"This is just great." Ian sighed.

"I always wanted to see a frost giant," Trist said, trying as always to make light of the situation.

"Have you ever wanted to get squished by one?" Ian asked him.

"Well no, not really. I kind of like myself to stay

unsquished. I look much more handsome that way."

Ian rolled his eyes and turned back to the castle. He looked lower down at the cliff on which the castle was standing. He scanned back and forth, then he looked back at something in the wall.

 There! On that far wall there is something that looks like it might be a door. If I can only get across, I might be able to get in without having to pass those guards.

"Look over there guys," Alexa said, pointing to the same door Ian had seen.

"How do we get over there?" Chloe asked quietly.

"Maybe Trist can levitate us over?"

"Do you have a death wish? I levitated an inch and nearly passed out! There's no way I can levitate four of us across that!"

"Okay so scratch that idea," Ian said.

Maybe...maybe I can control the wind. Like I did back with the Frostlings.

He waved his hand, summoning wind to him, and pointed to a little rock and then to the door in the cliff side. He crossed his fingers and waited. Slowly the rock lifted up a few inches and moved along the ground. It flew under the cliff bridge over to the little door. Then it hovered there for a few seconds before he let it drop.

That is a long way down…And I'm significantly heavier than a rock. Maybe if I try hovering for a second? There's no way I'm just jumping off a cliff and hoping the wind catches me. Although really I don't want to jump off a cliff even if I know the wind will catch me…But if I just start hovering the others will notice and they'll want to come with me.

"Wait here for a second, I'm going to try something." He whispered to Tristan. He figured Trist was less likely to protest than Alexa.

Ian slowly eased himself over closer to another boulder. He slid over to it when the wolves were looking somewhere else. Several more stealthy boulder swaps later he was near the edge of the cliff. Ian focused on the wind again and hopped. The wind caught him and he stood hovering a few inches off the ground. It took a lot more concentration than he would have liked, and he would have to go pretty fast, but it would still get him to the other side. He stared down and took a deep breath.

Oh stars that is so high! I don't know if I can do this. What if the wind gives out while I'm halfway across? I can't believe I'm doing this! This is the worst plan in the history of plans. I'm going to die. Oh stars I'm going to die.

He started breathing faster, his heart racing and butterflies in his stomach. He sat down for a second and closed his eyes, focusing on breathing deeply.

"Stop being such a baby. You have to do this." He told himself firmly.

He waved his hand slowly. The wind rushed over to him, and he pointed reluctantly to himself and then to the door. He rose a couple of inches and started floating across the gorge toward the door.

Don't look down Ian, just don't look down. I am going to die!

As he was floating to the door on the far side, he couldn't help look down. At least fifty miles below him he saw a thin ribbon of blue that he assumed was a river. His head spun, and his hands started shaking, causing the wind to jostle him in the air. He looked away quickly and swallowed hard. He floated faster until he was by the door and hovered there trying to open it. He tugged, pushed, and pulled. He was getting more desperate the longer he was off the ground. If he stayed here hovering much longer, he would probably scream. He pounded on the door in desperation. The door suddenly swung open when he put his hand on a little rock sticking out of it. He fell inside the passage behind it with a soft thump. Sitting on the rocky floor of the tunnel, Ian tried to control his frantic breathing and stop his head from swimming. His heart was pounding and he was shaking slightly. He took a deep breath and slowly crept back to the doorway. Then he stood, about two feet away from the edge, and looked out at his friends. They had gotten all the way over to the cliff edge and were gesturing to him to bring them over next. Ian slowly shook his head. He pointed at them and then at the path. He made his fingers walk across an invisible path and then made them sit down. Alexa glared at him and shook her head. Ian shrugged and turned into the passage.

There is no way I'm bringing them over here. They'll just be in danger. This is my kingdom, if anyone is going to die trying to get it back, it's going to be me. Besides they can't really use their magic all that well.

He turned when he heard a muffled scream behind him. Trist had attempted to levitate across after all but had fallen and was now dangling precariously over the edge with one hand on the ledge above. Chloe and Alexa were holding on to him tightly. Ian waved his hand and quickly pointed at the three of them and then at himself. He sighed. They were going to kill themselves trying to get over to the door if he didn't just bring them. They slowly floated over to him. Watching them float across was almost as nerve-wracking as floating himself over. If he messed up they would fall, and it would be his fault. Alexa had a smug expression on her face. He sighed in relief and dropped onto the ground as they landed in the passage next to him. His hands were sweaty and shaking slightly. He stuffed them inside his pockets to hide them.

"Happy?" he asked them shakily.

"Yes." Alexa said, grinning.

Chloe and Trist didn't look happy, but their faces were

set with determination. Ian was obviously stuck with them. He wasn't too mad about it though. He was actually happy to have them there, although, there was no way he was going to tell them that.

Oh well. It'll be nice not to have to go alone.

They crept cautiously up the passage, stopping to peer around each corner before moving ahead. None of them knew exactly what to expect, and it made them all more than a little jumpy. After about five minutes like this, Ian heard a thumping noise overhead. He jumped, crashing into Alexa, then relaxed when he realized that it was only the frost giant above them. He picked himself up and reached a hand down to Alexa. She ignored it, stood up and glared at him.

"Sorry," he apologized. Forcing himself to relax a little and take a deep breath, he moved on slowly down the passage. They moved carefully along, listening to the sounds above them to try and figure out where they were. About seven minutes after they heard the giant, Trist found a small dirty lump. They bent over to investigate it. Ian picked it up and it hung limply from between two fingers. He tipped his head and looked at it sideways.

"Maybe it's a towel," Alexa suggested.

"Or it could be a blanket," Chloe said softly.

"It's a toy." Trist said, shaking his head at the other

suggestions.

"How can you tell?" Ian asked skeptically.

"Guys, I can recognize stuff made for fun. I'm the expert on fun!"

Ian looked at it again. This time he could tell that it was supposed to be a stuffed animal. "Some little kid must have lost this thing ages ago." he said, setting it down carefully on the floor so it wouldn't spread mold in a cloud of dust.

"I wonder whose it was. They were probably so sad when they lost it." Chloe said.

"I don't know. It doesn't really matter though. We're supposed to get to the castle to stop Lilith. Not identify junk in the passageway." Alexa pointed out.

"Alexa's right, come on let's go." He was frustrated with himself for getting so side-tracked by a toy and letting Alexa take the lead. He was supposed to be leading here. It was his castle and his kingdom they were fighting for, after all. He took a deep breath and tried to stifle his frustration.

Come on Ian, you're just getting stressed. Don't take it out on Alexa, she's just trying to help.

They all walked slowly forward. Around the next corner they heard loud voices that sounded close but sort of muffled, as if they had sacks over their heads. As they walked, the voices kept getting louder as they reached the end of the tunnel. There was something dark and soft blocking the end and beyond the dark soft thing, people were arguing. Actually it was more like one person yelling and one person whining.

Ian got down and lifted just the tip of the cloth blocking them from the other people. The voices became clearer so that they could understand what they were saying, although they still sounded oddly muffled and echoing.

"But I want them found now!" he heard one voice scream.

"Your Majesty we've searched the whole of the Winter Woods. Those children are nowhere to be seen. The only things we've found are a couple of wolf statues that they've left behind," the other voice pleaded.

"A couple?" Alexa whispered. Well she tried to whisper but she was loud all the time, so really it was just a little quieter than Ian's normal voice.

"Shh!" Ian hissed.

"I'm being quiet." She protested, but she also dropped her voice.

He listened cautiously for a minute before sighing with relief. The people outside didn't seem to have noticed an extra voice.

"Statues?" the first voice said. There was something

familiar about that voice but it was still too muffled to figure out exactly who was speaking.

"Yes Your Most Evil One. They have frozen some of your Shadow Wolves."

"Some! I thought you only froze one." Alexa said.

"Shush!" Ian and Trist whispered.

The voices had been talking, and Ian hadn't heard because of Alexa's noise.

"Two," the second voice said in reply to a question they hadn't heard.

"Two of my wolves frozen! I want them brought in for de-freezing immediately.

"Yes Most Powerful One. How will we de-freeze them though?"

"Leave it to me."

"Yes of course."

"Now I have questions that need answering. Bring me the prisoner."

"Yes Milady, of course."

There was a scraping noise. Ian peeped out the corner of the cloth and saw that a small man was backing away, bowing repeatedly. He tried to see who he was bowing to, but the person was hidden in the large silver gilt chair directly in front of the cloth.

"I need those children found! They are the only things stopping me from claiming this throne and then all thrones forever!"

Ian almost gasped but stopped himself just in time.

That's Lilith! Although honestly that makes sense. Who else was I expecting it to be? So that means that chair is the throne of Winter. She's sitting on my throne! Hey! Why is my crown so cold? Stars that's cold! Is it because I'm close to the power charm or is it like some kind of anti-Ian defense spell? I'd better take it off just in case.

"Guys the room beyond this thing is the throne room. Lilith's on the throne right now. I think she has the power charm with her. Now how are we going to get it?"

"How about we run out there and grab it really, really quickly." Alexa said.

"How about not."

"One of us could distract her while you grab the power charm. I'm good at distracting people." Trist said, bouncing slightly as he spoke.

"That might work if I knew where the power charm is, but since I don't know where it happens to be and am only working on a guess, I don't think that would do anything." Ian said.

"Except get us all killed," Alexa pointed out helpfully.

"Yes except that isn't our goal Alexa. Strangely enough our goal happens to be the exact opposite; to avoid being killed while getting the power charm." Ian said sarcastically. He ran his hands through his hair, tugging lightly on the ends, as if trying to pull an idea loose.

"Well yes, but it wouldn't do nothing." She insisted.

"I wish we could turn invisible. Then we could sneak out and get it and no one would get hurt," Chloe said softly.

"That would make it was too easy," Alexa scoffed.

"But no one would be in danger."

"Where's the fun in that?" Trist pouted.

Ian rolled his eyes and then decided that they needed to do something soon, before they were found arguing and it was too late to do anything.

"Either you start doing something Ian, or I will." Alexa warned.

"Ok. I'm going to go out there and try and see if I can find the power charm. If I see it, I'll come back and we can make a better plan."

"Are you sure that's a good idea? That sounds dangerous." Chloe said, concerned.

"No I'm not. Any other questions? No? Good, here I go."

This is a really bad idea Ian. Hopefully it will keep Alexa from running out and trying to do something even worse though. If she got caught it would only complicate things. Of course, if I get caught it won't make things any easier either. Better me than her though. It's my kingdom, not hers.

Ian slipped slowly and silently from under the cloth. Looking back, he discovered that they had been hiding behind a large black tapestry with a white snowflake in the middle. Ian turned his attention back to the throne. He crawled over until he was sitting right next to one of the really large arms of the throne. Then he held his breath and slowly slid up until he could just see over the edge of it. There, right in front of him, was Lilith wearing a huge gaudy crown covered in snowflakes and a dress that was a shade of green that reminded Ian of poison. The look she was giving the door across the room matched it perfectly. Ian looked for a snowflake anywhere else on her except the crown and found none.

This is way too easy. Oh, except there are at least twenty different snowflakes. Never mind this is not easy at all. What does the power charm even look like anyways? What about Chloe's book? It might have a picture.

He tried to signal to Tristan to look in Chloe's book for the power charm picture. Trist just looked at him. Then his brown eye disappeared to be replaced by Alexa's storm-cloud gray one. He pretended to read a book and then shrugged and made a sort of snowflake by crossing his fingers in a strange way. Alexa raised her eyebrow at him and Chloe's eye was the next to appear. She watched Ian go through his silent sign again. Then she mouthed the word 'what'.

"Find a picture of the power charm in your book," he mouthed silently as clearly as he could.

Chloe nodded and her eye disappeared. A moment later, there was a picture of a small silver snowflake in the eye hole. He looked at it and then at the crown again. One snowflake centered over Lilith's forehead matched the picture exactly. Unfortunately, at that moment, his foot slid over too far and bumped into the throne, making a loud bang. Lilith looked down startled and then smiled.

Shoot!

"Well, well, well look what we have here. A little lost prince. What are you doing here, looking for mommy and daddy? Aww poor wittle princey poo."

Excuse me what did you just call me?

She reached over and grabbed his arm tightly. Despite her fragile looks, she was strong, and her grip pinched his arm tightly.

This is definitely by far my worst plan ever. Even worse than floating across the gorge. I should have planned more! What was I thinking?

"You've been causing me a whole lot of trouble lately,

freezing my wolves and sneaking around, stirring up rebellions no doubt. I thought that you would be a little more trouble to deal with, but I don't think this will be difficult at all. Thank you for coming here and saving me some time." she said, her nails cutting into his skin, making him bleed.

Chapter Nineteen

He swallowed hard and tried to come up with something to do. Then from behind the tapestry, Ian heard Alexa yell something.

Why is Alexa yelling? Oh no! What is she doing?

"Whoever hits her the most wins!" she hollered over her shoulder at Trist as she burst out from behind the tapestry, and throwing something at Lilith. It hit her square in the face and she let go of Ian with a loud exclamation of surprise. Ian jumped back from her hastily. The crown she was wearing was flung off of her head and Ian heard it slide to a halt up against the opposite wall with a sharp clang.

"Hey! No fair, you got a head start. Lexie you cheater come back here!" Trist hollered, kicking at a backpack that was caught on his foot, and throwing several objects of his own, that variously bounced off of the throne or Lilith.

"Be careful! What are you doing?" Chloe anxiously called after them, clutching the abandoned bag to her chest.

"Whoo hoo! I'm winning!" Alexa said, hurling another object, which Ian recognized as her fork.

"You cheated! You said go after you got up! Plus I got caught on Ian's backpack."

Ian focused, trying to shut out the noise of the others and summon a wind. He just hoped it would work inside a building. He let out a sigh of relief as he felt it brush past him from the tunnel. The wind scooped up the fallen crown and deposited it in his hands. He grabbed the power charm, and twisted. It snapped off of the crown easily, and Ian realized that it had just been fastened there loosely. He flung the crown away and held the power charm in his hands, gasping as he felt a sudden rush of power flow over him. Magic tingled in his fingers, and he stared at the power charm in amazement, temporarily distracted from everything else. Then he snapped back to attention when Tristan shouted. Lilith had recovered, and was now firing off spells at Tristan and Alexa, who dodged wildly. Alexa screamed as a spell flew over her, just missing her head.

Ian griped his power charm tighter and gestured towards Alexa and Tristan, imagining a solid wall shielding them from Lilith's attacks. A thin translucent sheet of ice seemed to sprout up out of the floor. It didn't look very strong, but it held when Lilith's spells bounced off of it. Lilith turned towards him with a feral grin.

"You want to play games Prince? Fine, let's play." She slid off the pedestal beneath her throne and stomped her foot. It hit the floor with an unnaturally loud bang and a crackling circle of dark purple and black magic swept out around her. He jumped, the wind catching him and he hovered above the floor. Chloe screamed and jumped back against the wall, and Alexa and Trist flinched when the ice wall in front of them shuddered and cracked slightly.

Ian fired a freezing spell at Lilith from the air, and then landed, firing another. It collided with one of Lilith's spells in midair, exploding in a blinding spray of sparks. Lilith laughed, the sound sending a chill down Ian's spine. She was just playing with him. There was no way he could hold his own against her for very long even with the power charm since he had no idea how to fully use it.

I need a way to end this fast...I don't think I can actually do anything to hurt her, but maybe I can at least get her out of Winter. Somewhere far away, where she can't hurt anyone, at least for a while. We need time to regroup and get stronger before we are ready to actually take her on.

He met Alexa's eyes through the ice wall and held

up a finger to her, to wait. She quirked her eyebrows up at him, and nodded, digging through her pack for something. Ian quickly flicked his hand out in a circular gesture, focusing hard on his intend, getting rid of Lilith. The wind rushed past him again, starting to whip around Lilith. She looked powerful and intimidating, her dark hair snapping around her and her laughter ringing in his ears.

"Nice try little Prince, but a little wind won't scare me."

She stalked forward, a little slower because of the wind, but not seeming very inconvenienced by it. Ian stood and waited as she came closer, watching for the perfect opportunity. One more step and she was only a few feet from the ice wall guarding Alexa and Tristan.

"Alexa now!" Ian shouted, collapsing the ice wall.

With a shout like a battle cry Alexa threw something at Lilith that hit her solidly on the back of her head. Lilith's neck snapped forward, and she screamed loudly in pain and fury. Ian shot a freezing spell at her while she was distracted and it connected with a bang, freezing her instantly. Ian knew it wouldn't hold her for long, he could already see the cracks forming. He gestured at her and the wind picked her up and carried her out the room, flinging open doors energetically before it. As the sound of the wind howling through the castle faded into the distance so did Ian's energy. He sagged slightly, and let out a sigh of relief. There was silence for a second and then Alexa and Tristan started talking at once.

"We did it!" Alexa said, pumping her fist in the air and jumping up ecstatically. "Did you see that? I hit Lilith in the head twice. I knew my amazing softball talent would come in handy someday."

"And then Ian was like, bang, and the wind was all like, whoosh, and boom! She was gone!" Trist said, talking and gesturing wildly.

Chloe ran up to the others. She was extremely pale, and she clutched a backpack to her chest.

"Alexa what were you thinking? You could have died!" Chloe said.

"But I didn't. Neither did Trist or Ian. Stop worrying Chloe."

"Chloe it's okay. Alexa's fine. Everything worked out," Ian soothed.

"Besides, I saved Ian. Why aren't you lecturing him about dangerous behavior?"

"I wish you'd both just...oh!" She stomped one foot in frustration. "You scared me. Please, just be more careful!" She flung her arms around Alexa and squeezed her tight. Alexa looked startled and patted Chloe on the back a bit awkwardly.

"I'm just so glad you're alright." Chloe said, sounding a

bit stuffy.

"Of course I'm alright, Chloe. Did you see me hit Lilith? I'm amazing!"

Chloe stepped back, laughing a little and rubbing her eyes.

"What did you throw at Lilith anyways? It looked pretty heavy." Ian asked curiously.

"Oh, some can of food I think. It was the heaviest thing I could find." Alexa said carelessly. "So, now what?"

That's a good question. Now what do I do? I need to do something about Conner and the other Shadow Wolves. Something to fix whatever Lilith has done to Winter.

"Hmm that's easier said than done," he said quietly.

"Well hurry up and fix it already," Alexa said impatiently, as if she had read his mind.

"Excuse me, fix what?" Chloe sniffed, rubbing one eye, obviously not thinking along the same lines as the other two.

"Lilith's spells."

"That's easier said than done." Ian repeated, louder this time.

"Why? What's stopping you now that you have the power charm?" Alexa clearly thought Ian was thinking it through too much.

"Alexa, I don't know how to," he said with as much patience as he could muster, which wasn't much under the circumstances. Plus he never liked admitting that he couldn't do something.

"Well don't think about it, just do it. Wave your hand and think about Lilith's spells being undone or something," Alexa said, vaguely waving her hand in the direction of the door Lilith had gone through.

"No, that won't work! I don't even know what she's put spells on and what she hasn't."

Alexa rolled her eyes and whispered something into Trist's ear. Tristan giggled, and Ian guessed it wasn't very nice, but at the moment, he didn't care.

Ugh! Alexa is so frustrating! She thinks that if you want to do something, you should just do it. She never thinks of the consequences. What if I wave the power charm around and do something horrible with it? What if I wave it around and it slips and gets lost or stuck somewhere? What if I...ok...maybe I am thinking this through too much...

"Give it here," Alexa demanded.

Ian sighed and handed the power charm over to Alexa. She stared at it and then handed it over to Trist who was bouncing up and down and begging for it. Trist looked at it and then held it out to Ian.

"No power button." Trist noted, nodding wisely.

"No, really? I didn't notice that." Alexa said, her voice dripping with sarcasm.

Ian rolled his eyes at the two of them, not really concentrating on them as much as thinking about the problem, then took the power charm from Trist.

He studied the palm-sized silver snowflake carefully, feeling along the thin silver lines and the tiny crystal embedded in the center. Absently he stared at it, trying to make some sense out of his whirling thoughts. His reverie was broken by Trist, who had picked up his bag and started to put it back on.

"Hey!" he yelped and dropped it on the floor.

"What's wrong? Did you get hurt earlier?" Chloe asked worriedly.

"My bag's freezing!" Trist said, looking accusingly at Ian.

"What? Oh I put my crown in there earlier because it was cold, and I didn't know what it was doing. Here I'll get it."

Trist gingerly picked it up by the strap and handed it over to Ian. Ian took it and reached carefully into the front pouch. His fingers brushed something as cold as ice, and he guessed this was his crown. He grabbed it and started to pull it out, but then stopped as if frozen. The moment his hand had closed around the circlet, an icy breeze had rushed in the open doors. It swirled in the center of the room until it made a sphere that was barely visible, glowing light blue in the center of the room. Then with a blinding flash, it solidified into a small pale blue ball floating a few feet from the floor. Quickly it started to spread, bringing with it a sudden drop of temperature.

"Did you do that?" Alexa asked Ian.

"I don't think I did, at least not intentionally."

"Then who did?" Trist asked.

"I don't know."

"Umm, it's spreading. Is that good?" Trist asked nervously, he bounced backwards a couple of feet to avoid touching the spreading blue light.

"It feels like your magic Ian." Chloe mused.

"What do you mean, it feels like his magic?" Alexa asked skeptically.

"I don't think it'll hurt to touch it Trist." Ian said after studying the spell seeping over the castle. "And anyways, we can't avoid it."

As he was speaking the light swept over them and the rest of the room completely. The temperature dropped noticeably, and it felt like there was a slight tingle in the air. Ian shivered sightly.

They turned and watched the blue light sweep out the open doors and into the rest of the castle.

"What is it doing?" Chloe asked.

"No idea but it's really cold now. Hey do you think it'll snow in here? We could have a snowball fight with Lilith's guards." Trist said, rocking back and forth on his feet.

"Yah Trist. It'll definitely snow inside a castle," Alexa scoffed.

"Great, when do you think it'll start?"

Ian wasn't quite sure if Trist was ignoring Alexa's sarcasm to annoy her or if he really expected it to snow. With Tristan, he was never quite sure. He wondered what the spell was actually doing.

"We need to find somewhere that I can see the whole kingdom at once."

"Okay why?" Alexa asked.

"So then we can see what the spell is doing." Ian said shortly. He was feeling strangely tired all of a sudden. Wondering what was wrong with himself, he shook his head and put it down to the craziness of the day.

"Sorry for not being a mind reader." Alexa said, rolling her eyes.

"Ian are you okay?" Chloe asked.

"I'm fine," he snapped.

"Oh...okay."

Ian shut his eyes and sighed. Opening them a second later, he attempted to calm down. "I'm sorry Chloe I'm just tired. Come on let's go."

Ian strode out of the room, trying to cover distance as fast as he could. As tired as he was he couldn't help noticing the halls were amazing. The walls were lined with tapestries and paintings of what Ian guessed were past rulers of Winter. There were also statues of wolves and other creatures that looked like they were either made of crystal or ice, Ian wasn't sure which, placed like sentries at each side of the few large wooden doors in the passage. He took the first flight of stairs they came to, taking the steps two at a time with his long strides. They were a speckled marble that had a dark navy blue carpet running down the center to make them safer for climbing. At the top of the stairs was a long passageway, a lot like the one they had just been in downstairs except that this one had a lot more doors heading off of it. He went down the hall and peered into one of the rooms. He guessed that this was Lilith's. It was very fancy and looked like a room from a fairy tale. Well, the room belonging to the villain in the fairytale. The canopy bed had a torn black gauzy curtain and lots of vibrant green colored pillows. Each one of its four corners had small gargoyles perched on the top of carved wooden skulls. They screeched and flapped their stone wings menacingly. The walls had shelves that looked like they were edged with writhing snakes made of copper. They were overflowing with strange looking potions in jars and old evil-looking leather books with tarnished gold locks. There were two doors, each in a different wall. One looked like it would probably lead to Lilith's closet. The other Ian hoped would be a balcony that overlooked the kingdom. He opened the door and looked out upon a view of an ice blue castle and partly-blue forest. He leaned on the railing to try and see all the way to the edge of the kingdom, but it was impossible. The mountain almost made a complete bowl around the castle so that he could only see what was directly in front of him. All other views were blocked by towering mountain slopes. What he did see of his kingdom wasn't promising. The spell had spread all the way down the mountain and into the forest. It might have been just finishing the shadow wolves' territory, but it couldn't have made it much farther than that. Looking around for some clue as to what the spell did, Ian glanced down into the courtyard. He blinked and rubbed his eyes then looked again. The Shadow wolves were attacking the giant. Even as he watched, the giant bellowed and ran, breaking the large wooden doors and bounding up the mountain side toward a distant cave. Then the wolves let out a loud howl, lifting their noses to the sky and the setting sun. Ian saw that they each had a glowing blue something around their necks. He could see it even though everything else was covered in a thin blue light because of how bright they glowed. Suddenly a wave of dizziness swept over him. He clutched the railing for support and sank down slowly until he was sitting, leaning against the balcony railing. Now he knew that the spell was definitely his. No other reason explained why he was suddenly so tired and dizzy. He rested his head on his knees and took a deep breath. The spell was moving fast. Five minutes later it looked like it was over halfway done, and Ian looked like he was almost ready to pass out. Even with the power charm to help tap into his magic, he was still having a hard time maintaining both the spell and his consciousness.

Suddenly a scream tore Ian out of his thoughts. He jumped up and turned around to face the door, balancing himself on the railing with one hand. He opened the door slowly and peered into the dimly lit bedroom, one hand gripped tightly on the power charm and his crown. When his eyes adjusted to the gloom he saw in horror that the gargoyles had come to life and were attacking Alexa! Chloe had been the one who screamed. Ian raised his hand that held the power charm and pointed at the gargoyles, willing them to freeze, but nothing happened.

"Ow!" Alexa reached one arm up to cover her face and grabbed a gargoyle with the other. It wiggled and scratched at her while the others attacked furiously. She smashed it to the ground. Ian took a deep breath and tried again. This time he managed to freeze one and almost collapsed from the effort. Shaking his head to clear it of the fuzz that covered it like a blanket, he tried it again. This time one more gargoyle crashed to the ground with the sound of shattering ice. Ian sank down onto the floor and tried to calm his loud ragged breathing. He watched in a rather detached way as Trist gave a loud shout and threw a book at the last gargoyle. His vision started to blur and dim, and the voices of the other three sounded distant and echoed slightly. He heard someone calling him but couldn't figure out who it was. He shook his head slightly and then collapsed on the cold hard stone floor.

Chapter Twenty

He woke up later in a strange bed. At first he thought he was back in one of the hotels he and Nanna had stayed at and that his adventure had been a crazy dream. Then he sat up and realized that he definitely wasn't in a hotel and he definitely hadn't been dreaming. He was inside one of the bedrooms in the Castle of Winter, and he had a splitting head ache. He lay back down on the bed and rubbed his eyes sleepily.

"Where did the others go?"

He jumped when someone actually answered his question.

"Your friends are in other rooms nearby Your Majesty. I believe they are all still asleep." a pompous voice announced.

Ian sat up and looked around for the speaker. He had sat up too quickly and felt a rush of dizziness that made him reach his hand down on the bed for support. When it passed, he saw a tall thin man standing at the foot of his bed.

"Who are you?" Ian asked struggling to get out of his tangled covers and pointing his finger at him ready to freeze him if he made one wrong move.

"I am Nathaniel, the castle steward Your Highness. I apologize for startling you, but I am glad you are awake. I trust you are feeling well?"

"I'm fine." Ian said.

"Very good sir, now we can move on to more important matters. Shall I have someone send up a tray of breakfast for you?"

"Yes please." Ian said.

Nathaniel walked over to a small panel in the wall by Ian's bed. He pressed a round blue button and Ian felt it give off a small pulse of magic.

"Please send up a tray of food for Prince Ian." He said. Then he pressed the button again and the magic aura around it faded. "Now Sire, there are several matters of business that will need your attention. I believe that the General will be wanting a word with you later. She has been leading the rebellion against Lilith, and will no doubt wish to inform you of what has been happening in your absence. However, I am more concerned with the preparations for the victory celebration."

In my absence? He makes it sound like I've been on vacation or something...Wait, celebrations?

"Victory celebrations? What victory celebrations?" Ian asked aloud.

"The ones that we will be organizing in honor of your return and the defeat of Lilith." Nathaniel said patiently.

"But why? I mean, I don't know much about ruling a kingdom but now that Lilith's gone aren't there more important things to be doing?"

"Certainly Sire, and the General and I will help you to oversee those. But it is just as important for the people of Winter to have a proper celebration now that Lilith is gone. We have been at war far too long. The people need something to celebrate." Nathaniel explained. "Trust me Sire, a victory celebration is just what Winter needs right now."

"Alright." Ian said skeptically with a small shrug.

Just then there was a knock at the door and Nathaniel turned to open it, revealing a woman holding a tray of food. She brought it into the room and then stood staring at Ian for a minute, smiling.

"Thanks." Ian said, feeling self-conscious under her direct

stare.

"It is an honor Your Highness. We have been waiting so long for you to come home to Winter." She said, with a curtsy. She set the tray of food down on a desk by the window and then slipped back out the door.

These people have been waiting for me...because I'm the prince. Oh stars, I'm the prince. Prince Ian. The one that people have been waiting for to come rule Winter, rule them. I don't know anything about ruling a kingdom! This is not good...I hadn't even thought about this part. Jsut get to the castle and defeat Lilith, not rule an entire kingdom afterward! Stars what am I going to do?

"Sire?"

Ian jumped slightly when he felt Nathaniel's hand on his shoulder, snapping him out of his internal panic.

He turned to face the castle steward, who looked a less stuffy and formal than he had before. He smiled at the Ian reassuringly.

"Your breakfast Sire." He gestured and Ian shifted his attention automatically to the plate of food he was pointing at.

The smell of maple and cinnamon wafted up from a big pile of pancakes, warm and sweet. He sat down at the desk, inhaling deeply.

One thing at a time Ian. Breakfast first.

The General will be back later this evening, she is out meeting with her captains. When she returns then we can start discussing what needs to be done to repair the damage done by Lilith. For now Sire, we only need to be concerned with the preparations for your celebration. Shall, I send the royal tailor up after your breakfast or would you prefer to start on the other preparations?"

"Why the royal tailor." Ian asked, his fork hovering over his first fluffy pancake.

"For your new clothes, Sire."

"Umm...you can send up the royal tailor." Ian said, figuring at least that would buy him a bit more time before he had to start making royal decisions.

Nathaniel bowed and left Ian alone to enjoy his breakfast. In addition to the large helping of fluffy cinnamon pancakes he also had several sausages and a small bowl of deep purple round berries that Ian discovered were extremely sweet, if a bit unusual. After breakfast he waited for the arrival of the royal tailor who would apparently be making Ian new clothes. He decided to look around the room. It wasn't fancy but Ian liked it. The walls were plain stone with no tapestries, and the floor was bare stone as well except for a single blue rug in the center. There was one window with thick blue velvet curtains tied back framing the view of distant snow covered pine forests stretching out into the distance beyond the castle walls. Near the window was the big wooden desk where he had eaten breakfast. At the foot of the bed was a heavy wooden chest and at the other end of the room were a large wooden rocking horse and a small wooden sword. He figured he was in a little boy's room. He got up and walked toward the rocking horse, but before he could look closer there was a knock on the door.

"Come in," Ian said glancing toward the door.

In waddled a tiny fat man holding a pincushion and some thread. The smile he was wearing made Ian slightly uncomfortable, and he slid his back up against the wall. After the man came Nathaniel, holding rolls of fabric in every shade of blue.

"If Your Majesty would please stand here we shall begin," the little man said in a squeaky high-pitched voice, pointing to a spot on the floor in front of him.

Warily Ian walked forward until he was standing in front of the little man and then began the longest, most tedious part of the whole adventure.

Half an hour later he sighed with impatience.

I've been prodded with so many pins, I'm surprised this outfit isn't covered in blood. This is so boring. Can't that tailor make up his mind already and be done? He's been humming that same song forever. He's even more annoying than Trist.

"And to think I thought waiting for the others in that park was boring. What exactly is the point of this?" He said aloud.

"Your Majesty must have new clothes ready in time for the festivities next week."

"Ouch!"

"Sorry, sorry. If Your Majesty would please just hold still, I wouldn't pin you."

"I was holding still! Besides, why do I need new clothes for one celebration?" Ian protested.

Nathaniel was standing nearby holding a roll of blue fabric and looking faintly amused by the whole situation.

So much for this being easier than other preparations... Ouch! These pins are crazy sharp!

"Your Majesty! You simply must attend the festivities in grand new clothes befitting your station. They are in your honor after all. It is no small thing when the Prince of Winter saves his kingdom and claims his throne. You can't show up in your travel clothes." The tailor sounded horrified by the very idea.

"But the throne isn't mine. What about my parents? Why aren't they reclaiming the throne?"

"The witch removed the King and Queen from the castle a few months ago. We do not know where they are or

Sarah Wood

what has happened to them. You, as their only son and heir, now rule the castle and the kingdom." Nathaniel said, entering the conversation for the first time since coming in the room. He gave Ian a sympathetic look.

"Yes, hence the celebrations and the new outfit." The tailor concluded, grabbing some more pins. Nathaniel gave him a withering look, but he didn't seem to notice.

Ian realized that his eyes were watering and, without thinking, he lifted his hand to brush the tears away.

"Ouch!" He had forgotten that his sleeve was covered in pins. Now his eyes were watering, but it was more from the pain.

"I think that this is quite enough to be starting with, don't you Richard?" Nathaniel said firmly. The tailor who was apparently named Richard looked startled.

"But I've only just started." He protested. This time he noticed Nathaniel's pointed glare and sighed. "Oh, very well. Give me a few minutes."

He started to jot things down in a small notebook, and carefully pull the cloth and pins off Ian.

After a few more minutes the tailor seemed to decide he was finally finished and had everything packed up. Bowing low to Ian, he turned and left leaving Ian alone with Nathaniel.

"Thank you." Ian said, rubbing a spot on his elbow where

he'd been pricked especially hard.

Nathaniel smiled in faint amusement and gave a small bow. "Of course Sire. I think I can handle the start of the celebration preparations without you today to give you some more time to recover from your adventures." He walked towards the door.

"Wait, will you please take me to see the others." He wanted to check on the others and see how Alexa was after being attacked by those gargoyles. Plus he wanted to find out what had happened since he had been unconscious. Obviously something had happened between him getting three of the gargoyles and him waking up with a castle steward in his bedroom.

"Of course Sire." Nathaniel said with a little bow.

He led the way out into the hall with Ian following. They walked down the hall a little ways and then stopped in front of a door. Ian looked at Nathaniel questioningly, and when he nodded, knocked on the door.

"Who is it?"

"It's Ian."

"Oh, come on in Ian."

He opened the door and walked inside. Chloe was sitting on the edge of the bed talking to Trist and Alexa. Alexa was wearing a half-finished blue robe on top of her clothes and was busy picking pins out of it and dropping them on the floor. Her face and hands were badly scratched, but other than that she looked fine. He walked over and sat on the chest at the foot of the bed. This room was slightly bigger than his, but except for the lack of toys, it looked pretty much the same.

"How are you feeling?" Chloe asked Ian.

"I'm fine. How're you Alexa?"

"Someone sent the seamstress to my room, and she's been poking me with pins all morning!"

"I didn't send them! I've been poked for hours too. I meant if you were fine after the gargoyles attacked you."

"Oh yah I'm fine."

Chloe looked pointedly at her and she sighed.

"Thanks for trying to save me Ian."

Chloe smiled at her and nodded approvingly.

"Anytime Alexa. So what happened anyway?"

Trist started jumping up and down excitedly.

"I got the gargoyle with a book! Then someone was knocking on the door. Chloe tried to keep me from opening it, but I got around her. When I opened the door we were all like wow and no way and then." Trist was wildly hopping around and acting out his story.

"And then Alexa got to tell the story before Tristan messed it up," Alexa interrupted.

"Humph. I was telling it just fine Lexie."

"Well like Trist was saying, he got to go open the door. I would have but he was closer. Then when he opened the door this little man was lying face down on the floor. He told us the prisoners were waiting in the throne room, then looked up because some genius over here," she said pointing a finger at Trist, "said it sounded cool. Then the man looked up and yelped. He jumped up and ran down the hall shouting for Lilith. The shadow wolves got him when he tried running into the throne room. We followed him downstairs, we meaning Trist and me because Chloe was with you, and saw the shadow wolves get him. I figured that any prisoner of Lilith's was a friend of ours and slipped in while Trist distracted the guards. I saw two people in the throne room and ran up to see if I could get some help. What? You were unconscious on the floor, we needed some help. So like I said there were these two people standing there; and I ran up to them, but they turned around and one of them looked super scary, like she was going to attack us or something. The other guy grabbed her arm though. They asked who I was and what I was doing. I thought...Trist looked scared of the lady, so I decided to tell them that we were here to stop Lilith. I thought they might like that more than me telling them I worked for Lilith, so stop staring Ian. I don't think they believed me, but before they could do anything else two shadow wolves came in. One was dragging the weird little guy and the other one was dragging Trist, who, by the way is lots weirder than that other guy."

"I thought you said Trist was scared of the lady," Ian said mischievously.

"Alright so maybe I was kind of...startled...by her. Anyway, they dropped them, and then one of them walked up and whispered to the two people. The woman nodded and turned to me. She asked me about the spell that you set off, so I told her that it had just happened. Yes Ian, I didn't tell them it was you. Then, before there were any more questions, Trist blurted that we were attacked by Lilith's baby gargoyle monsters and that you were unconscious in her room. Then the other shadow wolf talked to the two people. He told them that only the true prince could have broken Lilith's spell. Then all four of them looked at me so I told them who we really were, including you, and the lady went running up the stairs with the man right behind her. The shadow wolves bowed to us, then one of them led us up to some rooms. I think the other one was still guarding Lilith's weirdo. I told them I had to get Chloe, but the wolf said he'd get her for me. I went into my room and fell asleep. Then this morning, someone came in and looked at my scratches. They told me I was fine, which I already knew, and I told them so. Also someone brought in the best pancakes I've ever had. People in your castle sure know how to do breakfast, Ian. Anyway, then when they left this annoying seamstress came in and poked me for hours with tiny pins until I told her to get out. She didn't listen at first, but then I told her that I was going to be sick and she left. Then Chloe and Trist came in and we talked for a while until you joined us. After that Trist tried to give his horrible account of what happened but I took over and now you have heard it from the expert."

"Who were the two people?"

"Oh it was the general and..." she was interrupted by a knock on the door. It was Nathaniel again.

"And him," Alexa finished, pointing at Nathaniel.

"There is someone at the door that claims to know you. He looks rather sinister. We've brought him into the throne room. What shall we do with him Sire?"

"I'll come down and see him myself. Just give me a minute please." Ian said to Nathaniel, who bowed and left. Then Ian turned to his friends. "Are you guys coming?"

"Definitely, it's probably Conner." Alexa said.

"We're coming too!"

They followed Ian out the door, jogging to keep up with him. He went down the first staircase he came to and ended up in another hallway. Looking both ways, he wished that he'd thought to ask Nathaniel to take them

293

to Conner. It would have made things a lot faster.

He must walk super fast. We only left like 2 minutes after him at the most...

"I know the way to the throne room Ian," Trist said.

"Really?" Alexa looked skeptical.

"Yah follow me."

They followed him down the passage for a little while, past statues and tapestried walls. Then Ian saw a portrait of a particularly ugly little man he'd seen yesterday. He realized where they were and sped back up to his normal pace. In less than a minute, he was standing in front of the large wooden doors into the throne room. He didn't know how to get to the front door from here or even if Conner was there or somewhere else waiting, but he figured someone in there should be able to tell him what he wanted to know.

Should I go in? I might interrupt something important like a meeting or something. What if I'm not supposed to go in there? Wait, you're the Prince genius. You can go wherever you want to.

Alexa slid the door open on its well-oiled hinges.

"Are you coming?"

He made up his mind to just go in and play it by ear. Striding forward with Trist and Chloe, he entered the throne room. At first no one seemed to have noticed their quiet entry. They were all clustered around a low table that was set up in the center of the room. There was a large shadow wolf that Ian recognized as Thunder Growl, a tall man in armor who Ian guessed was a guard and a little Frostling who was shooting venomous glances at the other two. Then there was also Nathaniel, who had managed to make it down before them, and a tall woman who must have been the general.

"Excuse me." Chloe interrupted softly.

They looked over at her with disapproval. Then they saw who she was and also who she was with.

"Your Majesty," the general said, bowing low.

Ian could see why Alexa would have found her unsettling. She had a very intense stare.

"Your Majesty what are we to do with this boy?"

Ian looked where she pointed and saw, in a corner surrounded by five guards, Conner. He was sitting in a miserable heap and didn't seem to have noticed their entry.

"Conner!" Chloe ran forward and the guards stepped back in surprise. She reached Conner, pulled him up and hugged him. He looked rather startled, and Ian laughed at his confused expression. Turning to the rest of the people there, he got ready to tell them about Conner.

"You know this person," Nathaniel asked, confused.

"Yes that's Conner. He helped us to save Winter."

"Are you sure Sire?"

"Positive. Why?"

"I request a quick moment with you, Your Highness," the general said.

Ian followed the general, Nathaniel and Thunder Growl off into the farthest corner from everyone else.

"Sire you know who this is?" Nathaniel asked incredulously.

"Yes I just told you who he is." Thinking that maybe they needed a bit more persuading he told them all about Conner, purposely skipping the assassin part and explaining instead all the help he had been to them. Thunder Growl looked approving.

"Then he did not betray you in the end."

"No he chose to be frozen rather than abandon us," Ian said with a sideways glare at Nathaniel, who had been looking warily over at Conner.

"Sire, we trust your judgment of course. It's just that Conner is, or perhaps was, one of Lilith's assassins. The son of two guards who betrayed Winter to work for Lilith. You will have to pardon us if we are hesitant to trust." Nathaniel explained.

"It is one of the side effects of being part of an underground rebellion." The general agreed.

"He chose to help us, whoever Lilith trained him to be or whoever his parents were, it doesn't matter. I trust Conner with my life. He's already saved me and my friends multiple times." Ian said calmly.

Nathaniel and the general exchanged glanced and Nathaniel looked a bit guilty when he glanced back at Conner.

"I never even thought to check..." He muttered under his breath as Ian left the small counsel and strode over to the corner where the four others were clustered.

"You can go now." Ian told the guards, who then bowed and left, looking a bit nervously behind them as they left. "You look great Conner."

"Thanks. You were right; it's not pleasant being frozen," Conner said with a wan smile.

"No it definitely isn't."

"How are you now though?" Chloe asked.

"I'm okay now Chloe. A little tired but it beats the other options." As if to prove his point he yawned and swayed slightly.

"Let's get you to a room." Ian said.

Alexa and Trist grabbed Conner as he almost fell over.

"Nathaniel, will you take Conner to a room please?" Ian requested. Nathaniel bowed and led Conner out of the room with Trist and Alexa still holding him up. Chloe ran over and followed.

Chapter Twenty One

"Now I have some questions." Ian said, turning back to the general.

"Of course Your Highness. There are several matters of some importance that I need to discuss with you as well. I think we might be a bit more comfortable in a smaller room however."

Ian nodded and followed as she led the way out of the throne room. One door down, she entered a room. It was a smaller room with a large table in the very center. There were about fifteen chairs around the table. The walls were lined with bookcases and maps. The maps all had little moving dots on them, or notes like fortress or needs strengthening.

"This is the meeting hall," she explained. "We had a lot of war counsels in here before we lost the castle. My name is Celia, I'm the general of your army, captain of Winter's defense, and up until yesterday the leader of the rebellion."

"Nice to meet you. Will you please explain what happened to my parents?" Ian said as he sat down in one of the chairs.

"To do that we'll have to start a little farther back with Lilith's parents. About a year before you were born, our island was in the middle of a war. It ended suddenly when all eight of the season's rulers combined their powers and trapped Lilith's parents. Neither of them was willing to give up their magic or their ambitions so the kings and queens had to execute them. Lilith was young however, and they chose to spare her, thinking that she might have a change of heart. Instead they kept her in a secret underground prison deep in the middle of the island where no one ever went. They thought that she would be safe there, that she'd never escape, but they were wrong. A year later, she broke free of the prison and escaped. At first nothing happened, and we all thought she must have left Four Seasons for good. Then we heard rumors that she was still hiding in the middle of the island, creating a massive army with her powers. We sent out scouts but found nothing. So we waited. Another year passed full of waiting. Then that fall there was an attack on Spring. They managed to ward her off with help from Summer and us, but it was too close. Not long after the attack on Spring, there was an attack on

Summer. Again she was defeated there, but not before she sent someone to sneak into the castle and steal the power charm. Her servant was a traitor to both Summer and Lilith though, and kept the charm for himself. Furious, she disappeared back into the wilderness in the middle of the island. The rulers decided to meet and discuss plans for capturing Lilith. They met at the edge of Winter, almost at the border with Autumn. While they were talking, Justin the king of Summer arrived. He had been attacked on his way through Winter and had discovered that the castle was under siege. He ran to find the others and warn your parents. They, Justin, and Garen, the king of Autumn, ran back to the castle. Your parents found Lilith in the throne room. They attacked her, but she was too strong. She had more power than anyone had realized. While the other rulers were busy in other parts of the castle, she defeated your parents, took the power charm and locked them in the dungeon. Before they were captured, your parents managed to get a message to the other rulers telling them to escape the castle while they could."

"Wait what happened to the rulers from Spring?"

"Only the Queen of Spring came to the meeting in Winter. She was taking her daughter off the island to keep her safe. Queen Marie left for Winter Harbor when the other rulers were defending the castle."

"But they helped when Spring was in trouble!"

"Yes they did."

"That's not right. My parents sent me away to keep me safe, but they still stayed to help."

"Different people have different circumstances, so they make different decisions. Try not to judge when you don't understand the whole situation. There hasn't been much communication between the four kingdoms since that night, so it's probable that we don't have the whole story."

Ian sighed. After a minute he asked, "What about my Grandmother? Is she here?" He tried to ignore the voice in his mind telling him that if Nanna were here at the castle she would have come to find him by now.

Celia looked very somber. "I'm sorry Your Highness, Lady Adair died during an attack against Lilith. I know it's not much consolation, but she died a hero."

It felt like the ground had just dropped out from under Ian's feet. He felt numb, staring in disbelief at the general's sympathetic face in front of him. Although he had known that Nanna's death was a possibility ever since he found that village, it was easy to ignore with everything else going on. Besides, Nanna was always there. Always pestering him to put his scarf on and close the windows. Always chasing strange men away with her umbrella. And now she wasn't?

Nanna...gone? Really gone? She can't be. What am I

going to do? Oh Nanna...

Hot tears filled his eyes and he shook his head desperately, hands covering his face. In his mind he could picture her as clear as if she was there with him. Of course if she actually was here she'd probably give Ian a good poke with her umbrella for moping and remind him that he has responsibilities.

He took a deep shuddering breath, and looked back at Celia who was looking both sympathetic and slightly uncomfortable.

"What happened?"

"It was during the raid 11 days ago. It was just supposed to be a distraction, Lady Adair felt that Lilith was getting too close to finding out where you were hiding. We were trying to buy you more time, keep Lilith's attention on us. It worked too well. We raided three of her guard posts near the castle, our largest raid yet, but we were followed back to the village we were using as a temporary base. At first it was just her soldiers, and we were doing alright but suddenly Lilith was there and things got much worse. We called Lady Adair and with her help were able to organize ourselves a bit more, but we needed to retreat. Lady Adair and I each took a group and split up, so that at least some of us would get back to our camp. Lilith found the group Lady Adair was leading however. She fought valiantly, driving Lilith off temporarily and giving the others time to escape but she was fatally wounded. When she was brought back to camp it was too late. Her last thoughts were of you. She wanted me to tell you how proud she was, and how much she loved you."

"Thank you for telling me." Ian said quietly. "What else did you need to discuss with me?"

Celia looked a bit startled by the sudden change in subject but she nodded.

"There are several things that we need to discuss Your Highness, but none of them are pressing. They can wait until tomorrow."

"Thank you. I'm going to head back to my room then."

"Do you want me to show you the way?"

"No, I'm sure I can make it on my own." He actually wasn't quite sure about his ability to find his way through the maze-like corridors, but he wanted time alone to process what he had just learned. He started off through the halls, trying to remember which way would lead him back to his room. Unfortunately, every hall looked pretty much the same. He couldn't even find the staircase.

My room is on the second floor. How am I supposed to find my room if I can't even find the stairs. I'm so tired. At least being lost is a distraction...

Twenty minutes later he finally had to admit that he was

lost. Frustrated with himself, he kicked the wall hard with his foot. It made a loud banging noise followed by a scraping sound. Startled he backed up against the far wall and watched as the portion of the wall he had kicked slid open to reveal a dark space behind it. There were magical lights in the main part of the castle but this room was completely dark, as though the lights couldn't penetrate it.

"Hello?" Ian said, flexing his fingers and getting ready to cast a spell.

He hoped he wouldn't have to do any spells right now though, because he got the feeling that his magic was still recovering. He stared into the darkness feeling apprehensive. It felt like some hidden evil was lingering in the room, hiding from him but watching his every move. He shivered, hoping that Lilith didn't have anything extremely dangerous in there that he had just unleashed. Now there were two options that he figured he had. One was to leave and get help, which might give anything inside the room a chance to escape and wreak havoc before anyone could stop it. Two was that he could go in there and face it himself. He didn't really like that idea much but it seemed like the best thing to do; so taking a deep breath, he strode into the darkness. Groping around with his hands, he found a switch and pulled it down. The room was instantly lit with a sickly-green light, and the door behind him slid shut with a snap. He turned toward it and pounded on it with his fists. Nothing happened, except now his hands hurt from banging the seemingly solid stone wall. He cursed himself for being so stupid and turned to assess his situation. The room was small, barely big enough to qualify as a walk-in closet. On the wall were flickering green torches that had lit up by magic when the switch was pulled.

"The switch!" he exclaimed out loud. He searched the wall near the door and found a small switch built into the wall. He flicked it up and the door slowly slid open an inch and stopped.

"Password?" a low voice droned.

"Um Lilith?" Ian tried.

"Incorrect," the voice said and the door snapped shut again.

Ian tried to flick the switch again but it was frozen in place. "Great she has protective spells on this place. Wonder why though," he mused. The place didn't look that important. At one end was a door and the other end was a small desk and chair. There was nothing special about the room, but Lilith obviously thought it was important enough for a protective spell and a hidden door.

Who puts protective spells to keep people from getting out though? Shouldn't you need a password to get in, not out? She probably hoped someone would come and get locked in her freaky closet...This is just what I needed tonight.

He walked slowly over to the desk. There was a small pile of papers lying on top of it. The top one had a small sketch of a stick shaped like a blossoming tree and some notes.

He sat down and leafed through the rest of the papers. Some were designs for a large castle that she must have been planning to build. One was a map of Winter with several areas circled or crossed out. He was glad they had gotten here and stopped her before she had made the changes. None of them looked like a real improvement.

Unfortunately the stack of papers didn't seem to tell him how to get out of this room he was stuck in. He sighed in frustration and wondered why on earth he'd been so stubborn and come in here by himself. No one would even know he was missing until morning. He couldn't see any vents to let in fresh air, and he hoped that they were just hidden well. Lilith wouldn't have wanted to suffocate if she stayed in too long. Although she probably would have liked people who stumbled on the door accidentally to suffocate and put a spell on the vents so they'd close if you didn't know the password.

"Shoot," Ian said quietly. He walked over to the door again and flicked the switch. It was thoroughly stuck however, and wasn't going anywhere fast. He worked on the switch for a few more minutes before giving up. He let out his frustration on the door by kicking it hard. Nothing happened except that now his foot hurt.

"I make it through wolves, Frostlings, an evil witch, and stone gargoyles and now I'm stuck behind a door. Seriously, why me? Couldn't Trist have found the door or better yet, Alexa? It would do her good to be stuck in here for a few hours. I should have put a shoe in the door or something."

He sat down and tried to think. All he could think however, was that he was hungry and tired.

"What time is it?"

Ian jumped as someone answered his question. "It is ten o clock," the low voice who had asked him for the password droned.

Is this spell set up to answer questions too? That would be way too convenient.

"What is the password?"

"Power."

Of course, it would be.

Since the switch was still stuck, he didn't know what good that did him, but now he'd know it if the switch ever moved. He stood up and attempted once more to slide it down but it wasn't budging. Finally in desperation he pounded on the door and yelled for help as loud as he could. No one came to answer his plea. Ian was half glad that they didn't. It would be extremely embarrassing to be stuck in a closet and calling for help when he'd just saved the kingdom and everyone thought he was a hero. Sighing, he sat back down. Then an idea struck him.

"What do I do to get out?" Ian asked loudly.

"Say the password."

"The password is power now let me out!"

The door slowly slid open a foot and then stopped.

"Second password?"

"Oh forget it."

He slid out of the room just as the door started to close. It snapped shut with an ominous clang behind him. Letting out a sigh of relief he walked down the hallway. It took him a little while longer to find his room and get ready for bed, but finally he was asleep.

The next morning he woke up, determined not to let anyone know he got himself stuck in a magic closet. He got dressed and went down to try and find some breakfast. While wandering around he bumped into Tristan and Conner.

"Hi Ian."

"Morning. Trist do you know where breakfast is?"

"No. This is your castle, shouldn't you know?"

"It's not like I have a map or anything."

"Umm guys? I know where the kitchens are." Conner said.

Tristan and Ian looked at Conner who looked slightly nervous.

"Ok. Lead the way Conner." Ian said.

"Breakfast here we come!"

Ian rolled his eyes at Trist and followed Conner through the castle. His friend looked a little jumpy, especially with Trist asking a million and a half questions.

He's probably nervous being back here. He must have been here before when he worked for Lilith. Now Tristan is practically interrogating him. Brilliant.

"Hey Trist, have you gotten visited by the tailor yet?"

"What? Oh yah. Yesterday afternoon. He kept poking me with pins. Then he was talking about different colors."

Now that he had been distracted, Trist started talking about other things. Conner shot Ian a grateful look. They made it down to the kitchen a few minutes after that. There were a ton of people bustling around, stirring and chopping and all sorts of things.

"Where did all these people come from?"

"They work here, Ian."

"I thought the castle was empty."

"No. Lilith can't magically make herself food. She still needed servants for that. Besides a lot of people came back when they heard what happened."

"Oh."

Trist was busy grabbing as many different pastries as he could. Finally the head cook chased him out, shaking a ladle at him. Ian and Conner smirked and followed their friend out of the kitchens. They found a quiet corner by a window and sat down behind a suit of armor to eat the pastries Trist snatched.

"So what are we doing next?" Ian asked.

"There's a big party! That's what's next!"

"I meant after the party Trist."

"I didn't really think about that. I'm more focused on the party. I mean it's a party for us!"

"I imagine we'll go to Spring right? With Chloe?" Conner said.

"I don't know Conner, I just got here. How can I abandon my kingdom after I just saved it?"

Conner shrugged.

"Exie ahs een alking aout yeaing oon."

"Trist, we can't understand you when your mouth is full of pastry."

"I said that Lexie has been talking about leaving soon."

"To go to Spring or Autumn?"

Trist shrugged. "Spring I think."

"Are you two going with?" Ian asked.

Trist and Conner both exchanged looks. For once Trist looked serious.

"I think we have to Ian. I know Spring isn't my kingdom, but I want to help my friends. Then I have to save Summer. The people of Four Seasons need us."

"I want to help. I caused enough damage working for Lilith. I want to help make things right."

Ian nodded. They finished their breakfast in silence. "I think I'll go check in with Nathaniel. He might need help getting ready for the celebrations." Ian said.

He got up and walked quickly away. He could hear Trist and Conner whispering behind him, but he kept walking.

Probably whispering about me. What am I going to do? I can't run a kingdom all by myself! I can't just abandon it though. But what about my friends? They helped me save Winter. I can't abandon them either. They're the only friends I've ever had. I'm just finally getting used to having friends. What will I do when they leave? What am I going to do?

Ian sighed and kept walking.

Asking Nathaniel if he needed help turned out to be a mistake. Several hours later Ian was about ready to make a run for it. The amount of preparations for this celebration was crazy! There was a lot more to it than Ian had thought. He had already been in several meetings with Nathaniel and the different committees in charge of various aspects of planning, and Ian couldn't see an end in sight. The first meeting had been to discuss location, apparently they were worried about having it at the castle. Since it was a celebration for all the people the committee claimed there wouldn't be enough space. Turned out they thought that people would be too nervous to come to the castle after it had been ruled by Lilith for so long. Nathaniel had pointed out that a celebration would help people feel more comfortable again. Everyone on the committee had argued for longer than Ian thought possible and then finally turned to him for the final decision. The other meetings after that had gone pretty much the same way. At the moment they were having a preliminary meeting with the decoration committee. This particular committee seemed to consist of two sensible individuals and two people who just liked arguing...

"The tables need to be in a circle, to represent unity and

help people focus on the dais and the thrones in the center." One woman was saying, waving a pencil around in the air to illustrate her vision.

"Don't be ridiculous, it the tables are in a circle some of them are going to be behind the dais where they can't see anything." A man argued with Pencil Woman, waving a diagram of his own plan in the air.

His plans consisted of many rectangular tables arranged in a pattern similar to a snowflake. Or at least he said it was a snowflake. Ian actually thought it looked more like a spider, but he hadn't mentioned that.

"Wouldn't it be best to draw out a sketch of the courtyard first? That way we could visualize where everything should go." Someone else suggested, and she gestured at a pile of paper nearby.

Nathaniel nodded slowly.

"Yes, I agree. However I always think best when I actually see the site. Perhaps we should just go down to the courtyard and make a rough sketch from there." Another woman agreed.

These two woman worked well together and seemed to know what they were doing, which Ian was very grateful for. Everyone agreed with the idea of going down to the courtyard and as they all got up to head out Nathaniel consulted his lists.

"Sire, we have one more meeting for this afternoon."
Then turning to the rest of the committee he said,
"Crown Prince Ian and I have other matters to attend
to at the moment. Outline your rough plans for the
positioning and we'll meet here tomorrow at the same
time to go over them."

The four committee members nodded to Nathaniel,
bowed to Ian, and left. Pencil Woman and Snowflake
Man were still gesturing and arguing as they left the
room. Ian sighed.

"What's next Nathaniel?" He asked.

"The royal tailor has requested an appointment to talk
about your new clothes, Sire." Nathaniel said.

Not again!

Ian sighed, and let Nathaniel lead to way.

Luckily Ian escaped half an hour later, not having been
poked once. The royal tailor just wanted to talk about
color and style, neither of which Ian really cared about.
Once he had gotten the tailor to realize that he didn't
want anything fancy or elaborate the rest of the meeting
hadn't taken long.

Ian wandered around the castle hallways, not really
feeling like talking to anyone. People bustled along the
hallways though, cleaning up dust and the messes Lilith
left in the castle. When he walked by many of them

would stop and bow, staring at him as he walked.

I need out of here...Where could I go? There's probably less people outside...

Now with a direction in mind, Ian strode down the hallways, staring straight ahead and trying to ignore the people gawking at him. He found his way to the front door. There were two human guards and a shadow wolf talking off to the side of the huge doors. They all jumped to attention when they saw Ian, bowing and opening the doors for him. He slipped outside and the sudden change in temperature took his breath away.

"Maybe a cloak or a jacket would have been a good idea..." He muttered under his breath, rubbing his hands together quickly and breathing on them. He hesitated on the top step and glanced back at the big doors behind him.

Not yet...It's freezing out here but at least I feel like I can take a deep breath.

He looked around, and off to the side of the castle he saw part of a building. He figured it would be a warmer inside there and set off towards it, hoping that it would be empty. He slipped inside stamping his feet to rid them of the snow. Warm sweet musty air rolled over him and he realized he found the stable. Nanna had taken him to riding lessons for a few years when he was younger, and the smell of horses was unmistakable. Though the stable was large it was mostly empty. He walked down the straw strewn path glancing into the empty stalls. He could hear noises coming from the end of the stable so he knew it wasn't completely empty, but clearly it wasn't as full as it could be. He wondered what had happened to all the horses and if it had been Lilith that had done something to them. The four stalls at the back weren't empty though. Horses stuck their heads over their stall doors and snorted or nickered in greeting. Ian grinned, walking over to pet the head of a tall shaggy gray dappled horse.

"Hi there. What's your name?" He asked softly, glancing down at the nameplate on the door. "Mistystep, huh?"

"Who's there? Wait, Ian? What are you doing in here?" Someone called from behind him. Ian recognized the voice and turned to find Conner staring at him over the top of another stall door. The large black horse he was standing next to bumped his nose into Conner's side, trying to regain his attention. Conner rubbed his neck and slipped out the door, turning back to Ian.

"Hey Conner. I didn't know anyone else was in here." Ian said.

"Yeah, I come here a lot. Blizzard gets grumpy when I don't give him snacks." Conner said, gesturing back at the large black horse.

"Do you ride?" Ian asked.

"I know how, but I don't get to very often. I think Lilith

was afraid I'd bolt or something." He admitted. "What about you?"

"Not in a while, but I used to talk lessons when I was younger. Later we moved around a bit too much for lessons. Nanna would still try to find me somewhere to ride though." Ian was lost in thought for a few seconds then he shook his head, struck with a sudden thought. "Hey, these are my horses now right?"

"Yeah. I hadn't even thought about that." Conner said.

"Want to go for a ride?" Ian asked.

Conner grinned. "I know where the tack is kept." He said, leading the way into another smaller room that smelled like leather and polish.

30 minutes later Ian and Conner were outside swinging into their saddles, Ian wearing a borrowed cape from Conner. Ian looked up at the sky.

"Can't stay out for too long, or it'll get dark. People will probably get worried." He said.

Conner nodded and urged his horse forward. Ian grinned and followed.

I forgot how this feels...Probably shouldn't go too fast though. It's been a while since I've ridden last.

The horses were used to the snow, and Conner knew were there were some good trails and soon the two of them were riding in the forest out of sight of the castle. They rode along in companionable silence for a while. Ian took a deep breath, and realized he was actually relaxed for the first time all day.

No one to stare or bow or ask me 5 million questions. I should have done this hours ago! This is a bit ridiculous... I'm the prince of a kingdom and a hero. Everyone wants my advice, or to thank me, or at least get to see me, and I'm hiding out in the woods...

Ian started laughing, and Conner looked at him curiously.

"What?" He asked, looking amused.

"Conner, we need to do this again tomorrow..." Ian said, calming down for a minute.

"That was a helpful answer..." Conner muttered. "Do you mean the riding or the hysterical laughter bit?" He asked sarcastically.

"The riding." Ian said, grinning innocently.

"Glad we got that figured out." Conner said, rolling his eyes and laughing. "Come on crazy, we should probably be heading back."

The two of them talked the entire way back. With everything that had been going on, Ian realized that he hadn't actually ever talked to Conner about anything that wasn't related to their quest. It was nice to be able to talk about more normal things. Well, non quest related things at least. Since Conner had been training to be an assassin and Ian was an antisocial bookworm with an overprotective grandmother their conversation tended to be a bit unusual still. When they made it back to the stable the stable master was there, talking to a new stable boy about his duties and he insisted on taking care of their horses for them. Ian and Conner thanked him and went off in search of dinner and then bed.

Chapter Twenty Two

Two days later Ian was sitting in another meeting with the decoration committee counting down the minutes until he could escape and go riding with Conner again.

Can't anyone make decisions by themselves? Stars and Moon why would I need to be the one to decide the color of tablecloths? Besides, those are all blue. Does it really matter which blue they pick?

There was a knock at the door and then General Celia came in and bowed to Ian.

"Your Highness, I need to discuss several important matters with you if you have a moment." The general said.

Trying not to sigh in relief Ian turned away from the

discussion of decorations, signaling to the committee to keep discussing without him.

"Yes, General?" Ian asked.

"In the meeting hall Your Highness." She said, gesturing towards the door.

Ian nodded and turned back to the committee again.

"If you'll excuse me, I have some things to take care of right now. I'm sure you'll all do a great job coming up with the plan for decorations. You can give your final plan to Nathaniel or myself for approval. Thank you." Ian said, trying to sound official.

He stood up, and the rest of the committee stood as well, bowing to him as he left. Ian stifled the urge to bow back or check that his crown wasn't crooked. Instead he smiled and then turned and left the room, the general following him. Once out in the hall she drew level with him as they strode down the hall.

"It's about the prisoners and traitors Your Highness. We need to figure out what we are going to do with them." She said, one hand resting on the hilt of her sword and a look of distaste on her face.

"Lilith's prisoners?" Ian asked, confused.

"No, ours. There are those in Winter who welcomed the arrival of Lilith. We have captured several of them, and I have some guards out looking for others but we need a better plan. And as King."

"Crown Prince." Ian interrupted her.

"Your Highness, in the absence of your royal parents." Celia tried.

"No one knows if they are dead. I won't be king until we know for sure. I can still make decisions in their absence as the crown prince and heir to the throne. Besides, I don't really know anything about ruling a kingdom." Ian insisted, stopping in his tracks to face her.

For a minute Celia looked like she was considering pushing the issue but a few seconds later she nodded and kept walking.

"Very well then, Crown Prince." She said, looking like she wasn't sure to be disapproving or impressed. She muttered under her breath, "Nathaniel was right."

Ian let out a quiet breath of laughter, remembering the similar conversation he had already had with Nathaniel about the topic of being crowned king.

"Regardless of whether you are acting as king or as crown prince you will still need to make a decision on this matter." Celia said after a moment. They arrived in front of the meeting room and Celia stopped to face Ian. "I know that you aren't very experienced, I will be there to advise you Your Highness. But the people will expect you to make the final decision."

Ian sobered, nodding. Celia studied him for a second longer and then she turned and nodded to the guards that Ian hadn't noticed were present before. They bowed to Ian and opened the door. There were about seven people seated around the large round table in the room. The only person Ian recognized was Nathaniel, sitting next to a woman with curly dark brown hair. There were gaps in the seating though and Ian guessed that there were people missing that would have been here 15 years ago when his parents held meetings like this. He also noticed that a couple of the people in the room were too young to have been in his parent's council.

Are the seats in this council type thing inherited or something? I wish Celia had given me a bit more information...I'll advise you is all well and good but I'm supposed to at least look like I know what I'm doing aren't I? Some names would have been a helpful place to start...

Ian made his way around the edge of the table, following Celia towards some empty seats. Celia stopped right behind a chair, but she didn't sit down yet. Ian took the chair next to her.

"Crown Prince Ian James Weylyn, ruling monarch in the absence of his parents the royal King and Queen." Celia announced, gesturing. The people around the table, who had stood up when Ian was walking around the table bowed to him. Celia gestured for him to sit down, so Ian sat and the rest of the people in the room followed his lead.

"I believe that introductions would be a good place to start. There are a few new members to the council, as well as yourself, would you agree Sire?" Nathaniel asked.

Feeling incredibly thankful for Nathaniel, Ian nodded.

"Very well, I am Celia Thorne, General of Winter's army and Captain of the Castle Guard." Celia said.

The next two seats by Celia were empty. Next was Nathaniel.

"Nathaniel Icelyn, Castle Steward. And this," He gestured at the woman sitting next to him, "is my wife Noelle."

She smiled. "I'm the Chief Historian."

"Maria Evelyn Jackson, daughter of Lady Sylvia Ann Jackson. Representative of the Northern Corner of the kingdom." Said a young woman sitting next to Noelle. She looked a bit stiff and nervous, like she would have liked to start fiddling with the paper in front of her but didn't want to give a bad impression. Ian knew the feeling.

Next to Maria Jackson was an older man with gray streaked black hair and a short salt and pepper beard. He looked very serious.

"Lord Edward Sparks, Representative of the South Corner." He said, nodding his head solemnly at Ian.

There was another empty chair next to Lord Sparks, and then a young man with light brown hair and a scar along the left side of his jaw and cheekbone. He looked impatient, and a bit angry.

"Lord Jasper Douglas Coldin, son of Lord Douglas Randolph Coldin. Noble representative of the Western Corner of the kingdom." He said.

 The next chair was empty as well, and Ian wondered who had sat in all these uninhabited chairs and what had happened to them. There were only two people left at the table, a man and a woman sitting next to each other, and then one more empty chair.

"Owen Frost." He smiled at Ian, looking a bit wistful. "I was friends with your father Robert. You really look just like him."

"Thanks." Ian said, smiling and rubbing the back of his neck a bit self consciously.

"Eira Frost. Your mother Tira's friend." The woman next to Owen Frost said.

Celia straightened when the woman introduced herself.

"I didn't know you two had gotten married." She said, sounding a lot less professional and serious than she normally did.

Eira grinned. "2 years ago. We wanted to keep it secret, safer that way."

"I told you," Noelle said, smirking at her husband. Nathaniel just smiled and shrugged.

This is so weird...

"Shouldn't we get back to the actual reason we are meeting?" Lord Jasper said shortly.

"Of course, "Lord Sparks said. "But where is the representative from the East? What happened to Lucia?"

"Lady Blanche, " Lord Jasper said contemptuously, "was a traitor who served Lilith. She is in the dungeon awaiting punishment for her crimes."

"Lucia? I never would have thought...how could she?" Lord Sparks asked, confused and upset.

"Which you would have known, if you hadn't locked yourself away like a coward in your manor all these years Lord Edward Sparks." Jasper Coldin continued, his voice rising.

"Now you listen young man, just because I wasn't fighting every soldier of Lilith's that I could find doesn't mean that I wasn't fighting her. But I had a family to protect." Edward Sparks said heatedly, turning to face Jasper Coldin.

"My father died fighting Lilith, and protecting our family." Jasper shot back.

"So did my mother, but you don't see me insulting

anyone." Maria Jackson spoke up.

This is getting out of hand...I need to get things back under control before we're all fighting.

"Lord Coldin, Lord Sparks we are all on the same side. If you have personal issues to settle please wait until after the meeting." Lord Sparks looked slightly sheepish. He turned back towards Ian and straightened his papers. Maria Jackson also turned away from Lord Jasper and settled back into her chair. Lord Jasper still looked irritated, flashing a slightly mutinous look at Ian. Ian chose to ignore him. "Celia, what is the first order of business?" Ian asked loudly. Celia stood and addressed the room.

"As Lord Sparks and Lord Coldin have pointed out we now have several empty seats in the council that need to be filled. The Royal Mage, Hope Vale is unable to be at this meeting, but she will be back at the castle soon. That leaves two advisory seats, the position of Treasurer, and the Representative of the East." She said, and then sat back down.

"Sire, I have a suggestion for the position of Royal Treasurer." Nathaniel said.

"Yes Nathaniel?" Ian asked.

"I believe Thomas Childe would make a good Treasurer. He has been in charge of the finances for the rebellion and has done an excellent job with the limited resources that we had at that time."

Ian saw that several of the other council members were nodding in agreement and even Jasper Coldin looked approving of the suggestion.

"Alright, I trust your judgment on this Nathaniel. Thomas Childe sounds like a good choice. Thank you. Does anyone have any other suggestions?" Ian asked.

The room fell into a contemplative silence.

"Charles Evergreen. He was a crucial leader in the rebellion against Lilith. He should be made the new Representative of the East." Jasper Coldin suggested.

"Charles? I know he was a good leader in the rebellion, Lord Coldin, but he's a little hotheaded for a leadership position like this." Owen Frost said.

"He doesn't have any respect for authority." Edward Sparks pointed out.

"That's not always a bad thing." Jasper Coldin muttered looking at Ian.

Ian held his gaze and stared him down determinedly until Jasper looked away.

What is this guy's issue? I'm not letting him intimidate me just because he's got an attitude issue.

"Any other suggestions?" Ian asked.

"Joesph Silverson might be a good choice." Lady Maria ventured after a minute.

"He's also a good leader." Eira Frost said, nodding in agreement.

Nathaniel and Noelle were also nodding approvingly.

"The people love Joseph, he would be a very popular choice." Noelle said.

"Joseph Silverson isn't a noble. That position has always been held by someone of noble birth." Edward Sparks said slowly.

"Well, maybe it's time for some traditions to change." Lord Jasper snapped.

"Noble birth isn't a requirement for that position." Noelle informed them. Then she turned to Lord Sparks with a slightly disapproving frown on her face. "There have been many times when the positions of Representatives have been given to people outside of the established noble class."

Ian tuned out Noelle's gentle scolding, looked at Celia and then at Nathaniel. They both nodded slightly and Ian returned his attention to the rest of the room again. Noelle finished speaking and Ian cleared his throat before anyone else could start talking.

"The position of Representative of the Eastern Corner of the kingdom of Winter will be given to Joseph Silverson."

Ian said.

"Have you decided who you will choose as your two personal advisers Sire?" Nathaniel asked.

Oh shoot. I'm supposed to choose who gets the last two seats? My personal advisers...Drat. I don't really know anyone here yet...except Conner! Conner would be a great adviser. And maybe people would stop avoiding him like the plague. That only gets me one adviser though...

"Actually," Noelle spoke up, "As Crown Prince you only have one personal adviser and are supposed to rely on the advice of the council and the King and Queen's advisers."

Thank the stars!

"But we'll still have one empty seat." Lord Edward pointed out.

"It is only temporary." Nathaniel said, looking contemplatively at Ian.

"I'm sure that this council can run effectively even if it is a few seats short for a while." Celia agreed.

"Then I would like to appoint Conner as my personal adviser." Ian said.

"Conner? Who is Conner?" Jasper Coldin asked scornfully.

"Conner Randol?" Celia asked, looking startled.

Nathaniel leaned down and murmured something into his wife's ear. She nodded and smiled over at Ian.

"Prince Ian has informed us of how important Conner Randol was to his victory over Lilith." Nathaniel said.

Oh good...Nathaniel is going to back me on this.

"I don't know of this boy." Lord Sparks said hesitantly.

"I'm sure that we will all meet him at the next council meeting Lord Edward." Noelle said smoothly.

"Well, with that taken care of should we move onto the next order of business Your Highness?" Celia asked, having gotten over her surprise at his choice.

Ian nodded and they started discussing what should be done with the prisoners. 3 hours later they still hadn't come up with a solid plan and Ian was starting to get a pounding headache. Jasper Coldin was insisting on severe punishment for all who had supported Lilith in any way. Edward Sparks was disagreeing with everything Lord Coldin was saying, and the two of them had to be stopped from arguing every time they talked to each other. Maria Jackson seemed to fall somewhere between Lord Sparks and Lord Coldin's views but she was too quiet for Ian to really know what she was thinking for sure. Noelle was particularly good at getting Lord Sparks and Lord Coldin to stop arguing but it took up most of her attention so she hadn't contributed many ideas either. Celia, Owen and Eira all had experience with leadership in the rebellion, and they both had practical ideas for how to go about tracking down any of Lilith's remaining supporters. Nathaniel had been working as a spy for the rebellion from inside the castle and so he had information on Lilith's supporters. But he was also sympathetic to those who had been forced to serve Lilith through blackmail or had been too scared to really oppose her since he had interacted with those people for so long.

"My father..." Lord Coldin was shouting.

"Yes, yes we all know about Douglas's sacrifice." Lord Sparks interrupted him. "But that doesn't mean that you can trample justice in your path for revenge."

"Justice?! Where is the justice in letting traitors and murderers live?" Lord Coldin asked, shooting to his feet and gesturing wildly.

"Lord Coldin, no one is saying that those who served Lilith willingly shouldn't be punished. But you cannot punish everyone who wasn't an active part of the rebellion." Noelle interjected, trying to diffuse the situation again.

"Everyone's situation is different." Maria agreed quietly.

That's it. Alright this has gone on for long enough. I need out of here.

He gathered up the papers in front of him and then smacked them down on the table with a sharp crack.

"Alright." He said loudly. The room fell silent as everyone turned to look at him, looking a bit startled at the sudden sound. "Celia, as general of the army you are in charge of finding and capturing any remaining spies and servants of Lilith that are still in Winter. Owen and Eira Frost can help you with that. I'll leave the details of the plans in your capable hands." He turned to look at Noelle and Maria. "You're right Lady Jackson, everyone's situation is different and so everyone will be given a fair trial where the punishment will be decided for their individual crimes. Lady Maria, Noelle Iclyn, and Lord Sparks will be in charge of overseeing the trials. Any decisions that are contested will be brought before the entire council to decide. Lord Coldin and Nathaniel, you will inform Joseph Silverson and Thomas Childe of their new positions and help them to learn their new responsibilities. I will inform Conner myself. Are we all in agreement?"

Everyone nodded, to Ian's immense relief.

"Excellent. Then you are all free to go."

Everyone nodded and started filing out of the room in little groups, discussing plans.

Ian let out a sigh of relief and slipped out to go find Conner.

He tried looking for Conner in the stable, but there was no sign of him. Then he tried the kitchen, and several of the hiding places that Conner had told him about. Finally he decided to ask a guard who told him that Conner was down at the pond ice skating with Chloe, Tristan, and Alexa. He asked where he could find a pair of skates and then followed the guard's directions down to the pond.

As Ian walked down the path to the pond he could hear his friends before he saw them. Tristan's infectious laugh came ringing through the cold air. He turned the corner and saw a large frozen pond that had been partially cleared of snow. It shone in the pale sunlight. Chloe was gliding gracefully along the frozen surface of the pond. Tristan was lying spread eagle on the ice, his clothes covered in a thin layer of powdery white. He was laughing hysterically as he reached an arm up towards Conner who tried to pull him up. Alexa had found two large sticks and appeared to be attempting to use them as sort of walking sticks. She was very slowly but very determinedly making her way along the edge of the clear surface of the pond, wobbling occasionally.

"Ian!" The now standing Trist called out excitedly. "We're skating! Come on!"

"Some of us are skating. Some of us are just falling." Conner teased, pointing at Trist.

Trist just grinned and waved Ian over. Ian walked over to the edge of the ice and eyed his skates warily. He hadn't ever been ice skating before.

These things don't look that stable...I'm going to fall flat on my back.

"Come on!" Trist called, wobbling closer to Ian.

Ian sat down in the snow and laced up his skates. Then he stood up, wobbling a bit. He looked at the ice closer. Now that he was closer it really didn't look that smooth. There were frozen leaves and twigs embedded in the ice along with a fair share of ridges and divots. Now Ian was sure he was going to fall over. Conner and Trist had skated over to the edge to meet him though so he stepped out onto the ice cautiously. His foot started slipping forward and a few seconds later found himself sitting on the ice.

"Ow..." He muttered, grabbing Conner's outstretched hand.

Conner stifled a laugh and Ian groaned.

This is not going to go well...

An hour later Ian sat on the snow unlacing his skates. He had been right. Although Conner had tried to help him figure out how to skate, by the end of the hour he could barely make it halfway around the pond without falling over. His only consolation was that Tristan hadn't done much better than him. Alexa was a little more stable, but she had fallen quite a bit too. Chloe and Conner were definitely the best at ice skating. It was starting to get dark though, so the five friends headed back up to the castle to get warmed up.

15 minutes later they were all sitting in front of a blazing fire with cups of hot chocolate. Alexa was attempting to teach Chloe how to play checkers while Trist watched, alternating between cheering for each of the girls. Conner and Ian were sitting on the floor a few feet away watching when Ian remembered why he had gone looking for Conner in the first place.

"I had a council meeting today." Ian said.

"How did that go?" Conner asked.

"A headache mostly. But it turns out there's some empty seats in the council. One of them is for my personal adviser, and I was wondering...Would you be my adviser Conner? I know you're planning on going with the others to Spring, and that's fine. You wouldn't have to be here all the time. But I could really use a friend in there. I mean, Nathaniel and Celia are great, but they still expect me to be in charge all the time. And you've got good ideas, and you give good advice so I thought that you'd be a good choice. Unless you don't want to, I mean." Ian realized he was rambling and stopped talking, flushing slightly. He hadn't realized he was nervous about asking Conner until now.

"You want me to be a member of your council?" Conner asked, with a slightly awed smile. Then his expression fell. "What did the rest of the council say?"

"Well, Nathaniel, Noelle, and Celia agreed with me. And no one else argued. Besides, I'm the Crown Prince so they can't exactly complain about who I choose for my personal adviser." Ian pointed out with a smirk.

"Wow, me on the council? Are you sure?" Conner asked.

"Of course I'm sure." Ian said.

"Then yes. Thank you, Ian." Conner said, grinning.

"Conner, do you know how to play checkers?" Alexa interrupted. "Chloe is going to play cards with Trist."

Conner got up and joined Alexa at the small table and Ian wandered over to join Chloe and Trist in their card game. The rest of the evening the five friends relaxed and played board games together.

Chapter Twenty Three

A few days later Ian was startled to realize that it had been almost a week since he and his friends had saved Winter. The celebrations would start the next day. The past few days had been a blur of preparation. Ian had had a million question to answer, speeches to practice and more last minute clothes fittings. On top of that Ian had various members of the council cornering him to ask questions about their assignment or get his approval for their decisions. It was crazy. No one seemed to be able to make a decision without consulting one of the 'five heroes' as Ian and his friends were being called. People followed them around all the time asking if the cake should be chocolate or vanilla, which shade of blue the decorations should be, should there be a dance afterwards or not? Tristan had enjoyed the attention, bouncing around answering questions and helping decorate with crazy enthusiasm.

Chloe was shy and really didn't like all the attention, but she was so sweet that she hated ignoring anyone and so she often found herself surrounded by people asking her the most trivial questions. She would take the time to help all of them though until one of her friends came to pull her away from everyone. Alexa was loud and bossy, making sure everything was ready for both the celebration and their trip to Spring afterwards. Conner was still very jumpy and nervous around crowds. He tended to startle easily and seemed surprised that so many people thought he was a hero. Ian was glad that they hadn't needed to hold another council meeting yet since Conner would have to attend, but he was glad that people had stopped avoiding his friend. Currently, Ian was hiding in an alcove behind a suit of armor that Conner had told him about. He wasn't used to so many people and the endless meetings and people following him was getting to be too much.

I have about five minutes tops before someone finds me here. I probably shouldn't be hiding at all. After all, the celebration is for me as well as the others. I really should try to help...after they find me. I need a few moments to breathe. I need to think too. I still have to decide if I'm going or staying. I think Alexa is planning on leaving as soon as the celebrations are over. So the day after tomorrow. I could stay and try to run my kingdom, but I don't even know how. Couldn't someone else take care of it until my parents get back? Or at least until I'm older? The council could. Celia said they could run just fine with a few less members...So many people seem excited that I'm back though. I've brought back hope. Would it leave if I did? That seems a bit ridiculous. I think all this hero stuff is getting to my head. But should I really leave them after I just saved them? But what about my friends? I can't abandon them either. They all worked so hard to help me save Winter, even though it's not their kingdom. They are my friends. I can't stay here when they might need my help. What about me? Does is matter what I want? I want to go with my friends. They are my only friends and I can't lose them now. What am I supposed to do? I'm only 15. I'm way too young to save kingdoms, let alone rule one!

He was pulled out of his thoughts by a short woman asking him to come get his final clothes fitting. He sighed and followed her. The rest of the day was just as crazy and Ian hadn't been able to steal another minute to himself until he finally escaped into his room and fell into bed.

The morning of the festivities was bright and cold. Ian looked out his window and saw the courtyard had many tables, and chairs set up. There were also a lot of blue and silver decorations. Even though he would have rather skipped having a giant party he had to admit that it looked really nice. People were starting to arrive and they all seemed very excited. Nathaniel must have been right about the people needing something to celebrate. Soon he would have to go down as well, but for now he was just happy observing. Someone pounded on his door.

"Are you in there Ian?" It was Alexa. Ian was kind of surprised, because she had been avoiding him since he said he wasn't sure if he was going with them.

"Yes." Ian said as he opened the door.

"I came to get you. We're supposed to go down to the courtyard now."

"Thanks Alexa."

"Umm Ian..."

"Yes?"

"I wanted to say I'm sorry. I've been ignoring you and I shouldn't have. I know you have a kingdom to take care of now, and I probably haven't been making it easier for you. So I'm sorry." She said it very quickly and looked at the floor the whole time. Somehow Ian knew Chloe hadn't made her apologize this time.

"It's ok Alexa. Come on let's go down to the party."

The courtyard was crazy. It was so loud because of all the people talking and the music playing, Ian could hardly hear himself think. People were moving around talking and eating. It looked like absolute chaos. Up on a dais at the far end were five throne-like-chairs. Three of them were already occupied. Trist was balanced on the edge of his seat, bouncing up and down and looking around in circles. Chloe looked a bit nervous, being up in front of everyone, but she was still smiling and even waving at a couple of people who were loudly calling out their thanks. Conner sitting next to Chloe, and the two of them seemed to be discussing something they saw out in the crowd. He looked nervous but kind of excited too; like he couldn't quite believe he was up there. Ian and Alexa headed up and sat down on their chairs. There was a loud trumpet blown and everyone looked up at him. He froze and looked down at all the people. There were way too many people staring at him.

What am I supposed to do? What am I supposed to say? Why are they all staring at me?

He shot his friends a panicked look. Alexa rolled her eyes. "Let the celebrations begin," she mouthed quietly.

He stood up and nervously repeated what she had said. The he slunk back down into his chair.

Why was that so hard? That was harder than facing Lilith!

Tristan had bounced out of his seat the minute Ian had sat down. Now Ian could see his flaming red hair weaving through the crowd. Alexa jumped up and drug Chloe off the stage and towards the food tables. People were talking, laughing and eating. Ian decided eating was a great idea.

"Want to go get something to eat?" Ian asked Conner.

"Sure. Let's go catch up to Alexa and Chloe."

Ian and Conner followed the two girls over to the food. There was tons of food lining multiple tables. He grabbed a plate and piled on fruit, pastries, and bacon. Alexa had insisted that the celebrations be in the morning so that they could their finish preparations to leave that evening before bed. So the tables were filled with different breakfast foods. The four of them sat down at a table near the back of the room where Ian hoped they could get a few minutes to themselves.

"How long is this supposed to last?" Ian asked his friends.

"I don't know. Try to enjoy it though Ian. This party is for us." Alexa pointed out.

"Do we have to stay the entire time?" Chloe asked.

"Guys, smile everyone is staring at us." Conner said nervously.

They all turned and smiled at the crowd of people who cheered excitedly.

"Chloe you just have to stay till the dance. You can sneak back up to the castle after the first dance." Ian told her.

"Ok. Thanks Ian."

"When are we supposed to be giving our speeches?"

Alexa asked.

"After the story telling. Chloe goes first then Alexa, Trist, Conner and then I go last. I'll end my speech by opening up the dance floor."

There was another loud trumpet call and someone stepped onto the dais. The crowd quieted and turned to the front, and Tristan slipped over to them and sat down.

"I think they are telling the story now. Ian are you going to eat that donut?"

"No. Shh."

Captain Celia was up on the dais and she started speaking in a loud carrying voice. She told the story of their adventure to save Winter from Lilith. Ian didn't really pay attention when he realized that she was just telling their story. He had lived through it, he didn't need to be told about it. Alexa and Conner were playing tic-tac-toe on a napkin. He peered over and watched them. Alexa won 5 games and Conner won 9 before they ran out of napkin room. That was probably best though, because Alexa was getting very competitive. Ian hadn't known a game of tic-tac-toe could get so intense. They were still only half way through the story. He sighed quietly and closed his eyes. A few moment later Alexa was shaking him.

"What?"

"You fell asleep. The story is almost over. Then it will be time for speeches."

"Thanks." He was slightly embarrassed and hoped no one had noticed. Everyone else seemed to be paying attention to Celia telling the story on the dais though.

She ended the story and everyone started to cheer loudly. Alexa led the way back onto the dais and they all sat down in their throne chairs. Chloe nervously stood.

"Thank you for this party. It's been really nice. I'm glad I could help save you from Lilith. Thank you for helping me prepare to go to Spring tomorrow," she squeaked. Then she sat down and blushed bright red as people cheered.

Alexa stood next and gave a loud speech thanking them for their celebration and for the supplies. She bowed at the end of her speech before sitting down. Then Tristan stood and practically bounced in place as he excitedly talked about the fun he'd been having at the party. Conner stood up and nervously declared that he was glad he could help save Winter and fix the evil Lilith had done. Then it was Ian's turn.

He stood up and panicked for a second before realizing what he wanted to say.

I'm going to shoot myself later for not thinking this through more. Oh well. Here goes nothing.

"Thank you all for coming to the celebration. I am proud

to have been able to help save Winter from Lilith. I know that I had help though. I couldn't have done it without my friends. That is why I have decided that I cannot abandon them and their quest. I will be leaving with them tomorrow to go save the rest of Four Seasons. I cannot leave them to do it alone after all they have done to help me. While I am gone, Celia, the Captain of the Guard and Nathaniel, the steward of the Castle, will be in charge of running the kingdom. Thank you for your support and understanding. Now the dance will begin."

There was silence for a few minutes, but then the crowd cheered approvingly. Ian let out a breath he didn't know he had even been holding and sat down. All four of his friends were staring at him with their mouths open.

"What?" Alexa asked.

"You're coming with us?" Chloe said.

"I can't just leave you guys. You're my friends."

"I knew you'd come! I have supplies packed for you too," Trist exclaimed. "Come on, let's dance!"

Tristan bounced off the stage and asked a pretty blond girl to dance with him. She giggled and he led her to the middle of the floor. Conner turned to Chloe and blushed.

"Want to dance?"

"Thank you." She was blushing too as they went to dance.

Another boy from the crowd came up and boldly asked Alexa to dance with him. Ian sat on his throne looking over the dance, glaring daggers at people. He didn't like dancing. As he overlooked the festivities, he saw Alexa dancing with that boy. He pulled Alexa a little closer and Ian growled quietly.

If he tries anything funny I'll freeze him solid. Alexa is my friend and we're leaving tomorrow...Focus Ian. What do we need to do to get ready for tomorrow?

The celebrations continued as other people joined the dance, but the four friends left right after the first song ended. They had things to do to prepare for the next adventure. Even though they were all heading back out into danger, at least they would be together.

To be Continued...

www.ingramcontent.com/pod-product-compliance
Lightning Source LLC
Chambersburg PA
CBHW020329180626
46812CB00001B/108